D1236638

THE MAGDALENE VEIL

THE MAGDALENE CHRONICLES
BOOK THREE

GARY MCAVOY

Hardcover ISBN: 978-1-954123-03-8
Paperback ISBN: 978-1-954123-02-1
eBook ISBN: 978-1-954123-01-4
Large Print Edition ISBN: 978-1-954123-16-8
Library of Congress Control Number: 2021904086

Published by:
Literati Editions
PO Box 5987
Bremerton, WA 98312-5987
Email: info@LiteratiEditions.com
Visit the author's website: www.GaryMcAvoy.com

2.2LP

YOUR FREE BOOK IS WAITING

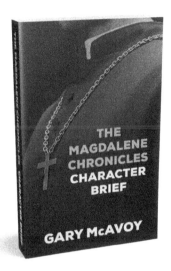

Download your free copy now of **The Magdalene Chronicles Character Brief**, containing brief backgrounds and other biographical details of all the main characters in *The Magdalene Deception, The Magdalene Reliquary*, and *The Magdalene Veil*—with my compliments as a loyal reader!

www.garymcavoy.com / character-brief /

BOOKS BY GARY MCAVOY

FICTION

The Magdalene Deception

The Magdalene Reliquary

The Magdalene Veil

The Vivaldi Cipher

The Opus Dictum

The Petrus Prophecy

The Avignon Affair

NONFICTION

And Every Word Is True

Harvest for Hope (co-authored)

PROLOGUE

JERUSALEM – CIRCA 33 CE

The unruly crowds lined both sides of the Via Dolorosa, most shouting, some spitting and heckling, many crying and wailing for the condemned Jew from Nazareth carrying a large wooden cross on his back. He would soon arrive at the hills of Golgotha, a section in the northwestern corner of Jerusalem outside the walls of the city, where his journey would end.

As he moved through the crush of onlookers, his face bloody and swollen from the beatings by Roman soldiers at his tribunal just moments earlier, one young woman took pity on the man, someone she knew. Stepping forward, she removed her byssus veil and offered it to him, so he could wipe away the blood and sweat of his burdens.

He held the veil to his face, taking in the soft, sheer, aromatic fabric smelling of myrrh, and after a moment of respite, handed the soiled veil, known as a *sudar*, back to the kind woman. Looking at it, she was astonished to find an imprint of his face had been imparted in vivid detail: the shape of his head, his tortured facial features, the stains of his blood—it was as if looking at a delicate painting. She took it to be a miracle.

As the man continued on his way, the woman followed

along, outside the horde of onlookers, until she came to someone she knew, someone she had been seeking, whom she knew to be the man's closest disciple. The woman was weeping uncontrollably.

"Miriam," she said gently, "I, too, grieve for Jesus. Look upon my veil, you will see his visage passed onto the *sudar* when he held it to his face. I want you to have this."

Miriam of Magdala gratefully accepted the veil, thanking her. "*Sas efcharistó*, Berenikē, for this gesture of kindness. I will place it in my Lord's tomb."

THREE DAYS AFTER THE CRUCIFIXION, Miriam of Magdala was the first to discover that the tomb was now empty. Soon, the apostles Simon Peter and John also came to see that Jesus' body was not there (John 20:3). They also observed two cloths where the body had lain: one was a large cloth which had been placed over their Lord's body. The other blood-soaked cloth was balled up and laying next to a rock.

Seeing this *sudar*, and knowing it to be the one given to her by her friend Berenikē, Miriam removed the cloth from the tomb and took it away, its facial image her only memento of her beloved Jesus.

～

RENNES-LE-CHÂTEAU, **France – 1937**

Ominous rumblings of an impending world war galvanized much of Europe as Nazi Germany grew restless under Adolf Hitler's unquenchable lust for expansion and domination.

Among the Führer's goals was the broad establishment of an Aryan race, one with, in Hitler's mind, historical roots that went back to the ancient Israelites—descendants of Abraham, Jacob, and Isaac—even identifying Jesus Christ as an "Aryan fighter" who fought against "the power and pretensions of the corrupt Pharisees" and Jewish materialism over spiritual values.

In support of Hitler's Aryan mission, SS *Reichsführer* Heinrich Himmler, the architect of the Holocaust, commissioned large-scale archaeological expeditions for years, predominantly throughout France but also in such disparate places as Iceland, for Nordic races were deemed Aryan as well.

A man obsessed by the occult, Himmler was consumed with acquiring the two most legendary sacred objects in history—the Ark of the Covenant and the Holy Grail. To this end he enlisted the aid of Otto Rahn, a writer of some fame whose book, *Crusade Against the Grail*, Himmler had embraced with a passion reserved for those of like minds.

Rahn was an avid student of the Cathar mythos—legends of a small and peaceful yet influential order whose beliefs and traditions rejected those of the Church of Rome. Rahn's own guiding principles in his search for the Grail were derived from Wolfram von Eschenbach's epic poem *Parzival,* from which Rahn had identified the last surviving Cathar fortress—perched strategically on the majestic peak of Montségur in the French Pyrenees—as the most likely resting place for the Holy Grail.

Funded by Himmler's think tank known as the Ahnenerbe—and in league with a mysterious Nazi occult group called the Thule Society—Rahn spent years searching the area—its churches, villages, even the labyrinth of caves snaking throughout the Languedoc region—to no avail. He never found the Holy Grail.

But while excavating a hidden room buried beneath the Church of Saint Mary Magdalene in Rennes-le-Château, France —a church that just two decades earlier had been overseen by a mysterious Catholic abbé named Bérenger Saunière—Rahn did find something of profound importance. It was a particular artifact contained in a small white alabaster box secured with an antique bronze hasp. Inside the box was a delicate ancient veil finely woven of rare byssus—also known as sea silk—on which appeared the full facial image of a man whose features clearly showed he had been beaten, whose cheeks and forehead suggested fresh wounds, and whose *peyes*—the side curls at the temples of Jewish men in the first century—were clearly visible. The image on the opposite side was identical, though in reverse to the image on the obverse.

Rahn was convinced he had discovered the legendary Veil of Veronica, which oral tradition claimed had been given to Mary Magdalene while Jesus walked the road to Calvary, where he would be crucified moments later.

Ecstatic over his discovery and certain he had something of acute historical value to present to his master, he returned to Himmler's Wewelsburg Castle fortress in Büren, Germany, and handed the alabaster box over to Himmler's deputy, SS Colonel Walther Rausch, who promptly gave it to Himmler, who secretly placed the object in the castle's hidden vault. Outside of ceremonial use by the mysterious Thule Society, it has never been seen since.

CHAPTER 1

PRESENT DAY

M ichael Dominic ran swiftly along the red clay path lining the Sarthe River in northern France, wiping back a thin sheen of sweat as he listened to the distant meditative Gregorian chant of the Benedictine monks at the Abbey of Saint-Pierre de Solesmes, a few hundred meters away.

He had been on retreat at the abbey for ten days now, just the respite of silence and prayer he needed from the rigors of his job as prefect of the Vatican Secret Archives. His friend and predecessor, Brother Calvino Mendoza, had retired seven months earlier, leaving the young priest in charge of the Church's vast collection of historical manuscripts, books, and ledgers comprising the official record of Church business for well over a thousand years. From its inception it had been known as the Secret Archive, but the Pope recently renamed it the Apostolic Archive, purportedly to demystify its purpose, since "Secret" had for centuries implied an aura of conspiracy to its contents—though not without justification. Dominic had arrived at this point in his career believing he had more than enough tools to fulfill his tasks: he was fluent in several languages and well versed in history. But the last year or two had shown him there was more to his place in the Church as Prefect than he had imagined. He'd faced dangers and disputes, with heresy and truth colliding. He had truly welcomed this retreat as a time to re-center himself.

The haunting chant grew louder as Dominic approached the abbey, echoes of it drifting through the surrounding trees and gardens of the monastery. Shifting to a cool down pace, he walked through a meadow of wildflowers and poppies, wild gladioli and orchids. The last rays of the setting sun cast an amber glow over the scene as butterflies danced around him in the warm spring air. Compared to the chaos of Rome it was a surreal moment—no honking cars or petrol fumes, no chattering tourists. Just the serenity of otherwise complete silence within the sounds of nature.

Tomorrow he would end his retreat, leaving for Paris and a brief visit with his journalist friend Hana Sinclair before heading back to Rome. But for what moments remained, he intended to take it all in.

"Excuse me," said a man with a thick German accent approaching him from behind. "By any chance, are you Father Dominic?"

The priest turned around. "By chance I am, yes."

"Ah, good. I was told I might find you here, near the trail."

Dominic appraised the man. About his age, early thirties. Good-looking in an Aryan sort of way, tall and well-built, with blond hair and angular facial features. He wasn't smiling, but his steady blue eyes told Dominic he was carrying some kind of burden.

"Is there something I can help you with?" Dominic asked. "How did you even find me here? Few people know where I am."

"Forgive me, Father," the man said, blushing uncomfortably. "I took great pains in locating you, for I believe you are the only one who can help me. I spoke to your assistant in the Archives who told me I might find you here.

"My apologies," he added, extending his hand. "My name is Jacob Rausch."

After accepting the handshake, Dominic spotted a bench in the garden. Encouraging Rausch to take a seat with a wave of his hand, he did the same. Then he waited for the man to begin speaking.

"Where to start…" Rausch said, looking at nothing in particular in the distance, his brow furrowed in thought. "What I am about to tell you may seem bizarre, but it is all quite true. Please bear with me as I explain.

"During World War II, my grandfather, Colonel Walther Rausch, was a high-ranking member of the Nazi party, assigned to the *Schutzstaffel*, or SS. He was not the kind of man one could look up to, for he did terrible things during the war. It is embarrassing for me to speak of such things, even now.

"At some point he became personal aide to SS Commander Heinrich Himmler, who, as you may know, was chief architect of the Holocaust and one of Hitler's most intimate confidants. Himmler was fascinated with the occult and its assumed influence in guiding tactical decisions over the enemy. He even hired thousands of tarot card readers in Berlin to supposedly learn how Allied powers were strategizing their wartime efforts. It seems ridiculous now, of course, but Himmler took it all quite seriously."

Rausch drew in a calming breath. "But more to my point. Himmler acquired an immense castle in Wewelsburg, Germany, not only to house his vast collection of mystical trappings, but to serve as the spiritual home of the Nazis' expanding empire."

As he listened to the man, Dominic's peaceful state of mind turned restless. *Nazis? Tarot cards? Shouldn't I instead be sitting in the chapel, listening to monks chant?* He'd discovered enough of Hitler's atrocities a couple years ago when he assisted Hana Sinclair in research about the Church's connections to Nazi gold. He didn't feel inclined to be swept into more of such dark—and dangerous—secrets of the past. Yet the man had gone to some trouble to find him here. He decided to let it play out—but not for long.

"As Himmler's most trusted deputy, my grandfather—I'll call him Walther for simplicity—was in charge of this collection, and indeed of Wewelsburg Castle itself. Nothing happened there that Walther did not know about.

"In November 1937 a man whom Himmler was very fond of, a medieval researcher and writer of some note named Otto Rahn, came to Wewelsburg Castle. With him he had brought an object—an artifact Himmler himself described as among the most important religious relics in all of world history. Himmler had given Rahn millions of Reichsmarks and a complete archeological team and security force to search for such objects, mainly in the area of southern France around Montségur and Rennes-le-Château. Apparently Rahn discovered something very special and brought it promptly to Himmler. He was ecstatic in having taken possession of this relic but swore my grandfather to complete secrecy. No one else was to know of its existence.

"Wewelsburg Castle had a special room they called Consecration Hall, a place where the number twelve figured prominently: there were twelve seats around a large table fashioned after King Arthur's Round Table; twelve pedestals surrounding the table, on which Himmler had placed the contained ashes of fallen comrades; and he appointed twelve SS officers as his followers, or 'apostles,' if you will."

Dominic was perplexed. "Why tell *me* of these things? What is this object Rahn found?"

Rausch looked directly into Dominic's eyes.

"I imagine there is no one alive who really knows. But to my mind there is only one thing it could be, of course," he said matter-of-factly. "The Holy Grail."

CHAPTER 2

D ominic looked at the man as if he were slightly insane. He stood up and glanced at the Tag Heuer strapped to his wrist.

"I'm afraid I have to get back to the abbey, Herr Rausch," he said. "It's nearly time for vespers."

"I figured that might be your reaction, Father. But, you see, you are already involved."

Rausch now had Dominic's attention, mystified as he was.

"What do you mean, I'm already involved? I've never heard of this before now."

"Well, I did not mean to imply that you personally were mentioned in the documents that led me here. But please, let me explain."

Dominic sat back down on the bench, his curiosity aroused.

"My father recently passed away and as the sole heir to his estate I inherited, among other things, the papers and property of my grandfather, who died in Santiago, Chile, in 1984.

"My grandfather was very active in politics and espionage during his twenty-six years in exile in Chile, and despite repeated efforts by Israel and Germany to extradite him for war crimes, he managed to evade expulsion through the courts due to his close relationship with Chilean dictator Augusto Pinochet. I am sorry to say, but Walther was a truly evil man, and quite deserved the punishment he avoided. As the inventor of mobile gas chambers, he was personally responsible for exterminating some 100,000 Jews, Roma, and other 'enemies of the German state' during the war." Jacob paused, and Michael could see furrows on his forehead, as if in remorse for the actions of someone of his own blood.

Jacob took a breath and continued. "I traveled to Chile a few months ago to take possession of Walther's estate and settle matters there which my father had failed to attend to over the years. In the process I discovered he had kept both a substantial account and a safe deposit box at the Santiago branch of a major Swiss bank, one that had catered to Nazis even before the war. With the proper papers, I went there to claim Walther's assets. But it was what I found in the safe deposit box that was both shocking and, admittedly, rather exciting.

"As it turned out, my grandfather was a prolific writer, and secretly documented a great deal of his covert work as a spy for both the West German and Chilean governments at various times.

"He also wrote profusely about his association with Heinrich Himmler at Wewelsburg Castle, and the bizarre events that went on in the Consecration Hall—strange rituals, intimate séances, and other occult ceremonies in which Rahn's discovered object was revered, much like Catholics venerate the chalice and Holy Communion during Mass. But Himmler's ceremonies, of course, were of a more pagan nature, dedicated to Aryan principles."

Heading back to ideas of the occult didn't settle well with Dominic. "This is all very interesting, Jacob," he said earnestly, "but once more, how does this relate to me?"

"You are the prefect of the Secret Archives, yes?" Rausch asked.

"Yes, of the Apostolic Archives, as I'm fairly sure you already know."

"Well, my grandfather was a close associate, even a good friend, to Austrian Catholic Bishop Alois Hudal who was based in the Vatican. Hudal helped set up the ODESSA ratline that served as an escape network for top Nazi officials fleeing prosecution, including Walther himself.

"At the end of the war, while the Allies were closing in on capturing Nazi leaders, my grandfather gave to Bishop Hudal Himmler's own personal journal describing the incredible powers of this object—powers described as true miracles—and the location where it was hidden. And according to Walther's diary, that journal is now in your Vatican Apostolic Archive, where Hudal placed it on the instructions of Pope Pius XII. And now we need to find it."

Dominic had been patiently listening to Rausch's story, but when he got to the end of it, the priest's mental radar lit up.

"Wait… you said Pope Pius personally instructed this bishop to archive Himmler's journal in the Vatican? That on its own seems rather strange—that the Pope himself would be involved in such a, well, fairly low-level archival undertaking, regardless of its author. It makes me more than curious."

"I'm glad I have your attention now, Father," Rausch said, encouraged by Dominic's change in attitude. "So, how do we go about locating this journal?"

"Slow down, Jacob," Dominic cautioned. He had chased other theories in the past, and fiction was filled with tales of the Holy Grail that held no reality. He didn't even know this man, let alone the veracity of any of it. "Is it possible to see your grandfather's diary myself first?"

"Yes, of course. It is back at my apartment in Paris. That is where I live."

"As it happens," Dominic said, "I'm leaving for Paris tomorrow, to visit a friend before heading back to Rome. Will you be there later this week?"

"Actually, I leave tomorrow as well." Jacob gave Dominic the address of a Parisian bistro where they would meet the following day. They parted company, and Dominic headed back through the gardens to the abbey. He'd found the peace and relaxation he'd needed this week. But now he contemplated the strange turn of events on his last day of retreat. And how it might shape his days ahead.

CHAPTER 3

H ana Sinclair sat across from Michael Dominic at a table for two on the quaint cobblestone alley of Le Procope Brasserie. Having opened its doors on the Left Bank in 1686, Le Procope was the oldest coffeehouse in Paris, conveniently situated near Hana's apartment in the Saint-Germain-des-Prés quarter of the 6th Arrondissement, and where she began her day every morning.

Her favorite waiter, a flirty Parisian named Sébastien, set down two cups of steaming café au lait along with a pair of warm croissants, winking at Hana as he retreated back into the shop, his snug uniform catching her eye.

"As crazy as it sounds, Hana, this Rausch fellow seemed serious. I did ask to see his grandfather's diary and he's agreed to share it. Would you like to join me? Sounds like something you might find of interest."

Hana took a cautious sip of the hot coffee. "Michael, you can't possibly believe Himmler actually found the Holy Grail. Wouldn't you think we would have heard about this long before now? Something that profound would be impossible to keep secret for all this time."

"Well, yes, I would agree," Dominic replied, "*if* the artifact

Rahn discovered had ever been seen by others. For all anyone knows it might still be in Wewelsburg Castle. Whatever it was, Himmler valued it highly enough to build a concealed vault for it there."

"As it so happens," Hana said pensively, staring distantly down the alley, "my editor has been pushing me for a new story with a historical slant. This might be just the topic I need. I suppose the old Nazi must have had some compelling things to say in his diary, Holy Grail or not. Sure, count me in. When are you meeting Jacob?"

Dominic smiled, anticipating his friend's interest in what could be an eye-opening look into history's darker side.

"We're meeting him this afternoon. On a hunch, I'd already told him you'd be joining me..." He looked at Hana hesitantly, hoping she wouldn't mind his presumption.

"Good hunch," she said, a sly smile curving her lips.

NOT FAR FROM Paris's main Gare du Nord train station, the Canal Saint-Martin neighborhood is home to an eclectic mix of bohemian artists, musicians, writers, and other like-minded Parisians who prefer the more tranquil streets and charming canals of the 10th Arrondissement to the more touristy areas of the city.

As Jacob Rausch sat at one of the sidewalk tables of Chez Prune bistro waiting for Dominic and Hana, a young man sitting on the canal wall played guitar beneath an aged linden tree, its dark green spade-shaped leaves offering shade on the warm spring afternoon, enhancing an already sylvan setting.

Rausch was nursing a local craft beer when Dominic and his friend approached the table.

"Bonjour, Jacob," Dominic said as he walked up to the German. After introductions and handshakes, the two took a seat at the table as Hana ordered both of them craft beers *un tango*—with a shot of grenadine, a French favorite.

"I'm so glad you could both make it," Jacob said enthusiastically. "What is it you do here, Hana, if I may ask?"

"I'm an investigative reporter for *Le Monde*," she said.

Rausch stared at her for a moment, a look of enlightenment slowly crossing his face. "Of course! I thought Sinclair sounded familiar. I remember a story you wrote—what, maybe a year ago now?—on the flow of Nazi gold involving several European Central Banks, a piece that prompted investigations into their post-war activities. Didn't you win an award for that work?"

Flushed with modest surprise, Hana replied, "Well… yes, as a matter of fact. The Albert Londres Prize. You've got a finely tuned memory, Jacob."

"I'm an insatiable reader," he admitted shyly. "Two newspapers a day, and usually a book or two a week. I've been a history buff all my life, which is why I'm so excited to be working with both of you on this adventure."

Hana looked at Dominic quizzically.

"Hold on," Dominic said, raising a hand, "let's not get ahead of ourselves. We haven't actually decided on anything yet. I invited Hana because she, too, is a student of history and might offer insights into your grandfather's diary. She's quite knowledgable about World War II, and especially certain financial and esoteric activities of the Nazis."

"I'd say their avid pursuit of the occult certainly qualifies as 'esoteric,'" Rausch noted.

"To be clear," Hana interjected, "the Nazi Party itself didn't broadly embrace esotericism, just many of its top officials and sympathizers, notably Heinrich Himmler, Rudolf Hess, Alfred Rosenberg and many others who had formed an occult group called the Thule Society. Its purpose was to validate the origins of the Aryan race. Hitler himself never showed much interest in the society's activities, though he was fanatically drawn to other pseudoscientific pursuits."

"Yes, my grandfather was also a member of the Thule Society. He wrote of it in his diary. So as you can imagine, I am quite anxious to find Himmler's journal to learn more about these activities, and find out the nature of Otto Rahn's discovery. How much of a challenge might that be, Father Michael?"

Dominic laughed. "You might think of it as looking for one particular grain of sand on a beach," he said. "There are millions of uncatalogued papers in the Apostolic Archive. We 'just' need something to point us in the right direction. Maybe Walther's diary will help in that regard. Are you ready to take us to it?"

"Yes, of course. I live just around the corner. Let's finish our beers and I'll take you there."

CHAPTER 4

Situated on the northwest bank of Canal Saint-Martin, Jacob Rausch's luxury apartment on the Quai de Valmy was a vision in tasteful opulence. Hana's seasoned eye for affluence quickly took in key features of the flat which identified its owner as a man of means—Old Masters oil paintings, white alabaster statuary, fine tapestries, fresh flower bouquets, and most obvious, hundreds, if not thousands, of books on long walls of shelving throughout the two-story space overlooking the shady-treed canal.

"You have a beautiful home, Jacob," she said. "How long have you been here?"

"Not long, a couple years or so. When he died, my grandfather left me a small fortune, and to be honest, I have always had lurking concerns as to where that money came from. I know he worked as a spy in Italy and the Middle East, and eventually for West Germany. And he was once the manager of a king crab cannery in Punta Arenas on the coast of southern Chile. But those activities can hardly account for the wealth he passed down to my father and me.

"Once Walther had died, of course, there was no one to ask

about its origins. But given his close activities with the Nazis, it's not hard to imagine that he may have come by his fortune in less than honorable ways. I bear some guilt for that to this day, strangely enough, though I cannot explain why, having no evidence one way or the other."

Dominic and Hana were silent on the matter, each having their own suspicions as to how such fortunes had accumulated for many top officials in the Nazi regime. This was not an uncommon occurrence for those eluding prosecution and grabbing what they could on their flight out of Germany, and particularly down to South America, where, as Hana well knew, Swiss banks had swept up massive dubious deposits from Nazi refugees, no questions asked.

As his two guests took a seat in the living room, Jacob brought out his grandfather's diary, setting it on the table in front of Hana. It was a well-aged, dark burgundy leather book with the name "**Walther Rausch**" and the runic "**SS**" lightning bolt insignia stamped in gold leaf on its cover.

A chill passed over Hana as she stared at it, and she visibly shivered before picking it up. She noticed several strips of paper had been inserted as various page markers.

"Were these already here, Jacob, or did you mark certain passages?" she asked.

"Yes, I did make note of the more relevant sections I thought might be important. Most of the diary is filled with musings of his work and duties, often complaining about his superiors and dire conditions during the war. His observations of Jews in the concentration camps were notable but not related to my own interests as regards Otto Rahn's discovery."

As she paged through the book to the sections Jacob had marked, she paused before reading them aloud, admiring the elder Rausch's finely formed, but difficult to read, Sütterlin cursive handwriting. Dominic sat back on the sofa, with Jacob sitting across from them in an armchair. Hana noticed a faint but pleasing scent of eucalyptus in the air, and the only sound in the room was the distant ticking pendulum of a grandfather clock in the entry hall.

She began reading the marked passages aloud, translating from the original German.

Wewelsburg – 12 Oktober '37

Telegram received from SS-Obersturmführer Otto Rahn in Montségur, France. He believes he is close to finding the Grail. Himmler delighted, anxious to acquire any relic but especially the Grail. Personally, I find the prospect absurd, but Rahn has Himmler's trust, and there is no question about his passion for the hunt.

…

Wewelsburg – 23 Oktober '37

Himmler commissioned installation of a hidden vault in the General's Hall, for storage of sacred artifacts of which many are already here. 'The Twelve' hold secret candlelight ceremonies at night, garbed in robes and masks. I make arrangements for them but am not permitted to participate. Chanting can be heard from outside the door. Very strange behavior.

…

Wewelsburg – 4 November '37

Rahn reported by urgent telegram that he found something of great importance. At Himmler's prior instruction, due to risks of interception, Rahn did not identify what was found. He returns to the castle in four days' time under a heavily armed Gestapo unit.

…

Wewelsburg – 9 November '37

The object Rahn brought back with him is incredible… I dare say even dazzling! It took Himmler's breath away (not something easily accomplished). The Twelve gathered again last night to pay homage to it. A Veil of secrecy. Even I am moved by its power to inspire awe.

…

"That's curious," Hana said, her brows furrowed with concern. "The object isn't identified here. Perhaps your grandfather was under some instruction not to reveal its true nature in writing?"

"That's what I thought, too," Rausch replied. "Which is why I believe we may find more in Himmler's journal in the Vatican Archives."

"There's something else here that I find odd," Hana said, turning back to an earlier passage she had read.

"His diary entries are clear and fluid throughout, with no shortcuts or abbreviations. But there is one section here that makes no sense. It simply reads, '*A Veil of secrecy,*' standing alone as its own sentence. It's completely out of context to the words surrounding it. And '*Veil*' is capitalized. Why would he do that? It seems like he's trying to convey some salient point here."

Dominic looked up at Hana, marveling at her ability to see beyond what was presented in any situation—to dig deeper into that which, to most people, might otherwise seem simple and straightforward. She continued reading.

Wewelsburg – 13 November '37

    Saturday—big event taking place tonight. The Führer himself is coming! It is a madhouse here as everyone scrambles to put things in order. Himmler's alabaster box and the artifact within will sit on the plinth of honor in Consecration Hall. Otto Rahn will be here along with Goebbels, Eichmann, von Ribbentrop, Göring, Speer, Boorman, Eva Braun… Where Hitler goes, his disciples follow. Castle security is on highest alert.

Wewelsburg – 14 November '37

    Himmler was instructed by the Führer to safeguard the sacred relic at all costs, that it might be invaluable in negotiations with the Vatican. I have no doubt Pope Pius would do anything to get his hands on the ■ ■ ■ ■.

"So, it's a 'sacred relic' kept in an alabaster box, though no mention of its size except that it would fit on a plinth, or pedestal," Hana remarked. "But this last part is crossed out. Obviously, he had identified what it was, then thought better of it. *Merde!*

"I have to admit, it's startling to read about Hitler's presence in the hand of someone who was actually there. Jacob, what was Wewelsburg Castle used for, and who were 'The Twelve'?"

Rausch resettled himself in his chair, eager to impart what he knew about the strange center of *Schutzstaffel* activity.

"Wewelsburg Castle is situated in Büren, a town in the German state of Westphalia, and was originally constructed in the 17th century. Today it is a youth hostel and museum, but under SS forces in 1934, well before the war, Himmler took control of the castle with plans to make it a school for SS officers. But he also had a vision for it as the headquarters of the Ahnenerbe, an offshoot of the SS dedicated to promoting the Nazi doctrine that modern Germans were descended from ancient Aryans, and were biologically superior to all other races.

"The Ahnenerbe—meaning 'ancestral heritage'—employed widespread propaganda campaigns to suit Hitler's racial theories and set in motion numerous archeological expeditions seeking evidence of broad Aryan ancestry, all in order to legitimize German expansion across Europe. This so-called evidence was largely manufactured by the Ahnenerbe in order to justify the Holocaust and its brutal extermination of Jews and other 'undesirables' in the years leading up to and during the war.

"As for the Consecration Hall, it was located in the north tower of the castle. It was a huge circular chamber with a sunken floor on which sat a massive round oak table with twelve throne-like seats—as I told Father Michael, think King Arthur and his legendary knights and you'll have some idea of what Himmler was trying to emulate. Beneath this round chamber Himmler had built a crypt where the ashes of fallen SS comrades were to be interred. But he had also constructed a secret vault somewhere in the castle—a vault in which to store the Holy Grail and other relics when they were found. To my knowledge this vault has never been found. I doubt that many people even knew about it after the war."

Rausch took a deep breath then reached for a glass of water, taking long draws on it before continuing. Hana and Dominic sat transfixed by his story.

"'The Twelve' were Himmler's highest ranking SS officers. They remained close to the castle when not on missions. But there were many Thule members, scattered through the top and lower ranks of the German military. The collective mission of the Twelve was the acquisition of the Grail, which Himmler was convinced could be found and brought to Wewelsburg. After reading Otto Rahn's book *Crusade Against the Grail*, Himmler had summoned Rahn to a secret meeting and soon after enlisted him in the SS, putting him in charge of the Grail expeditions.

"Keep in mind," Rausch continued, "that the Nazis went to great lengths to 'prove' Jesus was Aryan, not Jewish, and was descended from a long line of purported Aryans including Abraham, Isaac, and Jacob—the latter for whom I was named, by the way, at my grandfather's insistence."

Hana was mesmerized listening to Jacob's compelling history lesson. Her instincts flared at a strong story here, one she was becoming more keen to pursue.

"This Himmler journal you spoke of," she asked him, "how did Walther get hold of it? And how did it end up in the Vatican? And what of this 'Ahnenerbe,' what became of it?"

"As Himmler's closest aide, my grandfather maintained his confidential files and many of his personal effects at the castle. When it became clear Germany was losing the war, Himmler went to meet Hitler for the last time in Berlin in April 1945. Hitler had decided to remain in Berlin—where he soon took his own life, as we know—while all his top lieutenants had begun fleeing Germany through the Franciscan ratline and other means in order to escape prosecution by the Allies. Only a month later Himmler was captured by the British, and just prior to his interrogation he bit down on a cyanide capsule hidden in his mouth. He was dead within minutes. And Walther was now left with Himmler's most sensitive files, at least those that weren't burned by the SS.

"As I told Father Michael at the abbey where we met," Jacob continued, "my grandfather was a close friend to Austrian Bishop Alois Hudal, a secret Nazi collaborator and chief organizer of the ratline network. As you will soon read, Walther gave Himmler's journal to the bishop who eventually handed it to Pope Pius personally. I have no idea what compelled Hudal to do so—perhaps it was some measure of guilt or even sycophancy—but I later learned that the Pope promptly had the journal buried somewhere in the Archives. Perhaps its contents were too damaging to Pius's claimed Nazi sympathies, it's hard to say.

"As for the Ahnenerbe," he concluded offhandedly, "I think it was disbanded after the war."

Hana looked at Jacob for a moment, considering something. Then, returning to the diary, she flipped further ahead to the next sections Jacob had marked, now several years later.

Wewelsburg – 4 December '44

Himmler is at odds with the Führer over many things—the destruction of the Jews, the demolition of the camps—they do not trust each other, and Germany is losing the war. Things look very bad. Himmler wants to safeguard the relic from the others: Göring, Speer, even Hitler himself.

...

Wewelsburg – 23 April '45

Himmler has hidden the artifact in a secret place, leaving only a riddle on three slips of paper indicating its location. He gave one coded fragment to me, and Bishop Hudal told me he received one, but the whereabouts of the third is known only to Himmler himself. The writing on it means nothing to me. Why would he do this? The man I knew so well seems to be losing his mind.

...

Milan, Italy – 7 Juni '45

The war is over. Hitler and Himmler are both dead. For now I remain in hiding under the protection of Bishop Hudal, to whom I have given Himmler's journal. Before leaving Wewelsburg the SS burned all of the Reichsführer's remaining files, as was protocol in the event of capitulation.

...

Milan, Italy – 17 Juli '45

Hudal tells me he gave Himmler's journal to the Pope as a gift, since the two were very close.

...

Santiago, Chile – 12 August '58

My secret work collaborating with West Germany's intelligence community is a very great challenge. But the Mossad hunts me still. Friends protect me, but the threat is persistent.

...

Bariloche, Argentina – 22 Januar '59

Had a wonderful visit with my old friends Erich Prager and Johann Kurtz, both who live now here in Bariloche. A lovely reconstructed German village, reminiscent of home. He too is still hunted by the Israelis.

...

Santiago, Chile – 23 Mai '60

The Israeli prime minister today announced the capture of Eichmann in Buenos Aires! I fear for poor Adolf, they will not be kind to him. The net is closing in. We of the Brotherhood are always looking over our shoulders.

...

Aside from the pendulous ticking of the hallway clock, the room was silent as Hana closed the diary.

'There's just so much to unpack here," Hana said, a distant look in her eyes. Looking up at Rausch, she asked, "So Walther worked for West German intelligence?"

"Yes," Rausch replied, "for about three years. He also collaborated with Chilean President Pinochet's secret police, both posts relying on his expertise having worked in Himmler's Reich Security Office."

"And who was this 'old friend' Erich Prager he visited?"

Rausch paused before answering. "Prager was just a Gestapo interpreter based in Rome who handled Nazi relations with the Vatican."

Hana was pensive, even slightly disturbed as she looked down at the closed diary in her lap.

"And what of this April 1945 entry discussing coded fragments of a riddle? It says Walther himself was given one by Himmler. Have you found that yet, Jacob?"

Rausch casually glanced out the window, avoiding eye contact with Hana. "No, I haven't found anything like that among my grandfather's things."

Hana knew he was lying. She paused before saying what she was thinking.

"If we're to help you with this, Jacob, we all need to be forthcoming with anything we find and everything we know. Even the smallest details matter. Would you agree?"

Rausch stood up and looked at Hana. "Yes, of course I understand. I'm telling you everything I know." There was slight irritation in his voice.

"Well, in any case, I'm afraid I have to agree with Jacob, Michael," she said. "If there's even the slightest chance, we must try to find that journal. Despite Himmler's dabbling in the occult, whatever this object is seems to have drawn significant interest at the highest levels. Aren't you curious as to what it was Rahn found? Speaking for myself, I think there's great story potential here. But think of what it could mean for the Church."

"I am curious, yes," Dominic said. "But mainly because Pope

Pius himself was involved, which—apart from his presumed affinity toward the Nazis—just seems highly unusual. I'm intrigued now, and you know what happens when I get curious."

Hana smiled, knowing the hunt was on.

CHAPTER 5

"Where do we start?" Rausch asked with a renewed look of eagerness.

Dominic opened his mouth to say something, but Hana spoke before he managed to get a word out.

"If you don't mind my saying, I think it's important to understand what's in this for Michael, or for the Vatican really, should he involve himself in such a project."

"Actually, I was about to say the same thing," Dominic said, taking her cue. "I do work for the Church, after all, and the Archive is not open to just anyone. It is the Pope's personal and private library.

"I think if I *am* to be involved, the Church must be able to claim rights of possession to anything we find based on materials held in the Vatican. Is that a condition you are prepared to accept?"

Having considered this as an obvious outcome, Rausch agreed. "Yes, of course. I only ask that I be allowed to read Himmler's journal first."

"First?" Hana asked, surprised at the request. "Why first?"

Rausch blushed again, then tried to find the words to support his appeal. It took a moment to find his ground.

"Well, I... I just thought that since I brought this to you, I'd have some involvement in its discovery."

"I certainly can't say you'll be *first* to read it, Jacob," Dominic said. "It's normally a complicated process to gain access to the reading rooms, but I'll do what I can. You'll have your chance if I can manage to get you in.

"As for where to begin, I'll first search on Bishop Hudal and any of his correspondence with Pope Pius. That may take a while. Will you be here in Paris over the next few days if I need to contact you?"

"Actually, I'm returning to Chile for a few days this week, to further attend to my grandfather's affairs, but I can join you in Rome when I finish my work there. Meanwhile, you can reach me at any time on my mobile or by email." He exchanged contact details with Dominic.

"I can't imagine where this search might lead us all, but I am grateful you came to me. This sounds like the kind of research adventure Hana and I have had some experience with." He turned to Hana and smiled knowingly. "But for now, I must get back to Rome. Thanks for your time, Jacob. I'm eager to see where this takes us."

After saying their goodbyes, Hana and Dominic left the building, walking alongside the canal as they searched for a taxi back to Hana's apartment.

"Michael, there's something off about this. I can't put my finger on it, but Jacob is definitely holding something back, and his personal motivations are unclear. I'm just not sure we can trust him."

"Well, he did seem unsettled discussing that riddle fragment," he said. "But regardless, I've learned to trust your instincts. Let's just keep an eye on him for now. So, will you be joining me in Rome?"

Hana thought for a moment. "First, I need to do some research here at the French National Bibliothèque and the Shoah Memorial. Their archives on the Nazis and the Holocaust are unparalleled. Once I've got some foundational information to share, why don't I meet you in Rome and we can review what we've got?"

"I was hoping you'd say that," Dominic said. "Sounds like a good plan. As for Jacob, we can bring him in once we have a better idea of what we're dealing with."

As they got into the taxi that stopped for them, one thing kept running through Dominic's mind. *Why did Jacob want to be the first to read Himmler's journal?*

CHAPTER 6

The Richelieu Library of the Bibliothèque Nationale de France, a grand neoclassical structure in the heart of Paris's 2nd Arrondissement, houses over 225,000 manuscripts dating back to the Middle Ages, including a sizable repository of Nazi-era books and documentation.

After finding what she needed to start with in the catalog—a couple biographies of Heinrich Himmler, facsimiles of Bishop Alois Hudal's archives, and available records and correspondence of SS Colonel Walther Rausch—Hana settled herself in her favorite place, the architecturally-fabled Labrouste Reading Room. Along with its arbor-styled cast iron pillars, terra cotta domes, and frescoed walls, it also featured elaborate paintings of clouds, trees, and squirrels overlooking rows of black leather-topped reading tables. Its glass-paned ceiling bathed the room in natural light.

Hana paged through the first Himmler biography seeking details of Wewelsburg Castle and the SS commander's penchant for the occult. She paused over the many photographs of the castle: its unusual triangular footprint on the diminutive town's landscape, the many mystical halls within, and especially the tall forbidding tower at the north end. One image in particular caught her attention: a large runic "Black Sun" mosaic inlaid on the marble floor of the Generals' Hall in the North Tower, a dark symbol of Aryan brotherhood. She discreetly removed her phone from her bag and took a photo of it.

Reading further, she was surprised and unsettled to find that this decades-old SS symbol was still being revered in current neo-Nazi and white supremacist movements, something she needed to know more about for the task ahead, while also dreading what she might find.

She learned that Himmler had been Roman Catholic all his life, but left the Church when he embraced the German *Gottgläubig* movement. That movement despised religious institutions in favor of belief in a higher power—God as the divine creator. They believed that in His wisdom God put the Führer and his Third Reich in power, elevating the German nation as morally superior to all others. Himmler did retain his faith in Jesus Christ, but did not recognize the Church's influence in spiritual matters. He even decreed that all SS personnel—at their peak numbering nearly a million soldiers— must renounce their affiliations with any church under threat of expulsion from the ranks of the elite *Schutzstaffel*.

But it was reading about the strange and powerful Ahnenerbe that really got her attention, a history she had to share with Michael. Despite its exotic yet implausible mission, it had a significant foundational influence throughout the Third Reich. It made her wonder what life would be like today if Germany had won World War II.

HER WORK FINISHED at the Bibliothèque for the time being, Hana hailed a taxi for the ten-minute drive to the Shoah Memorial, Paris's Holocaust Museum and library. With over thirty million digitized documents and hundreds of thousands of original photographs depicting one of history's darkest events, she was certain to learn more about Himmler and hopefully Bishop Alois Hudal, Himmler's vile collaborator and post-war protector.

As she exited the taxi and made her way to the entrance of the Shoah library, Hana passed through a labyrinth of tall white stone walls in the Forecourt, on which were engraved the names of 76,000 Jews who were deported from France and savagely put to death at the most notorious concentration camps—Auschwitz-Birkenau, Sobibor, Lublin, Majdanek and Kaunas/Reval—all in just the two years from 1942 to 1944. She noticed several mourners reading the names on the wall, many of them old women dressed in black with headscarves, their hands clasping white kerchiefs to wipe away tears as they lightly swayed back and forth in prayer. She felt moved herself at the vast and unnecessary loss of life. In that moment, her mission strengthened. There was a great debt to be paid.

Entering the memorial she made her way to the archives, where she paged through the computerized index for the materials she was seeking, making notes of titles and location codes to give the librarian.

"Bonjour," she said as she approached the reference desk attendant, an elderly man wearing a black yarmulke with a

cascading white border. "I would like access, please, to this list of materials and one book."

The librarian peered closely at the list through thick bifocals, then silently walked toward the back of the stacks. A couple minutes later he came out with just the book, placing it on the desk. It was a worn copy of Bishop Alois Hudal's 1976 biography, *Roman Diaries: Confessions of an Old Bishop*.

"Mademoiselle, here is the book you seek, but the other materials are available in our digital archive. You may use one of the computers in our multimedia room." He pointed in the general direction to her right.

"*Merci beaucoup,* monsieur," she acknowledged, then set off to find a computer. Walking through the solemn space, she passed through the main exhibition gallery featuring all manner of Holocaust-related memorabilia: gruesome photographs of bodies piled high; scores of letters from victims to their families, many never delivered; thousands of photographs of deported children. The tragic reality of it all made her heart ache.

By the time Hana found the multimedia center, with its rows of redwood tables on which sat several computer stations, a sense of overwhelming sadness had taken hold of her. Knowing she would encounter even more desolation in the work ahead, she had to compartmentalize what she had seen and deal with the emotional impact later.

Launching the library's special search browser, she tapped in various search phrases for '*Heinrich Himmler*' and '*Walther Rausch*.' The number of results returned was formidable, so she narrowed her searches down using long-tail keywords such as '*Heinrich Himmler + Walther Rausch*,' which returned 124 results. *That's more like it*, she thought.

She scrolled through mostly old news clippings of Nazi propaganda: photos of the two men together at official ceremonies, one with both of them standing on the marble Black Sun in the Generals' Hall of Wewelsburg Castle, another of them surveying a concentration camp scene at Auschwitz, with scores of terribly gaunt Jewish prisoners lining the barbed wire fence separating them from the fat Nazis standing outside the perimeter. The guards were smiling and pointing, as if they were admiring animals in a zoo, a cruel contrast in human dignity.

Hana paged through the remaining results but failed to find anything of substance as it related to a religious artifact or mention of any other kind of unique discovery. There was further discussion of the Ahnenerbe, the strange organization Jacob had spoken of, which she read carefully while adding to her notes from the Bibliothèque.

Finished with the computer, she logged out, picked up her bag and Hudal's book and made her way to one of the more comfortable chairs in the reading room.

Opening the book, she first noted that it had been published posthumously, in 1976, since Hudal died in 1963. She wondered who had taken the time and effort to do something like this thirteen years after the bishop's death, and what the real purpose was. From what little she knew, Hudal didn't seem like the kind of historical figure that deserved the honor of a posthumous work.

She checked the table of contents to see if anything jumped out relating to Otto Rahn and Wewelsburg Castle. Finding nothing of either, she continued paging through the book, scanning various entries.

Though she was aware of Hudal's deplorable ratline and his collaboration with the Nazis, not to mention his falling out with the Vatican's own leadership over policy differences, much of what she read seemed to be of an unrepentant nature, some of it even galling. One passage she read in Hudal's own words made her sick with revulsion:

"I thank God that He opened my eyes and allowed me to visit and comfort many victims in their prisons and concentration camps and [to help] them escape with false identity papers."

The "victims" he speaks of here, however, were *Nazi* prisoners of war—and their "concentration camps" were Allied detention camps. Hudal cared little if anything for the Jews, but he was a brazen apologist for the Nazis.

In the center of the book was an insert of many pages featuring photographs on glossy white paper. As she paged through these, most of them of banal interest, she noted that the editor had included many items of Nazi memorabilia found among the bishop's possessions, including several examples of letters he had written.

Turning a page, she came across something quite strange. On it was pictured a single piece of paper in the odd form of an SS insignia, on which had been written several incomplete sentences in German Sütterlin cursive, where 'f's were long 's's and other letterforms had clustered ligatures and diacritical marks. She was tempted to tear out the page and take it with her, it was so fascinating—but there was already enough guilt and remorse in this sacred space. Instead, she took out her phone and snapped a photo of it.

Hana studied it carefully, curious as to why it was included in the book at all, since there was no description beneath it apart from its being found among Hudal's memorabilia collection. The fact that it appeared in the style of an SS symbol was a little creepy, she thought. She managed to translate what was written on it, but could make little sense of it.

…key to ope…
…door you can…
…always walk…
…sometimes but can…

…hat place…
…in the face…
…swings free to…
…and you now must…

...in hand you should ...
...center of the solar...
...face of God's...
...under the black...

She imagined it was some kind of 4-line verse in what looked to be three stanzas. *But why would it be cut off on either side, and unusually so? Maybe there were other fragments that joined both sides so that the entire message could be read. That seemed logical. Yet, there was something familiar here...*

Then it came to her—*This has got to be one of Himmler's coded fragments Walther Rausch spoke of in his diary!*

That she had stumbled on it so innocently had both shaken and delighted her. She couldn't wait to share this with Michael when they compared notes.

CHAPTER 7

A s he emerged from the elevator to the underground Apostolic Archives beneath the Vatican's Pigna Courtyard, Michael Dominic strode toward the index desk under pools of amber light high above that automatically detected his presence, lighting his path along the 53 linear miles of the massive section known as the Gallery of the Metallic Shelves, lights which then extinguished when no movement was detected. He knew by now that he simply had to keep moving, else find himself left in the pitch dark subterranean chamber where, for hundreds of years, the Church's archives had been maintained with no natural light to pollute its fragile inventory.

Sitting at the computer, he switched on the desk lamp then initiated a search on Bishop Alois Hudal. If there was anything on him—and more importantly, if it had been properly indexed, since millions of documents were sealed up in thousands of crates and still remained uncatalogued—he would find it here. His chances were good, since most extant World War II documents had already been indexed since the war.

The search results returned were encouraging. Dominic found many letters between Hudal and various members of the Curia, not surprising since the bishop's career was one of political turmoil, especially during and after the war. Hudal publicly praised Adolf Hitler and his intentions for the Third Reich, and was hardly discreet in his widely known opposition to Vatican policies. But he was a powerful representative of the Austrian Catholic Church, with a broad network of other influential clergy and political leaders, which went a long way toward retaining his post.

Even today many in the Church defended Hudal, claiming that a Pontifical Aid Commission had been a legitimate effort to supply a sort of papal mercy program for National Socialists and Fascists. In the process, hundreds of thousands of legitimate refugees were assisted, and that some Nazi war criminals simply took advantage of this, slipping in without Hudal's direct knowledge. Although Michael found that a difficult claim to believe considering the materials Hudal himself wrote of his infatuation with and support of the Nazi movement.

Hudal was especially close to *SS-Reichsführer* Heinrich Himmler, often advising him on matters of policy and strategies important to both the Vatican and the Nazi Party, and ultimately smoothing the way for Himmler's escape from Allied prosecution by way of the Franciscan ratline after Germany lost the war.

As Dominic paged through the correspondence, he discovered one letter in particular addressed to Pope Pius XII from September 1946, in which Hudal was gifting Himmler's last personal journal to the Pope, a year after the SS leader's death. No reason was stated for the offering, which Dominic found curious. *There must have been some purpose*, he thought. *But why? What did Hudal have in mind?*

At the bottom of the letter, beneath Hudal's cramped signature, was a papal notation in Latin, presumably to the Holy Father's secretary: *"Ponere in ephemeride Riserva."*—meaning "Place the journal in the Riserva." Beneath that was the Pope's own embellished signature, *"Pius pp.XII."*

The Riserva had long been the enigmatic closed section of the

Secret Archives where the Vatican's most sensitive documents were stored. No one was permitted inside the secured Riserva without the presence of the Prefect—Dominic himself, in this case—though one other key was held by whomever was Secretary of State at the time. Now that was Cardinal Enrico Petrini, who happened to be Michael Dominic's godfather and mentor throughout his life.

The priest stood up and made his way to the far reaches of the Gallery, following the spontaneous pools of light to the heavy wooden door of the Riserva. Reaching behind his head, he grasped a black leather cord from around his neck which held the key, then unlocked the steel-reinforced door and swung it open, switching on the light.

The vault was about six hundred square feet in size, with stacks of metal shelving along the walls and an enormous 17th-century *armadio*, or poplar cabinet, flush against the back wall. The floor, walls, and ceiling were composed of seamless cellular concrete with two low-level incandescent lighting fixtures hung from the ceiling. A vent on one wall maintained a gentle flow of conditioned air, and a gauge near the light switch indicated 35% relative humidity, ideal conditions for strict archival conservation.

Only the most highly-valued, secret, or potentially controversial materials were safeguarded in the Riserva. It was where Dominic had been instructed by the Pope to conceal the scandalous Magdalene papyrus only a year earlier, and where he had found, quite by accident, the telltale documents leading to its discovery. It was a room he was quite familiar with, his most treasured place in all the Vatican.

Except for the *armadio*, the room's contents were generally classified by year, then alphabetically. Working the shelves first, Dominic started with the section labeled "MCMXLVI"—1946 in Roman numerals, for the Vatican still operated largely in Latin— and began leafing through old file folders and thick binders of material looking for Heinrich Himmler's journal.

After some thirty minutes perusing the items stacked on the 1946 shelf, nothing even resembling a journal was found. That meant it was likely inside the *armadio*.

The great poplar cabinet, bearing the House of Borghese coat of arms in golden bas-relief—owing to that noble family's close historical ties to the Vatican, including one Pope and numerous cardinals—contained the most secret documents of the Church. *If Himmler's journal is in here*, thought Dominic, *it must be very special indeed*.

After its two adjoining doors creaked open, Dominic pulled a step ladder over from near the wall, needed to reach the higher shelves inside. On the lower section were a series of twelve wide stacked drawers, each three-inches high, used to store large flat documents such as maps, broadsheets, long palimpsests, and considerably sized documents. Such oversized documents included King Henry VIII's 1530 parchment dispatched by members of England's House of Lords to Pope Clement VII in support of the King's divorce from Catherine of Aragon. The three-foot-by-six-foot parchment had attached to it 80 red wax seals, signatories of the Lords' affirming of the King's request— which the Pope ultimately denied. That action led to Henry rejecting the Church's authority and installing himself as the head of the Church of England. Dominic was always moved seeing, and especially holding, this magnificent historical document, which was rarely shown publicly.

Starting with the top shelf he began searching for anything that gave the appearance of a WWII-era journal, as opposed to other obvious Curial books or sheaves of bound documents having unrelated markings.

It was only when he reached the third shelf down that he spotted a stiff black leather-bound, 3-hole pegged volume that looked like it might qualify as a ledger of some sort. Pulling it out from the depths of the cabinet he turned it face up. There, stamped in gold leaf, was the infamous name: "*H. Himmler.*"

Though Dominic was accustomed to seeing all manner of

intoxicating materials, the hair on the back of his neck stood up when he recognized what he was holding. Removing the book from the *armadio*, he placed it on the wobbly wooden table in the room and pulled up a similar chair, ready to explore the high-ranking Nazi's final years.

CHAPTER 8

Pulling open the black leather cover as he sat beneath the soft light, Dominic first admired its organizational elements: the yellowed journal pages lined with columns for date and remarks; Himmler's uncommonly precise handwriting, with a sharp up-and-down cursive as opposed to heavily slanted in either direction; his preferred use of a fountain pen with black India ink. This was a man who knew his lasting importance in history, albeit an evil one as historians would record. Men in particular—especially titans of war, politics and industry—set down their accomplishments with pride, how they viewed the world and their influence in it, while women who kept diaries typically recorded more subtle, emotional nuances of their lives and the people in them. Himmler's was filled with bold achievements and reflections on his largely unmitigated power and dominion over others.

Himmler began keeping diaries when he was just ten, having produced scores over his relatively brief life, since he died at age 44. Dominic had read that many of those journals had scattered to the winds, ending up in private collections or archives. The most recent ones to appear were discovered in Russian military archives in 2013, where they had been stored unbeknownst to anyone for 70 years, since the Red Army had confiscated them at the end of the war. Those typed diaries had been transcribed by Himmler's secretaries recording his official activities between roughly the same years as the journal Dominic now held, 1937 through 1945. In one, Himmler's dictation—or transcription by his assistants—easily moved from a jovial scene of having snacks with his men at a concentration camp, to ordering the mass murder of Jews a few moments later. In another entry, he ordered that fresh guard dogs be assigned to Auschwitz that were able to tear people "to shreds." The recorded entries in those diaries were nothing short of repugnant.

But the one laying on the desk before him had been written in the first person by Himmler himself, as Dominic had studied the man's handwriting style in preparation for his search—acute vertical strokes with broad angular descenders, evenly spaced. He had no doubt this was written in Himmler's own hand.

Dominic began reading, translating from German to English. For whatever reason, there were great gaps of time between recorded dates, and most of the entries were of an architectural or expeditionary nature. As he scanned the pages, several passages stood out, most of them written while Himmler was in residence at his beloved Wewelsburg Castle.

2 Feb 1935 - Berlin Headquarters
Met with Otto Rahn. A brilliant writer, he is fully informed on Grail legends with emphasis on Wolfram von Eschenbach's "Parzival." Appointed him to my personal staff to lead archeological expeditions.

...

21 Apr 1936 - Schloss Wewelsburg
Sent Rahn to Iceland with 20 SS troops to study the 13th-century Norse Eddas, essential to documenting the Aryan brotherhood.

...

12 Okt 1937 - Schloss Wewelsburg

Promoted Otto Rahn to Untersturmfuhrer. Sent him back to Montségur and Rennes-le-Château in the French Languedoc, on a mission to find the Grail.

…

9 Nov 1937 - Schloss Wewelsburg

Rahn returned from Languedoc expedition. There he discovered the sacred Veil of Veronica, brought to France by Mary Magdalene herself! It is said to possess incredible powers—bringing sight to the blind, and even raising the dead! It must have come from the tomb of Christ himself (John 20:3-7).

…

22 Okt 1938 - Schloss Wewelsburg

Reconstruction of the castle is in full progress, built by Jew prisoners from the nearby Sachsenhausen camp. Three chambers in the North Tower will be of special significance, the Hall of Pillars and the Hall of Dead Heroes, and both will have twelve symbolic marble columns. And the center of the Generals' Hall will feature our great runic symbol, the Schwarze Sonne. The Veil is now secured in my secret vault.

…

Dominic stopped reading and abruptly sat up. A shiver passed through him. *"The sacred Veil of Veronica"?!* He was stunned at the mere thought of it. He was certainly aware of the legend of Veronica and the offering to Jesus of her own veil to cleanse the blood and sweat from his face as he carried the cross on the road to Calvary. *Is this what Rahn actually discovered in Rennes-le-Château? Were even those legends true?*

Noting Himmler's reference to the Gospel of John, he reached for his bible, flipped to the New Testament, and read the marked passage, Chapter 20, Verses 3-7:

"So Peter and the other disciple started for the tomb. Both were running, but the other disciple outran Peter and reached the tomb first.

He bent over and looked in at the strips of linen lying there but did not go in. Then Simon Peter came along behind him and went straight into the tomb. **He saw the strips of linen lying there, as well as the cloth that had been wrapped around Jesus' head. The cloth was still lying in its place, separate from the linen…"**

Could the Veil that Himmler possessed really be one of the cloths found in the tomb?! Dominic also knew the legend of the burial linen itself, assumed by many today to be the Shroud of Turin, though that had its own questionable authenticity as a result of recent carbon dating.

Returning to the journal he scanned through the rest of the entries, most of which dealt with operational notations and such, still with large time gaps between entries, until he reached the very last record in the journal:

24 Apr 1945 - Berlin

In secret talks with the British to negotiate my surrender. Hitler is raving mad, relieving top generals of their commands, even me. Everyone is fleeing now. For my own safety I have given three coded fragments—one each to Walther Rausch, Bishop Alois Hudal, and Erich Prager—indicating the location of the Veil. They must be read together to decode the riddle. I only ask that my friends use it to take care of my family should any harm come to me.

Dominic was mesmerized. Can this get any more bizarre?

He knew Himmler was to die the following month—suicide by cyanide while in the hands of the British in May 1945. That these were likely his final written words was both riveting and repellent, apart from the shocking and unexpected mention of the Veil.

There was much to process here. He needed to learn more, and to speak with both Hana and his old friend Simon Ginzberg. Though it might be a long shot, he really wanted to find those coded fragments.

He closed the doors to the *armadio,* tucked the journal under his arm, then locked the door to the Riserva and headed back through the amber pools of light to the elevator, excitement spurring his every step.

CHAPTER 9

The ornate, sunlit Pius XI, or "Pio" Reading Room of the Apostolic Archive features a long row of Brazilian cherrywood reading tables, accommodating two patrons at each one beneath tall white domed ceilings. The walls on the lower floor of the long rectangular room house rows of books and document binders, above which are downlights casting an iridescent yellow hue across the shelves, as if patrons were sitting in a gauntlet of golden walls.

One of those patrons, a man with a small head of spare white hair but sporting a neatly trimmed Van Dyke, sat with his head bent over his work, thick reading glasses perched atop his aquiline nose.

Dr. Simon Ginzberg, professor emeritus in medieval studies at Teller University in nearby Zagarolo, had been a fixture in the Vatican Archives for well over a decade, one of the few scholars allowed virtually unrestricted access to the Archives' treasures. His primary focus of study, especially of late, had been researching the ambiguous advocacy Pope Pius XII may have had for the Nazis during World War II—Ginzberg's goal being not so much to upbraid the Church's role in history under Pius's reign as to simply shed light on it.

As he sat there, deep in thought while studying a set of Pius' recently released papers, the sound of approaching footsteps on the marble floor caught his ear. He looked up, then smiled broadly as he recognized his visitor.

"Michael! How marvelous to see you, my friend."

Father Dominic pulled a chair over and sat down, placing the Himmler journal on the table and clasping his hands over it.

"Good to see you're still at it, Simon," he said. "How goes the work?"

"Well, it's way too early to know anything concrete at this stage," Ginzberg replied, "but Pius certainly had an interesting reign as pontiff, during very troubling times. Truth be told, I admire the man a great deal, though from what I'm finding, there may be much to account for. As it is with all such grave historical matters, time will tell, eh? Now, to what do I owe the pleasure of your visit today?"

"Well, a few days ago I met a young man while I was on retreat in France…" Dominic began, as he unfolded the story about Jacob Rausch, his grandfather's role in the Nazi Party, Walther Rausch's diary, and its mention of Himmler's journal archived in the Vatican since the war.

"It's been locked away in the Riserva since Pius XII had it put there, Simon, and I just found it. I think you'll find the content more than interesting."

At the mention of Pius XII's involvement with Himmler's journal, Dominic now had Ginzberg's full attention. The old scholar's eyebrows shot up with interest. He leaned in closer.

Dominic opened the journal to the pages mentioning Wewelsburg Castle and the Veil and slid it across the table to Simon. As he read the words, one bony finger gliding beneath each sentence, his eyes opened wider. He looked up at Dominic, then back down again at the journal.

"This is an absolutely extraordinary find, Michael! I mean, yes, the journal itself is remarkable in a historical sense, of course. But do you really think Himmler possessed the veil reflecting the 'true image' of Christ? That would be incredible!

"As I recall," he continued eagerly, "three such veils are known to exist, but each has issues of provenance. One is known to be in a tiny Capuchin church in the Italian Abruzzi town of Manoppello, a sacred cloth locals call *Il Volto Santo*. The Holy Face. It has been there for some four hundred years, and bears an identical likeness to the same image revealed on the Shroud of Turin—which has its own authenticity in question.

"Another is the well-known Sudarium of Oviedo, in the custody of the Cathedral of San Salvador in Spain. While carbon dating put its age at around 700 CE, its historical presence has actually been documented as being much earlier, at around 570, but no sooner than that.

"And lastly, there's one in Rome, here in St. Peter's Basilica itself. But that one has questionable provenance at best and is even held by most to be a fake. In fact, many believe the original veil the Vatican once possessed was stolen hundreds of years ago and is actually the one found today in Manoppello. All of these are shrouded in some mystery or other, having passed through various hands during military conflicts or other dubious escapades. History is replete with those preoccupied with acquiring religious iconography.

"But, I have read scholarly works describing the legend of a woman named Beronikē, who wiped the blood and sweat from Jesus' face as he carried the cross on the Via Dolorosa, and Beronikē, knowing Mary Magdalene was Jesus's favorite disciple, had given the veil to her. This is not posed in the canonical gospels, of course, but the apocrypha do mention similar stories.

"In all likelihood, there was no person actually named Veronica. The most famous cloth bearing the likeness of Jesus was called a *'vera icon*,'" Latin for 'true image.' Over time, the popular lexicon mistook this as meaning the name of a person.

So, according to various traditions in many countries, *'vera icon'* has come to be 'Veronica.'

"If this is the same cloth found in the empty tomb by the Magdalene—who may have placed it there herself when Jesus was buried—then that brings this particular mystery back around full circle. But to think it may have ended up in the hands of such a monster as Himmler is beyond the pale! He did have a fanatical zeal for collecting religious artifacts, as evidenced by his association with the German medievalist Otto Rahn, and his expeditions sponsored by the Ahnenerbe and the Thule Society. But those efforts were undertaken to support Hitler's bold assertion that Jesus was Aryan, not Jewish."

"And what about these 'Norse Eddas' Himmler mentions?" Dominic asked. "What are they, and what significance do they have?"

"Well, nothing as related to the veil itself, but Nordic mythology served as the foundation of the Third Reich. Hitler had appropriated Old Norse symbolism in the form of the swastika and even the *Schutzstaffel's* runic SS insignia, both of which were derived from ancient Nordic symbology going back to the age of the Vikings, a strong, resistant race known for their large-scale raiding and conquest of Europe. These qualities impressed Hitler such that he moved mountains to establish German linkages to the noble Norsemen.

"The Eddas are a 13th-century set of two books that relate the mythologies of idealist perfectionism in Scandinavian culture. I can certainly see why Himmler would want to study them, to bolster Hitler's glorious Aryan worldview."

As always, Dominic was dazzled by Simon's wealth of historical knowledge.

His rheumy eyes sparkling with intrigue, Ginzberg removed his glasses and pinched the bridge of his nose as his mind absorbed what he had just read.

"These coded riddle fragments... Have you any idea yet

where they might be? Did your young Mr. Rausch give some clue as to his grandfather's own fragment?"

"I'm afraid he's been rather elusive on that point," Dominic said. "Hana feels he knows more than he's telling, but for what reasons we couldn't say. Not yet, anyway."

Ginzberg looked quizzically at the young priest, then smiled. "I sense you may be on to yet another adventure, yes?"

Dominic laughed and blushed. "You know me so well, Simon. This isn't likely something Hana or I can avoid at this stage. She sees a good story here, and if there's any chance I might be able to find the actual veil given to Mary Magdalene, well, I think you know my answer. I'll be meeting up with Hana here soon, let's see what she has to add."

THE MUTED PHONE on Hana's desk in her Paris apartment hummed with an incoming call. Looking over at it she saw it was from Michael. Smiling, she picked it up.

"I was just thinking of calling you," she answered. "You won't—"

"—You won't believe what I found!" Dominic said in a gush. They both laughed. "I assume you were about to say the same thing?"

"Yes, I was. If tomorrow's good for you, I'll catch the first flight to Rome. We have a lot to go over."

"Well, here's something for you to consider in the meantime. Himmler had apparently acquired the so-called *Veil of Veronica*, the legendary sweat cloth having Christ's image on it! *That's* the artifact he put in his secret vault at Wewelsburg Castle. It wasn't the Holy Grail. After spending time reading Himmler's journal —which I *did* find, by the way—I had a long talk with Simon. There is so much to share, Hana."

"Wait... Michael, you mean the actual veil itself? Do you think... well, let's not get into all this now; I'm meeting my grandfather here shortly. But I can't wait to talk. So, I'll see you tomorrow, probably around noon."

"Actually, why don't I just pick you up at the airport and we'll go to your hotel straight away?" Dominic said. "I'll take a couple days off work."

"Better yet!" Hana said happily. "It's Air France flight 1104, arriving Fiumicino at 11:35. See you then."

CHAPTER 10

Hana's grandfather, Baron Armand de Saint-Clair, had long maintained a suite at the Rome Cavalieri Waldorf Astoria, among the more upscale hotels in the Eternal City. Saint-Clair's banking business often brought him to Rome, and as a member of the Pope's elite *Consulta*, he also often met with the pontiff while he was in town.

Though the baron was traveling elsewhere at the moment, Hana also enjoyed residential privileges in the Cavalieri's Palermo Suite when she visited Rome, which is where Dominic took her after they left the airport in a car borrowed from the Vatican motor pool. As the porter unloaded her bags from the luggage cart, Dominic took a seat at the suite's elegant dining table and laid out his research: the Himmler journal he had brought from the Archives and the correspondence he found in Bishop Hudal's file.

"Care for a drink, Michael?"

"Just water, thanks. But let's keep a distance between liquids and these documents." He looked up at her expectantly. She knew the drill when he was working with rare documents. Hana sat down across from him, her own glass on the credenza behind her.

"Okay, what have we got here?" she asked, staring at Himmler's gold-leafed name on the black leather journal. "The history in that book alone has got to be captivating."

Dominic opened Himmler's book to the first page he had marked and slid it over for Hana to read. Like Simon, her face soon evolved from one of mild anticipation to rapt engagement.

"So, Otto Rahn actually did find something at Rennes-le-Château or Montségur, as the legends contend," she noted. "It's sure been kept secret all these years. Rahn died in 1939 and apparently never mentioned it after its discovery sixteen months earlier. At least nothing that became public, as far as I know."

"I expect the Nazis had something to do with that," Dominic said. "Himmler would have held him to absolute secrecy about the veil, probably under threat of death. Rahn did lose Himmler's confidence later, though, which may have precipitated poor Otto's demise on the frozen slopes of an Austrian mountain. He had resigned from the SS shortly before, but it's like the Mafia—nobody could just up and leave the SS without consequences."

"I barely remember the story of Veronica's veil from childhood," Hana said. "Isn't that the sweat cloth Saint Veronica pressed upon Jesus to cleanse his wounds on his way to the crucifixion?"

"Well, not according to Simon," Dominic said. He told her of Ginzberg's elaborate story of all the purportedly authentic veils and the mistaken oral tradition of Beronikē on the road to Calvary. He also showed her its biblical reference in the Gospel of John.

"So," he continued, "none of these can actually be proven to be the one, true image of Christ, at least not without further examination, but each cloth remains under such obsessive security by its caretaker—and faith being a much stronger inspiration than scientific analysis—that it's not likely to happen any time soon. For that matter, if we *do* find Himmler's veil—

and that's a big if—we'd put it through exhaustive testing ourselves."

Hana turned back to the journal to continue reading. When she got to the October 1938 entry, she stopped cold and looked across the table with a sudden recollection. "Michael, he mentions here a *'great runic symbol, the Schwarze Sonne!'* In German that's translated as *'Black Sun.'* In my research at the French National Library I found a Himmler biography with photos of Wewelsburg Castle, and one of them featured an inlaid runic black sun on the marble floor of the Generals' Hall."

She reached into her bag for her iPhone, launched the Photos app, and showed Dominic the haunting image of the Black Sun she'd taken from the book.

"There's something else," Dominic added, turning to the last entry in the journal and pointing it out to Hana. He waited for her expected reaction.

Hana read the passage—about Himmler handing out three coded fragments—then fairly leapt out of her chair, startling Michael. Which wasn't the reaction he had anticipated.

"I found one of those fragments! I'm sure that's what it was." She flipped through the photos on the phone until she came to the SS image. She showed it to Michael.

"This was in Bishop Hudal's biography along with other photos of his life and possessions. I had no idea what it was but decided to take a picture of it anyway. I'm glad I did."

Dominic looked at the photo, his face screwed up in confusion. "What does it mean? And why is it so strangely formed?"

"I transcribed what I could make of it. Here, read it yourself…" As she spoke she pulled out her notebook and slid it across to Michael. He scanned the gibberish.

"Obviously we need the other fragments to make any sense of this," he remarked. "It's amazing you actually found one. So we now have Hudal's, meaning Rausch's and Prager's are still in the wind."

"Michael, as I said before, I'm convinced Jacob knows more about his grandfather's fragment than he's telling us. I'd bet he's already found it among his grandfather's things. But why would he hold it back from us if he's seeking our help? So many things just don't add up."

She stared at the fragment on her phone, thinking. "This looks to be the middle piece, since there are obviously words missing before and after what's shown here. That would make this fragment the most essential, I'd imagine. But we need all three to at least read the riddle. Then there's the matter of solving it, of course.

"I'm going to call Jacob and just ask him straight up. It's morning in Santiago, he should be up by now."

CHAPTER 11

At the foot of the Andes Mountains bordering a mammoth glacial lake known as Nahuel Huapi lies the picturesque city of San Carlos de Bariloche, a jewel in the Patagonia region of Argentina.

Known for its charming Swiss alpine-style architecture and world-class ski resorts, Bariloche is home to upland geese and southern lapwings, local craft beers and fine chocolates, and copper-colored lenga trees overlooking crystal clear waters and vast valleys blanketed with the flush of spring wildflowers.

It was also home to some 9,000 Nazis who fled Allied prosecution at the end of World War II, and whose families still populate this largely German region of South America.

Perhaps its most famous Nazi resident—apart from the long-running rumors that Adolf Hitler himself had escaped to Bariloche on a U-boat from Spain—was SS-*Hauptsturmführer* Erich Prager, the senior commandant of the notorious 1944 Ardeatine massacre in Rome. In the course of protecting their city, Italian resistance fighters had killed 33 German SS police personnel, and Hitler vowed to retaliate by executing ten Italians for each dead German. On the *Führer's* command, Prager ordered the slaughter of 335 Italian civilians as revenge, including two he personally shot in the head.

After the war, Prager—assisted by the good graces of Austrian Bishop Alois Hudal—escaped to Vatican City, where Hudal provided him with false travel papers to Argentina. Settling in Bariloche, Prager, one of the world's most-wanted Nazis, had lived there as a free man for over fifty years.

THE CERVECERÍA PATAGONIA was hosting a lively crowd of mostly German tourists as Jacob Rausch and Christof Prager sat inside at a high-top table near the window overlooking the lake. They had both ordered local beers, and as the waiter set them on the table, white foam dribbling down the sides of the tall glasses fell onto their cardboard deckels.

"I may have already told them too much, Christof," Jacob said as he looked uneasily at his companion. "Father Dominic's friend is a reporter for *Le Monde*. She called and left a voicemail this morning, wanting to talk. The last thing we want is publicity. You should have seen how her interest sparked when I laid out the story. Perhaps I should not have mentioned the Ahnenerbe in such stark and adverse terms. What should I say when I call her back?"

Christof took a long draw on his beer as he listened, unconcerned about the reporter's curiosity.

"You may be worried for nothing, Jacob," he said, looking out across the lake. "The Ahnenerbe has always been and will always be. We are well-entrenched worldwide and will only expand. I doubt *Le Monde* will view that as 'news.' Call her back. See what she has to say.

"In the meantime, we must find the other missing fragments to Herr Himmler's riddle. The piece you found in your grandfather's diary is useless without the other two—the missing links to Himmler's Grail, or whatever it is, and the only way we can truly fund our mission in a major way. I have one buyer in mind who would pay enormously for such an artifact, if and when it can be found. If Hitler himself wanted it so badly, so will other discerning collectors."

Jacob handled his phone nervously, his thumbs sliding across the blank screen as he decided what to do. "I'll be right back."

He stood up, grabbed his ski jacket, and made for the door. Stepping outside he shrugged the jacket collar in closer, fending off the cold Patagonia wind blowing across the lake as he stood on the sidewalk outside the bar. He tapped the phone number shown on the voicemail message.

After two rings Hana Sinclair answered.

"Hana, this is Jacob Rausch, returning your call."

"Hi, Jacob, thanks for calling back. If you've got a few minutes I have something to ask. But first, some good news: Father Dominic found Himmler's journal in the Vatican Archives."

Jacob nearly jumped, he was so elated. "That's fantastic! When can I see it?"

"Well, he's afraid that won't be possible due to Vatican access restrictions, at least for now. There was a great deal of information we found in it, though, much of it utterly compelling. But there's something else: I discovered one of Himmler's riddle fragments, the one he gave to Bishop Hudal."

In the long pause that followed, his face froze with a mixture of elation and dread. His mouth dropped open, and his warm breath created a misty cloud in the chilly air. He turned to look at Christof sitting inside. Their eyes met, and at once Christof knew something important had occurred.

"What...what does it say?" Jacob asked her haltingly.

"Well, it's impossible to transcribe without the two missing fragments, and that's our next mission—finding your grandfather's piece and the other one that was given to this 'Erich Prager' your grandfather mentioned.

"My question is, are you sure you've looked everywhere for

something like that? It's on aged paper shaped in the form of an SS insignia, by the way, so it should stand out if you do see it. Maybe if you looked through Walther's things again you might find it?"

Jacob was momentarily paralyzed. He had to think quickly, to buy time, then speak with Christof as to what to do.

"It's possible I may have overlooked something, yes. I'll go back again, now that I know what I'm looking for, and see if I've missed it."

"That's a good idea, Jacob," she said. "And how do we find anything on Prager's associates? You're in Chile, right? Can you visit Bariloche in Argentina while you're there, maybe do some research? We *must* find those other fragments."

He needed a diversion. "Hana, I'm standing outside a bar in the freezing cold. Can I think about that and get back to you?"

"Sure, find someplace warm. But do give some thought to our dilemma here."

"Oh, one last thing," Jacob asked. "Is there a chance you could email me an image of that fragment, so I know what I'm looking for?"

Hana hesitated before answering. "Sure. I'll send a photo to you in a few minutes. Let's talk soon, alright?"

After exchanging goodbyes, they ended the call.

Jacob rushed back into the bar excitedly, yanked off his jacket and hung it on the back of his chair, then sat down, smiling at Christof.

"Father Dominic and Hana found Himmler's journal! She couldn't tell me much of what it contained, and they can't let me see it yet—something to do with Vatican protocol—but it did mention that the third fragment was given to your grandfather. So now I expect they'll be exploring that lead.

"But the best part is—Hana found the middle piece! Hudal's fragment! And she's sending an image of it to me here shortly!"

"Jacob, this is fantastic!" Christof said with a wide grin, which quickly vanished. "But we still need that third fragment. I haven't found it among my grandfather's things. I wonder what he did with it...."

Catching the waiter's eye, Jacob held up two fingers indicating another round of beers.

A few moments later his phone vibrated with an incoming message. He glanced up at his companion with a look of pride on his face as he opened the email app.

In it was the promised message from Hana, with an attachment. Tapping on the image opened it, filling the screen with a tiny picture in the shape of an SS insignia, as she had described.

But the low resolution image was so small that even enlarging it with his fingers made the highly pixelated writing impossible to make out. It was nothing more than a large muddle of black strokes.

Jacob and Christof looked at each other despairingly.

They needed another plan.

CHAPTER 12

Pleased with herself on the way she had minimized the image of the Hudal fragment—thus making it indecipherable—Hana had fulfilled Jacob's request while retaining control of the fragment she and Michael had decided to keep closely guarded.

The next step was learning more about Erich Prager. She had found much about him online—that after fifty years living in Bariloche he was finally arrested for war crimes, and spent the last 17 years of his life in Rome having been extradited there from Argentina in 1996. Years of court battles had taken place while he was under house arrest, but he eventually died in 2013 at age 100 from natural causes, before any final judgments on his case could be made.

Hana found it troubling that Jacob had downplayed Prager's role in the war, describing him earlier as *"just a Gestapo interpreter who handled Nazi relations with the Vatican,"* when he was evidently a widely recognized war criminal. *Why would he minimize Prager's vicious crimes?* she thought. If anything, wouldn't he have wanted to downplay his own grandfather's role and lay more blame elsewhere, like on Prager? Something to keep in mind.

But she was also curious as to what family may have survived Erich Prager, and what, if any, journals or memorabilia *he* might have left. This kind of job was better suited to someone distinctly equipped to investigate the more elusive details of a man's life.

Someone like her friend Massimo Colombo, director of Italy's domestic intelligence agency, the AISI. Surely, he might have contacts that could help.

"*Buonasera*, Max. It's Hana Sinclair. May I have the pleasure of your company over dinner, say, tomorrow evening?"

"Ah, Signorina Sinclair, it is so good to hear your lovely voice," Colombo answered suavely. "Dinner, you say? Well, that tells me you must be onto some new exploit—not that I would object to such a pleasant invitation anyway. Tell me, where and when?"

"How about eight o'clock at La Pergola in the Cavalieri? My treat, I insist."

"La Pergola? How could one refuse such a kind offer to the finest restaurant in all of Rome? I am at your service. I need only clear it with my wife. Fortunately, she is not the jealous type."

"She has nothing to fear from me, dear Max. And yes, this will be a business meeting. One I think you may find as compelling as I do. But more on that tomorrow. See you then?"

"I look forward to it, Hana, very much. *Grazie e buona serata.*"

"I'll have the Deep-fried Zucchini Flower with Caviar on Shellfish and Saffron Consommé as the starter, Stefan, and for the main course, the Loin of Lamb with Black Lentils and Ashed Buttermilk," Hana told the waiter confidently. "And we can share the Marinated Buffalo with Chervil Root appetizer."

Massimo Colombo, wearing his finest suit and polished shoes, stared at the menu nervously.

"Hana," he whispered to her across the small table, "I don't mean to be ungracious or ill-mannered, but our meals together will be well over three hundred euros! Are you sure we're in the right place?"

Hana smiled self-assuredly. "Not to worry, Max. My grandfather gives me a generous allowance. Besides, as residents we don't pay menu prices. Please, order whatever you'd like."

He leaned back in his seat, eagerly resigned to a moment of upscale luxury a government employee could ill afford.

"Then I will have as the *primo* course the Pumpkin Risotto with Sweetbreads, and for *secondo*, I'll go with the Pigeon with Black Salsify and Seasonal Mushrooms in Hay."

"Excellent choices," Stefan assured him with a winning smile. "Signorina Sinclair, I shall return with the wine list momentarily."

"No need for the list, Stefan," Hana said as the waiter turned back, "We'll have the Vietti Barolo. The 2014 should be fine."

"*Molto bene*, Signorina."

As was her tendency, Hana dispensed with small talk. "Max, the reason I wanted to meet involves a fascinating artifact Father Dominic and I are seeking, one that has come to our attention through old correspondence from a Nazi SS officer and a Catholic bishop during the war…"

As Colombo leaned in closer, Hana related Dominic's introduction to Jacob Rausch and his grandfather Walther's background, and the Nazis' dubious collaboration with Bishop Hudal. A few minutes into the story the waiter returned with the wine, prompting Hana to suspend her story while Stefan uncorked, sampled in his sommelier's tastevin, then poured the wine. When he left, she continued.

"Michael and I have done much research into these men, and both of us have uncovered some interesting things. First, of those fragments mentioned in Walther Rausch's diary, and which we later found confirmed in Himmler's journal, I actually found one of the coded pieces in Bishop Hudal's biography."

She took out her phone and showed Colombo the image of the SS insignia fragment.

"Now we just need to find the other two. It may be a long shot, but we think Jacob, for whatever reasons, may not be forthcoming with what he knows. We'll continue working with him on that, but there's now the matter of Erich Prager to deal with. I haven't been successful in researching him, and I'm hoping you might have certain resources that may be able to help us."

As Colombo pondered this, two waiters returned with the first courses, set each plate down with a flourish, and refreshed their wine glasses.

As he gently dug into his pumpkin risotto, the seasoned intelligence agent considered his response. "You say this Prager fellow is from Bariloche, Argentina? I do have a very dependable colleague in Buenos Aires, a good man with Interpol whose name is Javier Batista. He deals mainly in money-laundering and human trafficking across that country's notoriously porous borders, as well as the smuggling of drugs and firearms. He is also, I believe, closely connected with Israeli Mossad. He might be able to assist you. He has been with Interpol's National Central Bureau there for some thirty years. Javier would be well aware of the prevalence of Nazis, of course, given the large population who emigrated there after the war."

"Oh, Max, he sounds like the answer to our prayers," Hana said enthusiastically. "If you can introduce us I'd be immensely grateful."

"Let's see what he has to say first. If he is tied into the growing neo-Nazi movement in Argentina, which is affiliated with a political party called the Patriotic Front, then he may indeed know a good deal about your Erich Prager and whatever people he may have associated with. I will make that call first thing in the morning, Hana. I will do what I can to help you and Father Michael."

The next dishes arrived, again with a flourish of presentation. The intense flavors of the Pigeon with Black Salsify brought a look of ecstasy to Max's face, and as Hana slid a knife through her Loin of Lamb, she could only hope that Max's connections could be as satisfying as the meal they were both enjoying.

CHAPTER 13

Rosa Cruz sat on a wooden bench beneath the fat Palo Borracho tree in front of Interpol's offices in Buenos Aires. It was 2:00 p.m., her lunch hour, and she had picked up a grilled *choripán* from the local food truck, its juicy chorizo sausage tucked into a fresh *pan batido* topped with a thin layer of green chimichurri sauce.

As she savored each bite, her eye was drawn to the bright red blossoms on the tree above her. All Argentinians knew the legend of the Palo Borracho, reputed to once be a woman so in love with a soldier who had died in battle that, in despair, she had transformed herself into a magnificent silk floss tree in his memory, the blood of her dead paramour spreading through the flowers that were once her slender fingers. Everything had fabled meaning in the gaucho culture of Argentina.

"I thought I might find you here, Rosa," said the suave man approaching her. Javier Batista had the bronze weathered look of the legendary cowboys of that region, though he had never even sat on a horse, having worked in Interpol offices for the past three decades. A patch of gray at the temples of his jet black hair hinted at his sixty years, but he had the youthful vigor of a man much younger. His open-necked shirt revealed a

Star of David hanging from a silver chain on a dark mat of chest hair.

"*Buenas tardes*, Javier," said Rosa stoically, before taking her last bite of the *choripán*. "Pulling me back into work already?"

"*Si*, Rosita. We have a new project for an old friend in Italy and I'll need your help. But I'm afraid it involves your least favored immigrants to our beloved country."

Rosa looked at him with dismay. "No!" she cried. "Not the *Nazis* again! Please, Javier, can't you pick someone else this time? I hate dealing with those *bastardos*."

"Well, you won't actually have to 'deal' with them, since the subject of this investigation has long since died. We just need to find his living family."

"That's just as bad," she said, adding an old proverb her mother had drilled into her: "'Where blood has been shed, the tree of forgiveness cannot grow.'"

Rosa stood, dabbed her mouth with a napkin, folded her paper plate and dropped them both in a nearby trash bin. "Alright. Let's get on with it."

ONE OF SEVEN Regional Bureaus extending Interpol's global reach beyond its headquarters in Lyon, France, the Buenos Aires office was chiefly responsible for handling policing initiatives in counter terrorism, cyber-crime, corruption, and organized crime throughout all of South America.

As an Operations Specialist for the Command and Coordination Center, Javier Batista had long dealt with international fugitive investigations, forensic and criminal analysis. He was also involved in reviewing the growing neo-Nazi movements, particularly as it involved Argentinian subjects —and that alone was a burgeoning province of law enforcement. The Bureau found him especially suited to this area, for though his father was of early Argentinian descent, his mother hailed from a long line of Ashkenazi Jews who had settled in Argentina from Spain in the early nineteenth century. In a twist of historical irony—as Batista often reminded colleagues—following World War II Argentina had the largest populations of both Jews and Nazi immigrants in all of Latin America. His association with Mossad was never discussed, in line with that agency's inclination toward discretion and anonymity. He had an especially keen interest in this focus of his work and was glad to have the assistance of someone as capable as Rosa for his current research.

Settling back in at her desk, Rosa opened the email Batista had forwarded to her with what few details they had regarding the Erich Prager assignment, which was sent to him by his Italian colleague Massimo Colombo. She sighed seeing Prager's name, for it had crossed her desk before. She remembered producing a hefty background dossier for Prager's extradition to Italy in the mid-1990s—a very public affair at the time—but that wouldn't be on their computer systems now, meaning she had to go through the torturous paper archives in the basement. Shaking her head, she sighed again. *I'm getting too old for this mierda*, she thought, as she slowly made her way to the elevator and the archive room downstairs.

Two long rows of fluorescent lights hummed and flickered to life after Rosa flipped the wall switch in the empty room. Even on warm days the basement was cold and dank, with the musty smell of an old wet dog permeating the still air. Rows of drab gray file cabinets, dozens of them, filled the low-ceilinged room as she headed toward the "P" section of the alphabetized archive.

It didn't take her long to spot the Prager file, one of the largest in the drawer. Heaving it out, she slammed the cabinet shut, turned out the light and left the room. Returning to her desk, Rosa cleared a space for the work ahead and dug into it.

Seven thousand miles away the following day, Father Michael Dominic had just finished celebrating an early evening Mass in the Church of Santa Maria della Pietà, one of the nine churches and chapels on the Vatican grounds and his personal favorite, loved for its intimate reminiscence to his old neighborhood church in Queens.

Among the few congregants attending Mass was Hana Sinclair. As Father Dominic greeted each person leaving, Hana stood back, waiting for him to return to the sacristy, change out of his vestments, and join her for dinner.

As the last of those exiting the church had passed, Hana's cell phone buzzed in her purse. Retrieving it, she saw "Private Number" on the screen. She tapped the green button.

"Ms. Sinclair?" the voice asked.

"Yes? And who is this?"

"Ms. Sinclair, this is Javier Batista with Interpol in Buenos Aires. Our mutual friend Massimo Colombo asked me to do some research for you on Erich Prager?"

Hana perked up on hearing this. "Yes, Max mentioned you might call. Assuming he filled you in already, have you found anything that might be useful?"

"Oh, yes, and more than you were probably expecting," Batista said. "But we're dealing with far too much data for telephone and fax. I realize it's a long trip, but are you able to meet with us here in Buenos Aires? I do believe it would be worth your while."

Hana gave Dominic a look of eager anticipation, then made the decision for both of them.

"*Sí*, Señor Batista, we'll be on the first flight we can catch."

CHAPTER 14

The 14-hour Alitalia flight from Rome was long and tiring, and once they arrived in Buenos Aires just after dawn, Hana and Michael went straight to their rooms at the Alvear Palace Hotel and fell onto their beds for a quick nap before meeting with Javier Batista.

A couple hours later, now refreshed, they met in the hotel's L'Orangerie Restaurant for breakfast, waiting for Batista to join them as arranged.

As he sipped from a cup of steaming *cortado macchiato*, Dominic looked around at the meticulous splendors of the dining room.

"Don't you ever stay at a Motel 6?" he quipped.

"What's a Motel 6?" she asked in response, a sincere eyebrow raised.

"I guess that answers my question," he said, grinning. "Getting to know you has opened my eyes to a whole new way of living—at least among those in the one percent."

Hana flushed, grasping her friend's meaning. "My grandfather is a very generous man, Michael, but our family has enjoyed the blessings of generational wealth for over two centuries. And while we do live well, our foundation gives millions each year to many deserving charitable institutions, such as Doctors Without Borders and The Nature Conservancy. Such wealth has implicit obligations. Neither he nor I could think or act otherwise."

As Dominic appraised yet another side of this remarkable woman, the sound of approaching footsteps made them both look up.

"*Buenos dias, amigos,*" the handsome smiling stranger said as he stopped at their table. "Javier Batista at your service."

Dominic stood and held out a hand. "*Buenos dias,* Señor Batista. I'm Michael Dominic, and this is Hana Sinclair."

After shaking Dominic's hand, Batista took Hana's, held it up to his lips, and kissed the top of it while holding her eyes. "A great pleasure meeting you both, especially you, Ms. Sinclair. Max failed to mention your disarming beauty."

Blushing and taken aback for a moment, Hana found her voice.

"It is *you* who is disarming, Señor Batista. What a lovely introduction."

"Please, you must call me Javier. May I join you?"

"Of course!" Dominic said. Batista sat down, his eyes still fixed on Hana.

"I am so glad you were able to visit personally," Batista said. "There is much to go over in the Prager file. But first, let us order *desayuno*, or as you say, breakfast. I am sure you must be hopeful for a good meal after such a long flight, yes?"

After reviewing menus and the waiter having taken their orders, Batista warmed up the conversation with small talk before they got onto the main topic.

"So, this Erich Prager who is of such interest to you... May I ask what it is you are hoping to find? On Max's recommendation, of course, my office will be at your disposal. But knowing what you seek may help us refine our efforts together."

Dominic laid out the backstory—finding Rausch's diary,

Himmler's journal, Hudal's biography, the SS fragments and finding the middle piece—everything except mention of the actual veil itself, simply referring to the sought object as an "artifact of interest to the Vatican." As an intelligence officer, Batista knew not to inquire beyond what had been presented to him. There must be a reason for such discretion, he assumed. Perhaps a "need to know" sort of affair.

"Ah, an artifact, you say. In that regard I recall an incident that may be of particular interest," Batista said, "about a significant Nazi takedown a few years ago."

Batista looked up as if to recall the details. "It was June 2017, I believe, in what we called Operation Oriente Cercano. A confidential informant tipped us off to a shady art dealer, and during our inspection of his gallery in Béccar, a town north of Buenos Aires, we discovered a cache of illicit artworks for sale, art that had been listed in Interpol's database of stolen antiquities, much of it going back to the wartime era.

"After further investigation of the gallery's owner, we raided his home and found a hidden door to a secret room behind a bookcase. The room was filled with some 75 authentic Nazi artifacts—several bronze busts of Adolf Hitler, boxes of honorary Gestapo daggers, statuary emblazoned with swastikas, even musical instruments, and toys and puzzles for indoctrinating children. We believe all of it belonged to high-ranking Nazis who emigrated to Argentina after the war. The entire lot was taken into custody and is now in the Evidence Room of the local federal police office. Perhaps it is there you may find your missing fragment. I'm sure I can make arrangements for an inspection."

"That sounds like a solid lead," Dominic said, glancing at Hana. "How soon can we see these items, Javier?"

"Let me make a couple calls to make sure the objects are still in their Evidence Room, then I'll need to get special permission for a visit. Argentinians are most sensitive when it comes to our country's past affiliation with Nazi immigrants. But with you being a Vatican priest and a French journalist, this may offer stronger credentials than, say, a dealer in Nazi memorabilia. But I must tell you, the State does not want these items publicized, of that I am certain."

"Our goal is to find but one item, a simple piece of paper," Dominic said, "and all the Vatican needs is a photograph of it. We don't wish to take anything, and I'm sure Hana will respect your country's need for discretion."

Hana looked at him with a hint of irritation. She had just heard a fabulous story of hidden Nazi treasures and now was being dissuaded from writing about it?

We'll see about that, she thought.

CHAPTER 15

Having finished breakfast, Batista called for his Peugeot 408 from the hotel valet, then drove Hana and Dominic to Interpol's Regional Bureau headquarters on Calle Cavia, a mere ten-minute drive in the north part of the city.

The dingy tan and white fortress-like building took up an entire city block, and as Batista drove midway down the street, he reached up to squeeze a remote control clipped to his visor. A black solid iron fence jerked opened, exposing the driveway to an interior parking lot next to a three-story building topped with a crowded dish antenna array.

As they entered the narrow drive, Dominic noticed a row of inlaid spike barriers beneath the fence line, wondering when they might ever be used. It seemed an unlikely security precaution for a law enforcement building.

The three got out of the vehicle and Batista led them into his offices—an interior space that belied the building's shabby exterior, as if to camouflage the organization's more modern activities inside.

The room buzzed with activity, people chatting in small groups or carrying papers and digital tablets in all directions, gleaming flat screen computers on every desk, with a row of mainframes along the back wall. A small glass-enclosed SCIF, or Sensitive Compartmentalized Information Facility, was situated in the very center of the large room, where a secure meeting was taking place as Dominic and Hana walked by, following their Interpol guide to his private office.

Many heads turned toward Dominic and, seeing his white clerical collar, politely waved to him as he strode through the rank and file. It wasn't often they found a Catholic priest in their midst.

With no small measure of pride, Batista noticed Hana's wide-eyed impression taking in the scene.

"A good lesson in not judging a book by its cover, wouldn't you say?" he remarked, smiling. "Despite outward appearances, we are as well-equipped here as any First World country's intelligence service can be."

As he said this, he motioned for his assistant Rosa to join them in his office. She dutifully stood, picked up a bundle of folders and made her way to meet her boss and his guests.

"I would like you to meet my most capable assistant, Rosa Cruz. She has done most of the research on your behalf and will be able to brief you on what she has found."

After greetings were exchanged, the four sat down at a small meeting table in Batista's office.

"First of all, it gives me no pleasure talking about *Nazis*," she snapped frankly, needing to get that out on the table. Rosa Cruz was not one who hesitated speaking her mind.

Hana sensed the woman could use some support in front of her boss. "I quite agree with you, Rosa, probably for all the same reasons you do. It's unfortunate so many of them had chosen your country as their means of escaping prosecution. And we're here to see if even a small measure of justice can be wrought from their past sins."

Rosa looked at Hana in a new light, finding a political ally in her firm beliefs. From then on she directed her discourse toward Hana, with the others listening in.

"I expect you may already know much about Erich Prager's role in the Third Reich and his war crimes, so I'll present what we found about his family and associates here in Argentina. If you have any questions as I go along, just stop me. I've prepared this dossier for you to take with you, but I'll cover the highlights of it now.

"You are familiar with the Ahnenerbe, I assume?" Rosa asked.

Dominic and Hana nodded uncertainly. "Just barely," Hana admitted.

"Contrary to what most people think, the Ahnenerbe was *not* disbanded after the war; it just went quiet for decades. The organization actually has a large but discreet presence here in Argentina, sustained by neo-Nazis in collaboration with the fascist Patriotic Front party. Its goals are the same as they were under Hitler's regime—to advance the biological superiority of the Aryan race. They have enormous funding from many sources and their sphere of influence extends in all directions, like the head of Medusa—even inside the Catholic Church, Padre." She looked at Dominic as she said this. "Are you familiar with Cardinal Fabrizio Dante of the Metropolitan Cathedral here in Buenos Aires?"

Dominic reeled in his seat, shocked to hear Dante's name again, especially in a meeting at Interpol. Hana turned to him, her mouth slack, reflecting the same alarm.

"We are more than familiar with Cardinal Dante, Rosa," the priest said. "You could say he's been a thorn in our side for some time now." A thorn that could have cost he and Hana their lives only a year ago if not for the intervention of the Pope himself.

"Our intel shows he has strong connections with Erich's grandson," she continued, "a young man named Christof Prager, and several other Nazi-related families here and down south in Bariloche, a town near the Chilean border with a dense German population and thousands of Nazi descendants. Dante has been on our Watchlist since his arrival here last year. But, of course, the Church is very powerful in South America, so our monitoring activities have been rather circumspect in that regard."

"If you will excuse me," Batista said as he stood up, "I have a phone call to make. I will return in a few moments."

Still shaken by Dante's involvement, Dominic stood up to stretch his legs. "Rosa, Javier mentioned to us earlier about the Nazi memorabilia raid in Béccar. Was Cardinal Dante at all involved?"

"Not that we're aware of," she said, twirling a pencil in her hand. "But the gallery owner was believed to be a colleague of Erich Prager, so it's possible his family may have had some complicity. And that could lead back to Dante, but that's mere speculation."

Hana reached for her phone, calling up the Photos app and the SS insignia fragment. "Rosa, have you ever seen any images like this in your research?"

Rosa looked at it for a few moments. "No, nothing like that. Is that the item you are looking for?"

"Yes, there are two others we need to solve sort of a puzzle, one that could lead us to an artifact the Vatican would like to obtain." She knew she was stretching the truth a bit, but it didn't seem to matter in the larger context. Michael *did* work for the Vatican—and he *did* want to obtain it—and the object *would* likely end up at the Vatican, she reasoned.

The door to the office opened and Batista walked back in.

"Good news," he began. "The commandant of the PFA, our Policía Federal Argentina, has agreed to let us inspect the Nazi memorabilia in their Evidence Room. It is all still there."

"That's great news!" Dominic said, clasping his hands together. "Thank you both so much for your help. We are in your debt. When can we see these items?"

"We can leave right now, if that works for you," Batista said with a grin. "They are waiting for us."

"Perfect," said Dominic. "Ready when you are."

"Rosa," Hana said as she stood, "can we call on you again if we need additional information?"

"Of course, Señorita, I am here day and night, it seems." She glanced at Batista and rolled her eyes. They all laughed at her feigned burden.

"And this is for you." Rosa handed the dossier to Hana. "Take very good care of it, please. While not classified, it must be considered sensitive material."

"You have my word," Hana said, shaking hands with the woman.

CHAPTER 16

The forty-minute drive to Béccar, a suburb north of Buenos Aires along the shore of the Argentine Sea, was a pleasant one. Even though Buenos Aires was enjoying its autumn season in May, the temperature was a balmy 24 degrees Celsius, and Dominic was happy to be out and about. He had been missing his daily runs, and looked out over the passing landscape wishing there was more time to enjoy the pleasures of Buenos Aires.

Meanwhile, nested in the back seat with papers scattered around her, Hana pored over the Prager dossier. On a page marked "Subject's Associations," she discovered a few interesting facts about Erich Prager's post-war life in Bariloche. He had owned a small but popular German delicatessen called Graz, and became head of both the German-Argentine Cultural Association and the local German school. His closest friend and business partner was a man named Dr. Johann Kurtz, a fellow Gestapo officer and geneticist Prager had worked with in Rome during the war.

The Interpol dossier also noted that Prager still had a grandson living in Bariloche, a young man named Christof, whose occupation was simply listed as "community organizer." *What kind of a job is that?* Hana wondered. She made a mental note of it and continued paging through the other sections for any clue as to where the missing fragments might be found.

THE BÉCCAR DIVISION of the Policía Federal Argentina occupies a single-story red brick building in a residential neighborhood, taking up more than half of the long tree-lined city block. Turning off the two-lane street, Batista drove through an open chain link gate and onto a rough dirt parking lot marred by potholes, with several dozen cars parked haphazardly throughout the large field. Many had been sitting there for some time, Dominic noted, as evidenced by the piles of leaves on top of them from adjacent and now barren trees. He assumed it must also serve as an impound lot.

After finding a suitable space to park his Peugeot, Batista led his guests inside the building's back entrance, where the desk officer signed them in and escorted them to the office of the station chief, Capitán Carlos Portillo, a tall, heavy-set man with a bushy mustache and black hair slicked back with a pomade shine.

After introductions were made, Portillo asked his assistant to bring them fresh infused yerba mate, the traditional tea of Argentina.

"As I explained to you on the phone, Capitán," Batista began, "our friends here are seeking an item of special interest to the Vatican, one with some connection to the Nazis, and one man in particular who settled in Bariloche.

"As it may be among the artifacts you found in the raid from Operation Oriente Cercano, we would be most grateful to be granted a look at these items in your custody."

Dominic squirmed in his seat at the mention of the Vatican's "special interest," since nobody else even knew he was on the hunt for the SS fragments and, ultimately, the veil.

Just then the woman returned with a tray containing a bowl of ground brown tea leaves, a thermos of hot water, a calabash gourd and a long metal straw.

Portillo introduced his assistant, Maya, saying, "She will be our *cebador* for priming and serving the mate. This is a special ceremony that goes back hundreds of years, and it is our honor to share it with you."

Maya placed a portion of tea leaves into the gourd, filling it halfway. She then tilted and shook the gourd until the tea covered the inside, almost to its mouth. Gently pouring in the hot water from the thermos toward the bottom of the leaves, she explained, "This slow process awakens the tea, bringing out its vibrancy."

After a few moments of steeping, she placed the filtered metal straw, the *bombilla*, into the mixture, then held out the gourd for Hana to drink.

Knowing the ritual from past visits to South America, Hana accepted the bitter beverage and drank from the *bombilla*, respectfully finishing off the entire liquid she was offered, then handed the gourd back to Maya, saying *"Muchas gracias."*

Maya again went through the process for each of the others in the room, serving Portillo last. Each drank, returned the gourd to Maya, and thanked her, as was the custom.

"That was delicious mate, Capitán, *gracias*," Hana said. "My compliments to your *cebador*." Maya blushed and left the office with a proud smile on her face.

Portillo seemed pleased as well. "Now, let us take a look at what we found in our raid here in Béccar. After Agent Batista called, I immediately had all 75 objects laid out on special tables for you to examine." He led them down a long narrow hall to the far end of the building, where a wire mesh security door protected the contents of a wide room filled with all manner of objects and contraband on black metal racks and shelves rising to the ceiling.

Unlocking the door, Portillo held out his arm welcoming his

guests to the Evidence Room. Several tables had been erected in the center of the room, on which were placed dozens of Nazi-related objects, as was clearly obvious given the abundance of swastikas, SS insignia and iron cross emblems on most of the items. And, of course, the unmistakable bronze busts of Adolf Hitler. There was even a mannequin snugly fit with an SS officer's uniform, its gold-trimmed epaulets, battle medals and rank insignia gleaming under the overhead lights.

Portillo noticed Hana eyeing the mannequin. "On the open market," he said, "this uniform alone would sell for thirty thousand US dollars. There is a thriving market for all this material, even today, more than a half-century after the war."

Despite the warmth of the room, Hana shuddered at the massive iconography of the inherently evil movement that lay before her. Walking down the row of tables, she took in the larger pieces of memorabilia, wondering what kind of people collected such things. She noticed a similar reaction in Michael now standing next to her.

"Did you find any paper ephemera in this lot?" she asked. "Perhaps something that looked like this?" With that, she took out her phone and showed Portillo the SS fragment from Hudal's book.

Portillo examined it carefully, then shook his head. "No, not that I have seen, señorita. But then, I did not go through the albums or photographs myself. We had a forensics team do that after we discovered these items."

"You mention 'albums' and 'photographs.' May I see those?"

"Yes, of course." Portillo opened one of the cardboard boxes on a table and withdrew several scrapbooks containing photos, flyers, news clippings and similar paper collectibles. Hana picked them up.

"May I use this desk, Capitán?" she asked, as she walked toward a dingy gray metal desk that had seen better days.

Portillo nodded and held out his arm again in a flourish,

encouraging her to sit down. She gently set the scrapbooks on the desktop then took a seat in a folding metal chair and began paging through the albums.

"Michael, why don't you join me?" she asked. "Together we can make short work of this."

Dominic found a rusty folding chair leaning against the wall and pulled it over to the desk opposite Hana, then picked up another of the albums to examine. Batista and Portillo stood chatting quietly in Spanish in the opposite corner of the room so as not to bother the others.

Knowing what they were looking for, both Dominic and Hana turned pages quickly, not needing to admire or remark on the contents so much as to simply find their elusive prize. Hana knew it was a long shot, but felt they needed to turn over every stone while they had the opportunity.

The closer they got to the end of reviewing the scrapbooks, the higher their frustration rose. By the final page in the last scrapbook, Hana's initial encouragement had turned to dismay.

Dominic picked up the stack of books and returned them to the box Portillo had taken them from. Before dropping them in, however, he noticed a long white carton in the bottom of the cardboard box with an orange-and-red Kodak logo on it. He lifted it out, then dropped the scrapbooks back inside.

Opening the Kodak carton, he discovered it was a box of 35 millimeter transparency slides, the kind used in old projectors. He brought the carton over to Hana at the desk and sat down.

"Check this out. It couldn't hurt to take a look at these, though I haven't seen a 35 millimeter slide since I was a child. I'm sure we have some hidden away in the Vatican Archive somewhere, but they're pretty much an anachronism these days."

"Might as well," Hana said, as she removed half the color slides from the slim carton, with Dominic taking the rest. She angled the gooseneck desk lamp such that they could hold the slides over the light for inspection, which at least gave them some vague idea of the content of each 1-inch transparency inside its 2-inch cardboard sleeve.

It took them longer to analyze each one, since their minds had to interpret the practically microscopic images revealed on each slide. Some of them were truly horrific—photos of emaciated men and women behind barbed wire fences, obviously Jews and other prisoners in concentration camps, with dogs barking at them from the outside; proud young German soldiers standing next to tanks and other artillery, saluting the camera; groups of high-ranking officials in uniform, raising colorful steins of beer in front of a huge red flag with a white swastika emblazoned on it; and, strangely, photos of various official documents and even images of some of the very artifacts on the tables surrounding them.

As Dominic was looking at one slide in particular, he turned it one way, then the other. He held it closer to the light, pulling the slide in and out of his field of vision to better make out what he thought he saw. He looked up at Hana with an unmistakable look on his face that asked, *Is there something here?*

Taking the slide, Hana mimicked Dominic's analysis, squinting at the image she saw as she turned it back and forth above the light.

And there it was. One of the fragments shaped in a figurative "S," just like the first fragment. There was also what appeared to be writing on it, the part that was hardest to make out. But now she was certain. They had found one of the three riddle fragments.

Her mind went to work, fast. If they were to reveal their success, it seemed unlikely Portillo would simply hand it over, since this *was* evidence from a major crime bust. And it wasn't in such a position that she could simply take a photo of it with her iPhone—there would be no way to properly enlarge it. The authorities would never allow any of these items out of this room. If they left here without it….

Batista was still engaged with Portillo across the room. Subtly raising her hand to her neck, she dropped the slide into her décolletage.

Watching her, Dominic found himself in the midst of a dilemma. He realized, as she obviously did, that there was no other way to handle the situation if they wanted to find the veil, something of potential importance to the Church. He glanced at the table of so many symbols of that evil era. This was, after all, just one slide. And Portillo himself said he hadn't gone through the material.

Hana avoided looking at Dominic, her own conscience troubled despite the obvious necessity. "I think we're done here," she said with mock exasperation just loud enough for everyone to hear. She reassembled the remaining slides and dropped them into the Kodak container.

"Capitán Portillo, *muchas gracias*, but it looks like we've come up short in our search. We so appreciate your time and effort in helping us. How can we ever repay you?"

Portillo crossed the room and approached the desk, his hands held up in a slight gesture implying needlessness.

"You owe me nothing, señorita. It was a pleasure to be of service, though I am sorry you did not find the item you seek. I imagine it must be like trying to find a white cat in a snowstorm."

Hana laughed. "Yes, that's a perfect analogy."

Dominic stood and addressed both Portillo and Batista. "We're flying down to Bariloche in the morning. Might either of you have a contact with the police there in case we may need some assistance?"

Batista looked at Portillo, who smiled. "As it happens, my cousin Ramón is the *Jefe de Policia* of Bariloche. If anyone can help you, it is he. I will make the call to him this afternoon and introduce you."

"That's very kind, Capitán, thank you. If he is as generous as you have been to us, we'll be in good hands, I'm sure."

Hana just smiled thinking how the Capitán had been more generous than he'd intended to be.

CHAPTER 17

A s Javier Batista pulled his Peugeot up to the entry of
the Alvear Palace Hotel, he waved off the approaching
valet. Having said their thanks and goodbyes, Hana
and Dominic stepped out of the vehicle and headed straight for
the bar.

Taking a quiet table in a far corner, they each ordered a glass
of Patagonia's La Alazana single malt whisky, as much to relax
from the day's activities as to temper their excitement. After the
waitress delivered them, each raised their glass in a silent
celebratory toast, then took a long draw of the wickedly strong
amber liquid.

"Admit it, Michael, we were *very* lucky. What were the odds
of us finding that? Max knew Batista, then his good relationship
with Portillo… plus if you hadn't stumbled onto that Kodak box,
where would we be now?"

"It just shows the value of networking and what
perseverance we have when we put our minds to something. It's
not as if it hasn't happened before." They exchanged knowing
looks, thinking back to previous adventures together.

"Now, we just have to find a way to view the slide. It

distressed me to take it, but I was certain that they wouldn't have a projector in their lock-up. I didn't know what else to do."

Michael nodded. He wasn't comfortable with them taking it either, but it seemed the most efficient approach at the time. He would deal with his conscience later. For now they needed to see what that slide could offer them.

"Where would we ever find one of those old projectors?" she asked.

Dominic looked around the bar and through the door to the hotel's large lobby.

"Well, isn't this hotel also a conference center? They must have equipment for conventions and such stored here somewhere."

"Brilliant!" Hana cheered, reaching into her bra to retrieve the hidden slide as Michael abruptly took another chug of whisky. "We've got to see what this fragment says."

Dominic stood up. "I'll check with the concierge, see if they have anything useful." Walking unsteadily but with a warm glow about him, he headed outside the bar and, spotting the concierge desk, went over to inquire about a projector.

"Excuse me," he said in Spanish to the young well-dressed man behind the counter. "By any chance does your hotel have audio/video equipment available for use? Specifically, we're looking for a slide projector."

The young man looked at Dominic blankly, clearly not knowing what a slide projector was.

"*Uno momento, Padre*, I will check," he said respectfully as he picked up the telephone. Addressing the person who answered, he asked the same question. A moment later he smiled, gave the person instructions, and hung up the phone.

"*Si*, we do have such a thing, *Padre*!" he said proudly. "We would be happy to have it delivered to your room."

"*Excelente!*" Dominic said, giving the man his name and room number, and leaving a tip. "Just have them put it in the room. My companion and I are in the bar, but we'll be up shortly."

Pleased with his success, Dominic turned to head back to the bar. As he did so he failed to notice two men walking behind him engaged in conversation, and bumped into one of them. Looking up, he came face to face with the last person he would ever expect to find here.

Cardinal Fabrizio Dante.

The two men looked at each other stonily, both clearly jolted by the encounter.

"Father Dominic," Dante said simply, without welcome. "I must admit I'm surprised to see you here. What brings you to Buenos Aires? Are you here on Vatican business?"

Scrambling for words, Dominic managed, "No, just here on a brief holiday, Eminence." He looked over to Dante's companion, a policeman by the look of his uniform.

"Allow me to introduce Comisario Julio Borges, Assistant Chief of Police for Bariloche. We were just about to have dinner. Are you here with anyone?"

"Yes, I, uh, have a friend waiting in the bar," Dominic said. "And I need to get back now, actually. It was good seeing you, Eminence."

"And you, Dominic," Dante muttered, holding the priest's eyes a moment longer. Then he and Borges turned and headed toward L'Orangerie restaurant.

"I've got good news and bad news," Dominic said as he took his seat rejoining Hana in the bar.

"I hope the good news is that you found a projector," she said.

"That's the good news, yes."

"And…the bad?" she asked tentatively.

Dominic sighed. "I literally just bumped into Cardinal Dante.

He's having dinner here with—and you won't believe this—the *assistant chief of police for Bariloche!* His name is Julio Borges."

Hana's mouth hung open in shock. "You *cannot* be serious," she said rhetorically. "That can't be good." Hana was well aware that the only reason Cardinal Dante now served the Church in Buenos Aires was that his actions against Michael last year had vanquished him from what had been a rising career as Secretary of State within the walls of the Vatican itself. The man had been dangerous before. Blaming Michael for his career set-back, he could be even more dangerous.

"That's why I called it bad news. What do you suppose the two of them are up to?"

"Who ever knows with *him*," she fumed. "But I suspect corruption is at the heart of it." After pausing a moment, Hana continued. "Well, there's nothing to be gained by speculating on Dante's actions. We may need to watch ourselves in Bariloche, though. Hopefully Portillo's cousin Ramón isn't also in league with the cardinal. As the *chief* of police, he's obviously Borges's boss."

"Let's finish up here and check out that slide," Dominic said, done with the Dante enigma. "The concierge is having the projector delivered to my room."

They both downed the last of their whisky, paid the bill and headed for the elevator.

As PROMISED, the slide projector was sitting on the desk in Dominic's room when they arrived. Hana set down her bag and retrieved the slide as Dominic plugged the machine into the wall socket at some distance from a blank white wall. Removing the carousel, she dropped the slide in and placed the unit back into the projector, then turned the machine on. Dominic turned out the room lights.

The slide image appeared brightly on the wall, but the clarity was fuzzy. Dominic adjusted the focus ring until the picture was clear, then they both gazed at the SS symbol in full color.

Picking up her notebook, Hana transcribed the Sütterlin words she could make out, prepending them to the previous page she had interpreted from the first fragment, yielding a transcription that took on better comprehension:

I hold the key to ope…
The secret door you can…
I always run, walk…
I sing sometimes but can…

No head on which a hat to plac…
You always look me in the fa…
The key swings freely to and…
Remove it and you now must…

With key in hand you should…
The center of the solar…
The holy face of God…
Is resting under the black…

Given time to digest what they had just read, and read again, they both looked at each other.

"Wow," Hana marveled, then laughed. "Now that's not tantalizing at all."

Dominic was deep in thought looking at the riddle thus far. "So we have a *key* to a *secret door*? A key that *swings freely*? *The center of*, what, the *solar* 'system,' maybe? And *the holy face of God's* something? Could that be the image of Christ on the veil? Oh, this stuff drives me *mad!* You're the puzzle expert. What do you make of it?"

"This poses too many possibilities. We *must* find that final piece, Michael. We could spend the rest of our lives trying to interpret this!"

Then she had a thought. "There are two lines here that might make some sort of sense, if I'm right: *'No head on which a hat to place… You always look me in the face….'* They logically complete each of the sentences, and they do rhyme. The rest of it, not so much."

"Yeah, that's good," he said encouragingly. "Keep going!"

Hana looked at him skeptically. "I think I'm out of options, Father Dominic. Maybe we could use a little prayer right about now."

"Well, from my experience, it doesn't really work that way."

Hana grabbed her phone and took a photo of the wall-sized image.

Dominic then turned off the projector and unplugged it from the wall. Hana placed the slide inside her notebook to protect it from scratches and dropped it into her bag.

"Since Dante is in the restaurant, why don't we just order

room service then call it a night? Our flight to Bariloche leaves at noon tomorrow."

"Good idea," Hana said. "What would you think Argentine television is like?"

"Probably not as exciting as that slide," Dominic said as he pulled out room service menus from the desk drawer.

CHAPTER 18

Terminal C of the Ezeiza International Airport in Buenos Aires was abuzz with activity, as a cosmopolitan mix of business travelers and tourists herded luggage and children in all directions while soldiers in camouflage uniforms ambled the halls with Heckler & Koch assault rifles patrolling the terminal areas.

A voice announced on the loudspeaker that Aerolineas Argentinas flight 1684 to Bariloche was now boarding. Dominic and Hana, just finishing up their coffee and sweet *medialunas* in the café, collected their carry-on bags and made for the gate.

Before leaving the hotel Hana had made copies of her notebook page with the partially transcribed riddle on it, and Michael now spent most of the flight trying to make sense of it. By the time the jet touched down at San Carlos de Bariloche Airport two hours later, he was no further ahead than when he started, but it took his mind off the anxiety flying had always imposed on him. The Xanax he had taken in the café also helped.

As the taxi sped away from the airport terminal heading toward their hotel, Dominic took in the stunning views Bariloche afforded visitors and residents alike. To the east he marveled at the rugged flatlands of the Patagonian Steppe. To the west, the soaring peaks of the snow-covered Andes extending as far as the eye could see. And surrounding the city itself at the base of the mountains sat the glistening Nahuel Huapi lake. Its stunning natural scenery made Bariloche one of the top vacation spots for all Argentinians and visiting tourists from around the world.

After checking into the Hotel Cristal in the city center, Hana placed a call to the office of Ramón Santos, chief of police for Bariloche. After confirming their association with his counterpart in Buenos Aires, Carlos Portillo, Santos's assistant made arrangements for them to meet the chief later that afternoon.

In the meantime Dominic suggested they take a walk around town to enjoy the predominantly German architecture and cultural infusion. Much to Dominic's surprise, a corner kiosk outside the hotel was actually selling tourist guides to Nazi landmarks, given the town's historical association with thousands of such German émigrés. After buying one he reviewed their options.

"Hey, we can walk by Prager's old house!" he enthused.

Hana rolled her eyes and smirked, but since they had time to kill before their meeting, she didn't object.

When they arrived, they found a quaint alpine cottage with a tall white picket fence and a tidy flower garden—patrolled by a pack of menacing Doberman Pinschers guarding the yard, barking at passersby to deter those with a mind to linger and gawk.

Walking up the street they stopped in at a German bakery that doubled as a souvenir shop, selling such tourist tchotchkes as dolls of lederhosen-clad hikers, alpine hiking being a popular pastime with German travelers in particular. The smell of fresh baked apple strudel made their mouths water, so they picked up a couple slices to take back to the hotel.

As she was paying for the strudel, Hana asked the cashier if she knew of anyone in town named Christof Prager.

"Oh, *Ja*, Herr Prager comes in here often," said the plump

gray-haired woman, smiling as she handed Hana her change. "He, too, loves our homemade strudel. He's a good young man."

Hana was elated to learn this bit of information. She tried to further her luck.

"Does he live nearby, do you know?"

The woman's smile faded quickly. "I am sorry. Even if I did know, I would not tell a stranger. This is a small town where we value our neighbors' privacy."

Well, it was worth a try, Hana thought, as she and Dominic turned away from the counter and left the bakery.

APART FROM THE Argentine flag flying above it and a cluster of official police vehicles surrounding it, it would be hard to distinguish the Policía Federal Argentina's office from any of the other homes surrounding it on the corner of the residential block.

The door of the reclaimed white brick and redwood three-story building featured a wrought-iron rooster welcoming visitors, its significance lost on Dominic and Hana as they walked through the entrance to the front desk. A large poster of Lionel Messi, the iconic Argentine football player, hung on the wall.

"We are here to see Chief Ramón Santos, please. Father Michael Dominic and Hana Sinclair."

The petite young desk attendant checked her log. "Ah, *si*, Señorita Sinclair, *el jefe* is expecting you. Please, follow me."

The desk officer led them upstairs to the third floor and introduced them both to Chief Santos. He offered them seats, then mate, which they graciously declined. There was little time for ceremony now.

"We do not see many priests in this building, Padre," Santos said with a glint in his eye, "but I'm sure there are those in our jail who might wish to make a confession, something we pray for daily here."

Dominic laughed. "I am at your service, Capitán. But we come to you with a request for information." He turned to Hana to let her explain.

"First of all, thank you for seeing us. Your cousin, Capitán Portillo, was most kind to arrange for this meeting, so we'll take up as little of your time as possible. We are in your beautiful city for just a couple of days, and were hoping we might meet one of your residents, a young man by the name of Christof Prager. Are you familiar with him?"

On hearing the name, Santos's manner changed from affable to restrained in a heartbeat.

"*Si*, we know of Señor Prager. His family has been here for two generations. I must assume you know his grandfather's dark role in history?"

Hana looked at Dominic as she responded.

"Yes, *jefe*, which is why we are here." She explained the barest of details about the Rausch diary and Himmler journal, and their quest for something of interest to the Vatican. Again, Michael shifted in his seat, uneasy about the slight subterfuge.

As Hana spoke, the chief looked over Dominic's shoulder to see a man standing just outside his office door, his back to the wall, clearly listening to their conversation.

"Julio!" Santos called out. "Stop lurking by the door and come in to meet our guests."

The uniformed officer, not expecting to be discovered, entered the room, his face turning crimson.

"Señorita Sinclair, Padre Dominic—this is my assistant chief of police, Julio Borges."

Both Dominic and Hana jolted inwardly, hoping their reaction wasn't noticed at hearing that name. Then they stood and turned to greet the man, but Dominic's normally pleasant demeanor had changed in an instant. As he extended his hand, Dominic said, "Yes, we met just yesterday in Buenos Aires, in the company of Cardinal Dante." He and Borges held eyes apprehensively.

Hana, too, became reticent as she took her turn shaking hands.

"A pleasure having you here," Borges said with little emotion. "I hope I'm not intruding, *jefe*. May I join you?"

"Of course," Santos said, "these people are looking for Christof Prager, in a matter of some interest to the Vatican."

"I saw Señor Prager just this morning, walking along Avenida Perito Moreno with another man," Borges said. "Being tall and blond makes him easy to recognize."

"Might you know where we can reach him?" Hana asked.

Santos reached for a pad and pencil. "Rather than reveal such private details, what if I take your number, then contact Prager myself and have him call you? Would that be acceptable?"

"Yes, I understand, of course," Hana replied. She gave the chief her cell number. "Please tell him we just have a few questions."

"May I ask," Borges interrupted, "what it is the Vatican thinks Señor Prager has that merits such a trip all the way from Rome to Argentina?"

That's just the kind of question Cardinal Dante would ask, thought Dominic. And I'll bet the answer would go straight back to him.

"Much as you value privacy here, Señor Borges, the Vatican does as well," Dominic said politely. "We can take up the matter with Prager himself, with thanks for your understanding.

"In the meantime," he asked, gliding off the subject, "can you recommend a good restaurant here featuring Argentina's world-renowned beef? It is one of the other reasons we came here." He flashed a wide smile at the chief.

Santos laughed. "Yes, our beef here is the finest in the world, grass-fed on the fertile plains of Patagonia. I would suggest you try Familia Weiss, an old German restaurant that has been here over forty years. Their food is spectacular. Any taxi can take you there."

"Then Familia Weiss it is, *gracias*," Dominic said, standing up to signal the end of their meeting. Hana stood as well, and they all exchanged goodbyes.

As the sun set over the Patagonian mountain range to the west, the taxi Dominic had hailed sped through the streets of Bariloche as if there were no rules of the road. Hana hastily fastened her seatbelt as Michael held on to the seat in front of him, so startling was the ride. Arriving at the restaurant some fifteen minutes later, Hana paid the driver with trembling hands.

There was a line of people waiting to get in, which Dominic took to be a good sign of the cuisine. The architecture was that of a large Bavarian ski lodge: lofty A-framed roofs with bare beams of stripped wood supporting the arched ceiling inside, ivory drapes gracefully swagged between wooden columns, with a blazing fireplace and strategically placed lights casting a warm glow throughout. Packed with chattering patrons, this was clearly the place to be for fine dining.

A few minutes later, the hostess seated them at a romantic table near the fireplace. Once they were settled, Hana looked up at Michael, smiled whimsically, then they both laughed lightly.

"Oh, if only you weren't a priest," she said, blushing in the low light.

Dominic looked back at her with a sincere smile. "To be honest, there are times that I wish I wasn't."

Hana raised a hand to her hair, brushing several strands back over her ear, then looked around the room to take her mind off the tender moment that couldn't be.

As she did, she glanced at surrounding tables to see what others had ordered. The dishes looked delicious, and the aromas pouring out of the kitchen aroused her appetite.

It was only when she looked beyond the food and at the faces of people seated that she was shocked to find someone she recognized.

Several tables away sat Jacob Rausch, drinking beer and

talking to a tall blond man sitting across from him. Two thoughts stuck her.

What is Jacob Rausch doing in Bariloche? And is that Christof Prager with him?

CHAPTER 19

The Metropolitan Cathedral's administrative offices in Buenos Aires were quiet this time of night, but Cardinal Fabrizio Dante had stayed at his office late, attending to matters regarding major donors to his parish's operational fund. *There is never enough money*, he mulled. *I need to get out there and twist some arms.*

As he pondered the funding dilemma, his private cell phone rang.

"Yes?" he answered abruptly.

"Good evening, Your Eminence," a man said timidly. "It is Julio Borges here in Bariloche. I thought you might want to know that Father Dominic and his companion visited our chief of police today."

"And who was this companion, do you know?"

"A Señorita Hana Sinclair."

While not surprised, Dante was troubled by their combined presence in Argentina.

"So, Dominic and Sinclair are here together," he said apprehensively. "What was it they wanted, Julio?"

Borges filled him in on what few details he knew of the priest's mission.

"They are now looking for Christof Prager, the grandson of the Nazi war criminal. *El jefe* offered to make an introduction. As I said, this is something I thought you might wish to know."

"*Gracias*, Julio. You have done well in letting me know. Goodnight."

Dante disengaged the call and considered this new piece of information. Still holding the phone, he made another call.

"MICHAEL, don't look now, but wait a moment then check out who's sitting seven tables away by the window, facing us."

Dominic turned away from reading the menu and discreetly raised his head in that direction. His reaction matched Hana's.

"*Jacob Rausch?!* he whispered. "What the hell is he doing here? Didn't he say he was in Chile?"

"Look who he's seated with. Based on Borges's description, wouldn't you think that might be Christof Prager?"

"There's only one way to find out."

Dominic stood and made his way to Rausch's table. Several heads turned to watch him walk across the room, the appearance of a priest probably an uncommon sight in the busy restaurant.

As Dominic approached the table Rausch stopped talking and looked up. His face drained of color.

"Fa…Father Michael! What a surprise to find you here!" Rausch managed, spilling his topped-off beer froth as he set the glass down on the table.

"Hana and I were just saying the same thing, Jacob." He turned to point her out back at their table. Jacob's eyes followed his raised arm. Hana waved to him, her head cocked slightly downward. He waved back.

"I thought you were in Santiago," Dominic said, then looked at his tall blond companion. "Hello, I'm Michael Dominic." He held out his hand.

"Pleased to meet you, Father. I am Christof."

"Christof…," he hummed as if pondering something. "Christof *Prager*, by any chance?"

Prager's face took on a cautious look. "Uh, yes, that is my name."

"What a coincidence!" Dominic said in mock surprise. "Hana and I came to Bariloche looking for you." He turned and looked around the room. "It's a pity there are no larger tables for us to eat together. Would you mind joining us in the bar after dinner? Our treat, anything you'd like."

Christof was taken aback, uncertain how to respond. He looked at Rausch pleadingly.

"I suppose we could have a drink together, sure," Jacob said, meeting his friend's eyes.

"Great! We'll see you there in a little while, then. It was very good meeting you, Christof. I look forward to speaking with you."

Dominic walked the twelve paces back to their table and sat down.

"It's him alright," he said to Hana, picking up the menu to mask his eagerness. "We're all meeting in the bar after dinner."

"*Perfect!*" Hana said, looking at her menu as well. "Nicely done, Michael. Now, let's find that famous Argentine steak…"

WITH DINNER FINISHED at both tables, Michael and Hana met Jacob and Christof in the bar adjacent to the restaurant. After introducing Hana and Christof, the waitress came by to take drink orders.

"Christof, this is your town. What would you recommend?" Hana asked.

Christof was more animated now. "You must try Legui, the perfect digestif, especially after beef. It is named for Argentina's greatest jockey, Irenaeus Leguizamo, and tastes of cinnamon, anise and green peppercorns. A very soothing liqueur, not bitter at all."

Hana showed surprise as the waitress left to service their order. "You seem to know a lot about liqueurs."

"My father is a local winemaker, just outside Bariloche. Argentine wines are among the best in the world, and our family vineyard is well known, especially for its Malbec and Pinot Noir. I grew up learning about such things, naturally, and that is where I work, too."

A moment later the waitress returned with four large shots of Legui. After a toast, they all took sips, remarking on the sweet balance of the liqueur. After a bit more small talk, Dominic got down to business.

"Christof, has Jacob explained to you about his approaching me in France regarding his grandfather's diary?"

Prager feigned ignorance. He looked over to Jacob and said, "No, I didn't even know he had gone to France. But then, I expect he travels a lot."

"How do you two know each other?" Hana asked.

Christof looked at Jacob warily. "Our grandfathers were good friends during the war," he said. "Our families stayed in touch through the years, and Jacob and I got to better know one another."

Hana reached into her bag and brought out her phone, opening the Photos app. She held it while she spoke.

"When Jacob first shared his grandfather's diary with us in Paris," she began, "his hope was to find an artifact that Heinrich Himmler might have once had. We've done a great deal of research in that regard, and have come across something of a riddle, the solving of which could lead us to this artifact. The problem is, we only have two fragments of what looks like a three-piece puzzle."

"Two?" Jacob's eyes widened.

"Yes, we've been busy," Hana said, leaving it at that.

She held the phone down briefly for all to see the two images she had taken: the one from Bishop Hudal's biography, and the one from the slide found in the Béccar Nazi trove.

Jacob and Christof stared at the images eagerly, each quietly anxious to possess the two fragments they needed to complete the third, which Jacob had taken out of his grandfather's diary. They found themselves in a quandary, unable to ask Hana for full images without raising suspicion, while reluctant to give up their own lest they be left out of acquiring the prize.

Hana only allowed a few moments for them to see the image, not enough for them to get a good read of its contents. Withdrawing her phone, she returned it to her bag.

Christof looked up at Jacob. Jacob returned the gaze. *What to do?*

"I don't mean to be rude, but may we have a moment to discuss something?" Jacob asked.

"Not at all," Hana said, half expecting the reaction. "We'll be here when you return."

He and Christof stood and walked out of the bar and headed toward the restroom at the back of the restaurant.

"To my mind, it's pretty obvious they're discussing how to handle sharing the third fragment with us," Hana said to Dominic. "My money is on Jacob having it. I'd bet that fragment we found in Béccar was actually the one given by Himmler to Erich Prager. God knows how it ended up there."

"And I'd bet you're right," Dominic said, "since you usually are."

Several minutes later Jacob and Christof returned to the table, both of them more confident in their behavior. They sat down.

"First of all," Jacob said, "I must apologize for misleading you. I do have the missing third fragment."

Hana quickly glanced at Dominic, who flashed the barest of knowing smiles in return.

Jacob continued. "The reason we need this artifact is simple, but very important. Whatever it is, we believe there must be great value attached to it, especially since Himmler—and Hitler, for that matter—desperately wanted it for themselves. Assuming it can be found, our objective is to sell it to help Christof's father hold onto his vineyard, which he is on the brink of losing, a longer story I won't bother going into. I already have a buyer interested in acquiring the object. Even with what few details we know about it, this buyer is highly motivated."

"I should also mention," Christof interrupted, "that the second fragment you found once belonged to my grandfather. I happen to know he gave many such things to a friend in Béccar who was a collector of Nazi memorabilia. You obviously know of the raid on that man's home, an art dealer, since I imagine you found the fragment in police custody."

"In a roundabout way, yes," Hana said.

"In any case," Jacob continued, "we must come to some kind of arrangement, since we are now all in this together. If we pool our three fragments and solve the riddle my grandfather mentioned in his diary, then what will become of the artifact? Would the Vatican be willing to buy it, with the proceeds going to us?"

Dominic looked thoughtfully at each person around the table, lastly at Hana. Apart from the adventure, he reasoned, she was into this for the story, so she would have no resistance to such an outcome. The look in her eyes pretty much confirmed that, leaving the decision to him.

"I can't speak to the Vatican's ability or inclination to actually *pay* for something of this nature—whatever the artifact may be. After all, none of us really knows what it is we're dealing with here, nor really what may be involved to go about locating it."

Jacob looked pensive. "What do you suggest? I have revealed something I know to be important to the Church and I want to honor that, of course. Yet, please, you must understand my good friend's needs as well. And only together can we resolve the puzzle, correct?"

This was true, of course. Dominic had no way that he could ensure any financial return for this remarkable discovery. But he also certainly had the ear of Cardinal Petrini and the others in the hierarchy who would recognize that the value of this object would be well worth assisting a farmer in Argentina.

Dominic decided to trust them with knowledge of what they believed it to be. "Again, although I cannot speak for the Vatican, I am comfortable that they would recognize the value of compensating Christof for his contribution in what would have never been discovered otherwise. Now, as for the object, based on Himmler's journal notes he appears to have identified the artifact as being what's known as the 'Veil of Veronica.'" He went on to explain the history of the veil as he did for Hana earlier.

Jacob and Christof were both astounded at hearing this dramatic new information. Looking at each other, they both nodded in agreement.

"Alright," Jacob said. "Let's meet tomorrow at your hotel. I'll bring my fragment and we'll all work on figuring out the riddle."

He looked directly into Dominic's eyes. "If we can solve the riddle, we will leave the search for it in your hands, Father Dominic, and trust in your word that we will be compensated later."

CHAPTER 20

J ust as the bells of the nearby Cathedral of Our Lady of Nahuel Huapi struck 11:00 a.m., Jacob and Christof arrived at Hotel Cristal. They made their way to Dominic's room, where Hana had room service deliver beef empenadas and mate so they could enjoy lunch while planning their next steps.

Hana had the hotel's business center print out the two fragments from her iPhone, approximating their original sizes. All they needed now was Jacob's piece in order to complete the riddle.

"Again, I am sorry I withheld this," Jacob confessed, "but I did not realize how far you would get in your own research. So, now let's see what we have here."

With that, he withdrew the third folded fragment from his wallet and laid it out on the table next to the two Hana had printed and trimmed. When properly pieced together, the riddle was now apparent to everyone.

Hana retrieved her notebook and filled in the missing text. Now, finally, they had something complete to work with:

I hold the key to open free
The secret door you cannot see.
I always run but never walk
I sometimes sing but cannot talk…

No head on which a hat to place
You always look me in the face.
The key swings freely to and fro
Remove it and you now must go…

With key in hand you should explore
The center of the solar floor.
The holy face of God's own son
Is resting under the black sun.

They all bent over to read Hana's notepad transcription, but she read it aloud anyway, and read it once more.

"You notice it rhymes?!" she exclaimed. "Himmler must have written this first in English as a rhyming riddle, then translated it into German. What an odd juxtaposition. Why would he go to the trouble?"

Jacob had an idea. "Himmler had a fondness for codes, cyphers, and simply playing with words, and he was learning English. Maybe it was to confuse others about who the author was? If found, the fragments could appear to have been written by an English speaker who had it translated to German? Just one more ploy within a puzzle, is all I can guess."

Hana was struck by something she recalled.

"One thing I do recognize here is the 'black sun'—which I presume is the same image I found in Himmler's biography, the runic mosaic inlaid on the floor of the Generals' Hall in Wewelsburg Castle. It's *got* to be the same reference. But if there is a key to get into it, that's buried here somewhere in the riddle. Do any of you recognize the meaning of any of the rest of it?"

While Hana assembled the mate and passed around the empenadas, they each studied the riddle in silence, playing it over and over in their minds.

Dominic was the first to speak. "So, what is it that has a face we can look at, but doesn't have a head? And while it cannot talk, it is able to sing; and it runs but can't walk. What a bizarre concept. Who would have thought up such a ridiculous thing?"

"Well," Jacob offered, "a dog has a face but can't really wear a hat. And it can howl but can't talk…though it *can* run *and* walk. Besides, such a dog can't still be alive, unless it's a statue…" He realized he was fumbling in the dark.

Hana, ever the puzzle master, was frustrated. There was *something* familiar here, she just couldn't put her finger on it.

"Something about the '*key swings freely*' is related to the object. What swings?"

As they munched on the delicious empenadas and sipped their mate—rather than add the suffering of a ritual to their already strained minds—the bells of the cathedral struck noon.

Hana listened to the lovely chime, but as she did something triggered in her mind. Each *gong* of the bells seemed to shine a light on her thought processes.

She got up to reread the riddle. Then she dropped her empenada on the table and looked up with a broad smile on her face.

"Do you hear the *singing?*" she asked the group with a look of pride.

"What singing?" Dominic asked.

"The singing of the *clock!*" she responded. "Or rather the church bells, but a clocktower also *'sings,' 'runs,' doesn't wear a hat*, and we can *look it in the face!!* It's a *clock!*"

The others stood up and reread the riddle. As each finished, they looked up at Hana with new admiration.

"And a grandfather clock has a pendulum, which *swings to and fro*. So the key must be inside a grandfather clock, probably somewhere in the castle, and somehow attached to the pendulum."

"Hana, that is nothing short of brilliant!" Dominic said, clearly pleased by his friend's puzzling skills.

"Michael," she enthused, "this means the veil—*The holy face of God's own son*—is buried beneath the black sun mosaic inside Wewelsburg Castle. How are we supposed to get inside, which is one obstacle, with another being to actually open the center of the sun mosaic—assuming there's still a grandfather clock there and the key is still inside it—and then retrieve the veil, which obviously must be in the hidden vault Himmler spoke of? And Jacob did tell us the castle today is a youth hostel and museum. It's such a convoluted prospect! Any thoughts?"

"Whoa! Let's take this one step at a time." Dominic loved her enthusiasm, and her assessment of their obstacles was accurate.

But they needed to approach this logically. He reflected on all that Hana had just proposed. He got up to walk around the room, thinking as he sipped his mate, then turned and faced the group.

"I do have one or two ideas…."

CHAPTER 21

The blow to his chest had nearly knocked him unconscious, but still the others circled around him, pressing in for a closer look, an invisible shroud of testosterone in the air.

"Stand back," urged the man in charge, "give them some room."

Karl Dengler was surrounded now, but the focus of his attention was the man towering above him, the one who had put him on his back, the blade of a menacing halberd hovering inches from his face as the man's foot rested on his chest. Dengler considered his limited options.

Sergeant Dieter Koehl stood over the young soldier in a posture of domination. Looking down, he smiled at his opponent, then, retracting both his foot and the training halberd, reached out a hand to lift him up.

Dengler smiled back as he was hoisted to a standing position. "*That* was a great move, Dieter. I did not see it coming at all."

"You just need more years on the planet, little one," Koehl chided. Dengler punched his friend's shoulder playfully in reply. The others applauded Koehl's tactical mastery.

Next it was Lukas Bischoff's turn, going up against Dengler

in a test of judo combat as the Swiss Guards, tasked by the Holy See to protect the Vatican, continued its routine training session.

Facing his opponent, Dengler turned his body diagonally, knees slightly bent, his left leg further forward than his right. His abdominal muscles were tensed but not fully engaged, his balled hands held loosely in front of his face. Each man assessed the other's determination as they faced off, circling within the ring of onlookers. The hot room smelled of sweat.

In a flash Dengler dove for Lukas's legs, then suddenly twisted, bringing Lukas face down on the foam rubber mat. Dengler quickly moved on top of him into a *shime-waza* position, a strangling technique designed to render his opponent helpless. His right arm circling Lukas's throat, Dengler flipped him over, pulling his own arm in tighter, applying pressure to Lukas's neck thus reducing circulation to the brain which, if he'd continued, would have cut off breathing in seconds. On his back, with Dengler beneath him, Lukas was just about to lose consciousness when Karl whispered into his partner's ear *"Ich liebe dich."* Lukas tapped out, choking with laughter.

The group gave another round of applause, this time for Dengler, who pulled Lukas up from the mat then gave him a quick hug while running his hand through his hair in a discreet gesture of affection.

Assisted by the local *gendarmerie* at the Swiss Guard training camp in the Ticino canton of Switzerland, Karl Dengler, Dieter Koehl, Lukas Bischoff, and a few other fellow soldiers from Rome had been invited to serve as instructors for the spring session of training new candidates for the Pontifical Swiss Guard. Once their training was complete—comprising 176 hours of tactical military and personal defense techniques, along with rigorous marksmanship drills employing a variety of weapons— the inductees would be welcomed into the elite corps by the Pope himself on May 6, in a traditional ceremony held every year on that date since the Sack of Rome in 1527, when 147 Swiss

Guards died defending Pope Clement VII against the invading soldiers of Emperor Charles V.

"Dengler! Bischoff! Front and center!" shouted the drill instructor.

The two young men scrambled to the front of the group and promptly stood at attention, their chests heaving for air beneath sweaty t-shirts after the strenuous workout. Lukas was still a little wobbly from the chokehold.

"Gentlemen," the instructor announced to the group, "as you have just witnessed, Sergeant Dengler executed a perfect *shime-waza* within seconds, particularly notable since he was the smaller man. Once he had control of his opponent's neck restricting the veinal flow of blood and oxygen to the brain, Corporal Bischoff did not stand a chance. When properly applied, your opponent will usually become unconscious in less than 15 seconds, often half that time.

"It's a good thing they are friends," he concluded, to laughter by everyone. "Okay, off to the showers, we are done for the afternoon. Tomorrow is your last day of training, so get a good night's sleep."

"YOU NEARLY PUT my lights out today, Karl," Lukas said as they both savored beers in a nearby *gasthaus*, reviewing the day's activities. "There will be retribution, though, when you least expect it—like Cato and Inspector Clouseau."

"Promises, promises," Dengler teased his partner with a warm smile, enjoying the banter and his reference to the *Pink Panther* movies.

The cell phone in Dengler's pocket vibrated with an incoming call.

"It's Father Dominic!" he said to Lukas, tapping the green button.

"Hey, Michael! How are things with you?"

"Karl, it's so good to hear your voice," Dominic said. "Hana and I are in southern Argentina at the moment, but we'll be leaving tomorrow."

"Argentina?! What took you there?"

"It's a long story, but one I'll tell you when we meet up. You're still training in Switzerland, aren't you?"

"Yes, tomorrow is our last day and Lukas and I still have a few days off after that, so we were thinking of heading to Paris to visit friends."

"Karl, Hana and I have stumbled onto a pretty exciting artifact hunt, and we could really use your help. Instead of Paris for now, how about joining us at Wewelsburg Castle in Büren, Germany? I'll make it worth your while."

"Hold on, let me talk with Lukas…"

After a brief discussion, Lukas agreed, happy to oblige their friends.

"You've got a deal, Michael. Lukas and I will meet you there at, say, around noon the day after tomorrow? We'll be done with training and can drive there in my Jeep. We can stop through Paris when we're done."

"Fantastic, Karl, thanks so much. We'll be flying into Dortmund Airport near Wewelsburg tomorrow and find a hotel. I'll text you instructions where to meet when we arrive. I'm really grateful, my friend. And I promise you some excitement in a new adventure."

"We are always up for rousing new experiences," Karl said, looking at Lukas. "See you then, Michael."

CHAPTER 22

The sun had set hours earlier, and the large dark barn on a private estate on the outskirts of Bariloche was slowly filling up with people, mostly men, nearly all of them having blond hair and blue eyes, and all of them of German descent. Under a dim light over the entrance, two armed guards checked the identifications of each person approaching them, verifying faces and names on a clipboard checklist held by one of the young guards, Günther Fischbein, before allowing them to enter the building and join the assembly.

Inside, a hundred metal folding chairs had been set up, most of them filled by now. Several long red banners lined the walls of the barn, each with a large white swastika in its center. There was a stir of expectancy in the air as attendees murmured to the persons sitting next to them, waiting for the meeting to start.

When the checklist had been fully marked off and all registered guests were confirmed to be present, the guards closed the barn doors, remaining outside to patrol the grounds.

At precisely 9:00 p.m. Jacob Rausch and Christof Prager walked onto the makeshift stage. Each stood silently at parade rest for a few moments until all murmuring ceased, at which point they clicked their heels together loudly, raised their arms in an outward flat-palm salute, and shouted the words *"Heil Hitler!"* Everyone in the room snapped to a standing position, raised their arms, and repeated the salute to the *Führer*. *"Heil Hitler!"*

The meeting of the Ahnenerbe's *NaziKinder* had begun.

"… And that is why our current mission is so important," Rausch continued in his address to the gathering. "As the children of our honored forefathers, we will be the ones to recover Herr Himmler's precious veil bearing the true image of Jesus Christ. Such an object shall be instrumental in furthering the supremacy of our Aryan race, as Herr Hitler wished it to be."

As Jacob finished, he ceded the floor to Christof, who stepped forward. "We are even now putting a team together to obtain the artifact from Wewelsburg Castle in Westphalia in two days' time, using local collaborators in Germany. We are aware that a Vatican priest and his colleague are doing the same thing, but we hope to get there first. The veil must be returned to our people, and we will acquire it by any means necessary. The Ahnenerbe has important plans for it."

The room erupted in applause and repeated shouts of *"Sieg Heil! Sieg Heil!"*

"Christof, Günther and I will be leaving for Germany tomorrow to lead our team in this effort," Jacob said boldly. "In a few days we will return with the artifact, so the real work can begin. Stand with us then as you stand with us tonight. *Heil Hitler!*"

On cue, everyone gathered stood and repeated the salute, then again, and a third time. At that point, the meeting was adjourned.

As the assembled hundred chattered while making their way to the exit, a tall man in a black trenchcoat and felt fedora, with sharp facial features above a clerical collar encircling his neck, approached Jacob and Christof who had just descended the stage.

"An excellent speech, by both of you," he commended them. "As you know, I knew your grandfathers in their later years. They would be proud of you."

"Thank you, Eminence, I'm honored that you could attend our meeting, having come all the way from Buenos Aires."

"It was worth it," Cardinal Dante said. "I spoke with my good friend Capitán Portillo in Béccar about Father Dominic's interfering activities, and I very much look forward to your return with the veil. If there is anything I might do to assist, you have but to ask."

CHAPTER 23

At two hours before midnight, the gypsy compound outside the French town of Les Pèlerins was quiet. Most of its inhabitants had settled into their tents for the night, and the fires in the metal bins on which they had cooked their evening meals had burned out, with only glowing embers and wisps of wood smoke still lingering in the evening air of the forest encampment.

Gunari Lakatos, the *voivode*, or chieftain of the Roma commune was reading a book in his tent when his cell phone rang.

Surprised he would be getting a call so late, he answered cautiously.

"*Bonsoir, voivode,*" Father Dominic said with a smile in his voice. "My apologies for calling so late, but it is important we have a conversation that cannot wait."

"Father Michael!" Gunari said happily. "What a great pleasure hearing your voice, despite the hour. How can I help you?"

"Do you remember that favor you offered me the last time we met?"

Gunari paused a moment. "As you have just reminded me,

yes, I now recall that promise," he said affably, "and of course, I shall honor it whenever it suits your purposes. Shall I assume this is why you call me tonight?"

"Yes, Gunari, I need the good services of your talented sons, Milosh and Shandor, in a special operation we're planning in West Germany. It is not too far from where you are, and we will, of course, take care of all expenses, including transportation."

"Ah, but Milosh still has his beloved BMW Roadster—I believe you will remember the car he found 'abandoned' on our last adventure together, yes?—and I am certain they would prefer to drive it rather than take the train. As for other expenses, I will leave that to you."

Dominic smiled at the mention of the "abandoned" car. The Roma sons had been instrumental in assisting Michael in an earlier adventure. The car had been leftover spoils of the situation, and Michael had turned a blind eye to its origins or the brothers method of obtaining it. Now Michael gave him the necessary details, including when and where to meet, as well as a brief summary of the job involved. Thanking the gypsy leader, he ended the call.

CHAPTER 24

As the jet took off from Buenos Aires bound for Dortmund, Germany, Dominic reclined his seat to take a short nap, aided by the effects of the Xanax he had taken now kicking in. Hana had insisted on paying for First Class tickets for the long flight with multiple stopovers, which Michael did not object to given his concerns about tight spaces.

He had not gotten much sleep the night before as he struggled to lay out their plan to somehow break into Wewelsburg Castle and retrieve the veil. Using one of the hotel business center's computers, he had done a good deal of research on the castle itself, including available floor plans, hostel accommodation requirements, the adjacent museum's layout, and other details of the building to help in preparing for the operation. He printed out all documents to later share with his team.

He found that the grand Generals' Hall was essentially just part of the tour offered to castle visitors and was rarely used for other purposes. In one of the photos he found on the internet, he and Hana were thrilled to have discovered a grandfather clock standing against the wall near the Black Sun mosaic, and presumed that to be the clock from the riddle. They had to admit there were long odds involved, but that would be their first objective, exploring the pendulum for some type of key to the floor opening—if there even *was* a 'floor opening' of some sort. Looking closely at the photo of the black sun, they couldn't conceive of where such an orifice might be, much less facing the possibility of it having been discovered long before now. Or how to access it privately without arousing suspicion from the current occupants. There were so many variables in the scheme, each one resting upon another.

"Are we crazy for even attempting this?" he had asked Hana before they left the hotel for the airport. He wasn't exactly comfortable with this surreptitious approach, but whoever owned the castle now might not be as willing as Jacob to allow the Church to take possession of the veil, even if offered compensation.

"No doubt about that," she replied flatly. "But what is the worst that can happen, except possible prison time for breaking and entering?"

"This is going to be a long trip," Dominic sighed.

FINALLY ARRIVING in Dortmund at 6:00 p.m. the next day, they had arranged for a rental car for the one-hour drive to Wewelsburg Castle and the closest hotel that would serve as their home base. Before they left Buenos Aires, Hana had made arrangements for the four others on their team—Karl, Lukas, Milosh and Shandor—to stay at the youth hostel inside the castle. This was a crucial component of Dominic's plan, giving them easier access to the Generals' Hall, the grandfather clock, and the black sun.

Now all they needed was luck. A lot of it.

CHAPTER 25

Dengler and Lukas were waiting in the lobby of the Hotel Walz for Dominic and Hana to arrive when Karl spotted two young men walk through the entrance, appearing as though such a venue was completely foreign to them. At once he recognized them—they were the two gypsies they had worked with in the ski resort of Chamonix, France, many months earlier.

"Milosh!" Karl called out with a wide grin. Seeing a friendly face, the two Roma rushed up to Karl and both gave him a welcoming hug. Karl introduced his partner, Lukas, and the four of them took seats waiting for Dominic and Hana to show up.

"So, we will be staying at the youth hostel in the castle itself," Karl told the new arrivals, "where we'll have better chances getting the job done. Father Michael will have more instructions for us when they get here, but that's as much as I know now."

The four chatted amiably over the next half hour until they saw Hana and Dominic enter the lobby.

Everyone exchanged greetings, after which Hana checked in and got their room keys. They all then gathered in Michael's room to go over the operation.

Dominic had laid out the floor plan of the castle showing

which parts were public and which parts were closed off. The Generals' Hall was shown as a Restricted Area, which had good and bad implications: good, in that no one else was likely to be there while they carried out their mission; bad, in that if they were caught, they were subject to the laws of the castle's owner, the governmental District of Paderborn. The 400-year-old castle was deemed a historical monument, and the Historical Museum of the Prince-Bishopric of Paderborn was considered a national treasure, despite—or perhaps in tribute to—its villainous past.

"Karl," Dominic began, "you, Lukas, Milosh and Shandor will be staying in the east wing of the hostel. The house closes at 10:30 p.m. so all guests should be in their rooms by then. At 10:45, from the east wing on the second floor you'll all need to take the fire stairway here," he pointed down at the map on the table, "then make your way down to the Generals' Hall here," he moved his finger now pointing to the Hall, "where Milosh, you'll need to pick the lock to open the door and let everyone in. You have your tools with you?"

Milosh grinned and produced a multi-folded oilcloth in which were laid out several professional lock picking tools.

"Good. Lukas, you stand guard outside the door. If any of the staff sees you, just tell them you were looking for the kitchen for a late night snack or something. Do whatever it takes to get them away from the Hall.

"Now, as for the rest of you…"

Dominic gave each person detailed assignments for the balance of the operation. Each man understood their role and that time was of the essence.

"You guys better leave now to get checked into the hostel," Hana said, looking at her watch. "See if you can get a tour of the place and find a way to inspect the Generals' Hall if at all possible. That would be immensely helpful, to get a preview of what you'll be facing. For obvious reasons, Michael and I won't be able to join you, so you're on your own."

"When you're finished," Dominic added, "return to your

rooms, text me with an update, then get some sleep. Check out in the morning and meet us back here first thing. If you have any trouble, find a way to call us here." He opened a drawer and pulled out a sheet of the hotel's guest stationery and wrote down their room number on it, handing it to Karl. "Plus, you have my mobile number."

With that, the four young men left the hotel in the Jeep Wrangler and made their way to the Wewelsburg Youth Hostel five kilometers away.

CHAPTER 26

It was just past 9:00 p.m. when Dengler and his team arrived at the imposing castle, its massive dark shape in the moonless night dominating the skyline as the four young men approached on foot, having parked the Jeep in the guest parking lot. Two tall turrets framed a medieval bridge and gatehouse entrance, beneath which was a wide stone bridge over an empty moat, one that Himmler had intended to complete before the war ended. A light shone through the windows of a small balcony room extending out over the entrance, and the courtyard beneath the arched gate could only accommodate foot traffic, so narrow was the entryway.

Dengler led his team across the bridge, through the arched entry and into the brightly lit hostel office. A friendly German Shepherd stood up to greet them as they walked through the door, thrusting his nose up and whining to be petted, which each of the new arrivals did in turn as the dog took each of their scents. Lukas, who had much experience with dogs in the Swiss Army's K-9 Unit, spent several minutes playing with Fritzi, as the hostel manager, Frau Schneider, had introduced him to the group. There was a small bowl of dog treats on the counter.

Lukas grabbed a few, giving Fritzi one now and pocketing the rest by habit.

Having checked passports, made note of their vehicle in the parking lot, and taken payment for two dorm rooms—two men to a room—Frau Schneider gave each of them room keys and a map of the castle, circling where the rooms were located. She then explained the rules of the house—curfew by 10:30 p.m., no smoking, no partying or loud music—and absolutely no exploring of the castle without a staff member. They could have a tour tomorrow if they wanted, but it was too late for one tonight, since she was the only one on duty.

Though disappointed they couldn't get a tour, Dengler took her sole presence as a good sign their activity was not likely to be interrupted. The tower where the Generals' Hall would be found was far enough away from the office that she wouldn't hear them anyway.

Once the team left her office, Frau Schneider went back to watching TV in the back office, Fritzi resting at her heels.

FINDING THEIR ADJOINING ROOMS, Karl and Lukas took one, while Milosh and Shandor occupied the other. They all settled in until the appointed time.

"A little more comfortable than our tent in the forest, isn't it, Milosh," Shandor noted. His brother nodded, laying on one of the soft beds to test it.

"So, this is how the *gorger* live," Milosh said, referring to non-Roma. They had few opportunities to sleep anywhere outside their gypsy camps, since Roma were often on the move when forced by local authorities to leave their current dwelling places. Such is the plight of nomadic tribes throughout Europe, the only life the two young brothers had known growing up. The bed was a luxury they had rarely known.

· · ·

At 10:45 there was a quiet knock on the door. Shandor opened it, and Karl and Lukas walked in. Karl had a red backpack slung over a shoulder.

"Ready?" he asked. The other three nodded tensely.

Looking out into the dimly lit hallway to make sure it was clear, Karl led the others out of the room, and they quietly made their way to the fire stairwell at the north end of the hall.

Gently pushing the door open, they descended the stairs, going down two floors, then exited into a wide circular hallway that led to the Generals' Hall.

When they got to the entrance—two large wooden doors, richly carved in bas-relief—Milosh pulled out his tools and promptly got to work on the lock while the others shielded his activity. Within a minute the lock popped open. Everyone but Lukas slipped inside. He then locked and closed the door behind him and remained on guard in the dark hall.

The massive Generals' Hall was an airy, circular marble-floored chamber about thirty feet high and sixty feet across, featuring twelve floor-to-ceiling granite and brick columns framing twelve window alcoves, all surrounding the inlaid marble *Schwarze Sonne* mosaic at its very center—the same runic Black Sun Hana had shown them in the photo. Dengler's first impression was that the space looked more like a ballroom than anything else. But knowing of the strange ritualistic Nazi ceremonies that had once taken place here gave him chills.

Looking around for the grandfather clock, he spotted it against the wall near a door leading to the west wing. While Dengler went to inspect it, Milosh and Shandor's assignment was to determine what kind of special "opening" the Black Sun mosaic might possess.

At first glance there was nothing but smooth, flat marble, seemingly impenetrable. Cracking a green military-grade chem light Dengler had given them for illumination, they both got down on their knees to more closely examine the tiles. Perhaps there were cracks that one might use to lift the slabs out.

Inspecting every bit of it, nothing seemed to offer clues as to how one might access any part of the mosaic.

Holding the chem light closer to the center, Shandor noticed a tiny bit of compacted dirt on one side of the inner circular tile that clearly was not part of the design.

"Milosh, hand me one of your tools, like a small pin or screwdriver."

Reaching into his oilcloth for something suitable, Milosh produced a slim lock rake. Handing it to his brother, Shandor then poked at the dirt, scraping it such that the dirt came away in small chips of dust. Clearly now, this was a hole that had been compacted with dirt over many years, such that it had been firmly tamped down with other debris accumulated between the cracks of the mosaic.

He repeated the chipping process, then dug deeper, clearing out all the dirt after a few minutes, revealing a round hole about twelve millimeters deep.

Peering diagonally across the center tile from the hole, he spotted a similar round slab of compacted dirt, and began the same digging process. Before long, two half-inch holes had been revealed.

Shandor looked at Milosh and smiled as they both silently celebrated their discovery.

MEANWHILE, Dengler had no problem unlocking the tall glass door to the grandfather clock using just the pick on his Swiss Army knife. The clock simply required a standard skeleton key, which were easy to pick, a trick shown to him some months prior by his Swiss Guard special ops colleague Dieter Koehl.

He then snapped one of the chem lights, which flared a bright green. With the door now opened, he held the light inside searching for anything resembling a key of some sort. Finding nothing apparent, he more closely inspected the innards of the pendulum mechanism. He had to be careful not moving the hanging weights around so as to minimize any undesired clanging noises.

The time showed 10:57 when Dengler stopped the pendulum bob from swinging.

There were five pendulum rods attached to the large pendulum bob at the bottom—the lowest decorative part of the clock that swung back and forth. As he slid his hand up and down the back of each rod, each flat strut was smooth, with nothing resembling a key attached to any of them. His hand did pass over two metal knobs in the center rod—each about six millimeters round, twelve millimeters long, and a hand's length apart—but he thought nothing of it, assuming it was simply just some manufacturing grip, certainly nothing like a key.

As his frustration grew, he stood back, looking at the entire mechanism as if something would stand out as obviously out of the ordinary. *Where could it be?*

Turning, he saw Milosh and Shandor on their knees, looking up at each other and smiling.

"Psst!" he whispered. "Find anything over there?"

The brothers stood up and rushed over to Dengler.

"Karl," Milosh whispered excitedly, "we found two holes in the marble, each twelve millimeters deep, about six millimeters round, and maybe two hundred millimeters apart. That *must* be the key receptacle! So, you need to be looking for something with two protrusions, probably metal, that would be used to turn the marble plate in the center of the mosaic."

Dengler thought a moment—the two knobs his hand had passed over! That would roughly match the measurements Milosh had described. Thrusting his hand back to that spot behind the center pendulum rod, he felt them again. *That had to be it!*

Holding the light higher, he reached up to the hook on which the rods were fastened, and discovered each rod could be independently removed from the suspension spring at the top. Analyzing the mechanism, he realized the center rod served no purpose at all in the functioning of the clock! A special hook had been made for the center rod alone, its appearance masked by the adjacent pendulum rods. *Brilliant!* he thought, as he gently unhooked the center rod, carefully removing it from the rest of the assembly and pulling it out of the cabinet.

He looked at the two brothers. They all smiled eagerly as they made their way back to the Black Sun.

CHAPTER 27

O utside the door to the Generals' Hall, Lukas was still standing in the darkened hallway with his back to the entrance. A patient man by nature, he grew more anxious the longer he stood guard, uncertain how much more time his friends would need. Having nothing else to do, his mind became restless.

Then he heard a sound, and not a welcome one. It began as a low growl coming from the other end of the hallway, in the shadows. At once, Lukas was alert to the presence of a large animal. Whatever it was, it was slowly approaching him in the darkness, snarling quietly as it moved closer. It had to be a dog. He took a chance.

"Fritzi?"

The growling stopped. A moment later Fritzi advanced in the shadows, his tail wagging. Lukas reached into his jacket pocket and withdrew a couple of the dog treats he'd saved. He bent down to ruffle the dog's neck.

Then he heard footsteps approaching, and the light of a small torch cutting through the shadows of the hallway. It was Frau Schneider.

"What are you doing here?" she asked in scolding German.

"I, uh, was looking for the toilet and, um, got lost," Lukas responded in a louder than normal voice, so his colleagues might hear him. "I'm glad Fritzi found me, but I'm not sure he'd be helpful pointing the way. Could you show me?"

Frau Schneider looked at him skeptically, then shone her torch on the doors of the Generals' Hall. She walked forward, rattled the door handle to make sure it was secure, then looked again at Lukas.

"I will show you where is the toilet. Please follow me."

As she led Lukas away from the doors, Fritzi dutifully by his side, he tried to make conversation with the woman to allay any suspicions she might have.

"I am a Swiss Guard at the Vatican now, but I was once in the Swiss Army, and had a German Shepherd just like yours for our K-9 Unit missions. That's probably why Fritzi likes me."

"He likes everyone," she snapped. "Some guard dog *he* is." Then her tone softened. "So, you help protect the Holy Father in Rome?"

"Yes," Lukas replied, "it is a great honor to be in the Pontifical Swiss Guard."

"I am Catholic myself," she said, "and would love to have an audience with His Holiness. Is that something you could arrange?" She looked up at Lukas, smiling in jest.

He snickered. "Well, I can certainly say you'll be welcomed to join the faithful in St. Peter's Square…" Frau Schneider chuffed a harsh little laugh.

"*Ja*, that is what I thought," she replied, now a bit friendlier. They had finally reached the east wing where the woman pointed out the men's room.

"Here is the toilet, *mein Herr*. Now, no more exploring. Get some sleep."

With that, she headed back to her office with Fritzi while Lukas entered the restroom. *That was close*, he thought to himself.

Waiting a few minutes, he peered back out into the hallway, then snuck back to the west wing and the Generals' Hall.

. . .

A FEW MINUTES EARLIER, Dengler and the two gypsy brothers
heard the door handle being worked from the other side, along
with the sound of voices. Alarmed, they quickly dispersed in
silence, each taking cover behind one of the large stone columns
in the hall, waiting nervously for whomever was coming in to
discover them and blow the operation.

After a couple minutes, the voices receded. Obviously, Lukas
had taken control of the situation, whatever it was. When they
heard nothing but silence, they emerged from hiding and
continued their work.

With the pendulum key rod finally removed from the
grandfather clock, the team moved to the center of the Black Sun.

Dengler bent down, key rod in hand, and lined up the two
pegs in the matching holes on the marble floor. *They fit!* Using
the rod as leverage, he put moderate strength into turning the
rod counterclockwise, assuming the center tile was some kind of
screw-based receptacle cover. It did not budge.

Inspecting the round center tile, he noticed a circle of dirt
surrounding the tile, pointing it out to Milosh and Shandor. Both
of the brothers got to work using the picking tools, scraping the
age-old compacted dirt and muck from the now visually obvious
circular ring around the center tile. Decades of grime had settled
into the cracks, and it took some effort to clear it all out.

Once they were satisfied the ring was clean, Dengler tried
again to force the rod to open the tile cover.

This time it budged. It was a thrilling moment for them all.
They were so close now!

Dengler pushed and pulled the rod to loosen up the screw
thread. Slowly but surely, he made progress rocking it back and
forth. Eventually the grime fell away and he was able to make a
complete 360 degree turn. Four more full turns, and the lid came
free from the inner screw threads.

Each face looked up at the others expectantly. Dengler lifted

GARY MCAVOY

away the marble lid, likely the first time the lid had been removed since Himmler left Wewelsburg and later killed himself in 1945.

Setting the lid and key rod aside, they raised their chem lights and peered down into the hole.

In it was a small upright safe. Fortunately, not a combination lock, but an ordinary key lock. Milosh grinned, knowing he could make short work of it.

Unfolding his oilcloth and laying out his tools, he extracted a snake rake and a half diamond, two of the implements he figured this lock might require. He began inserting and manipulating them inside the keyhole.

Dengler asked in a whisper where he'd learn to pick locks.

"I'm a gypsy...it's in our blood!" Milosh said proudly. "Actually I learned from another Roma, a very experienced *voivode*. He once told me that 'lock picks are like fishing lures, but they are meant to catch the fisherman, not the fish.'"

A few moments later, the internal lock mechanism clicked, and the lid sprung free from its bolts. They lifted the lid.

Sitting inside was a single object, a white alabaster box. Dengler carefully removed it and set it on the marble floor. Shining his light into the safe, there was nothing else left in the cavity.

He opened the lid.

Inside the box was a bundle of sheer fabric of some sort, with various colors on it. He dared not disturb it, for Dominic had told him not to touch the veil if they found it, just to check and make sure it was there.

Replacing the lid, he put the alabaster box into his backpack, protecting it with a thick towel he had brought with him.

"Let's get out of this place," he said to the brothers. "We are done here."

Resealing the safe, Dengler returned the lid to the circular hole, and screwed it back into place. He then took the rod key and returned it to where he found it inside the clock. Once in place, he swung the pendulum bob at the bottom to restart the clock, reset the hands to the current time, 11:28, then closed the glass door.

Making sure there was nothing else left to reveal they had been there, they silently walked to the door, then tapped twice lightly to alert Lukas they were ready to come out, hoping Lukas was still there. Two taps came back from the opposite side, signaling all was clear.

Dengler opened the door, and all three emerged from the Hall. He then closed the door and locked it, making sure it was secure.

As they moved away, they heard the grandfather clock in the Hall behind them strike the half-hour chime at 11:30, echoing loudly through the empty marble room. Breathing easier now, the team quietly made their way back to their dorm rooms.

After settling back in his room, Dengler texted Dominic that their mission was a success. They would see them first thing in the morning.

CHAPTER 28

Early the next morning the team had assembled in Dengler's room for their departure. As they arrived at the hostel office, Frau Schneider was just about to leave her shift, making way for old Herr Becker to take over for the day.

As Fritzi ran up to Lukas for another treat, Karl and Milosh returned their room keys and retrieved everyone's passports.

"Where are you boys headed now?" the woman asked. "Are you just exploring our castles?"

"No, I'm afraid our holiday time is up," Karl said. "We now head back to Rome and our jobs at the Vatican."

She looked at the two long-haired gypsy boys with a raised eyebrow. Dengler followed her gaze.

"Oh, our friends here live in France. We just met up with them for a road trip in Germany for a few days."

That seemed to placate Frau Schneider. "Okay, then. *Auf wiedersehen*, boys. Do come back and visit us soon. Come, Fritzi, let's go home." She and the dog left the office.

After bidding farewell to Herr Becker, the men left the office and headed across the bridge to the parking lot. It was a warm morning and they were all in good spirits, their mission having been accomplished, and looking forward to sharing their treasure with Dominic and Hana back at their hotel for a celebration.

As they crossed the wide stone bridge, four men were approaching from the opposite direction. As they passed, Dengler smiled and gave them a quick informal salute and a "*Guten Tag*" greeting, which the three younger men—all tall, blond, athletic sorts—returned in kind. Dengler observed that the fourth man was quite older, not the kind who might typically stay in a youth hostel, and had the military bearing of a soldier. He was also wearing a trench coat, rather odd clothing for a warm spring day.

After loading their gear into the Jeep Wrangler and settling themselves in, Dengler drove out of the lot and headed for the Hotel Walz a few kilometers away.

"*Guten Tag*," Jacob Rausch said to the old man behind the counter of the hostel office. "We would like a tour of the castle, now if possible."

Herr Becker blinked behind thick glass lenses and looked up at the clock on the wall. "Well, the first tour of the day begins in about an hour. The tour guide is not yet here. You are welcome to wait."

"Our main interest is the Generals' Hall," Rausch said, ignoring the man's statement. "There is something we are looking for that is very important. Couldn't you just open that up for us?"

Becker stood his ground. "I am afraid not, young man. I must stay here in the office and there is nobody else to accompany you. Those are the rules."

The older man in the trench coat stepped forward and produced a wallet from his pocket, flipping it open to reveal a police badge and identification. The Ahnenerbe had tentacles spread throughout Germany, even in law enforcement, which came in useful for situations such as this.

"I am Constable Jäger with the *Bundespolizei*. I must insist you open up the Generals' Hall for us now, please. This is a matter of state interest."

Becker looked down nervously at the ID. "*Ja*, Herr Constable, of course I will comply, if it is that important."

Becker walked around the counter, placed a "Be Right Back" sign in several languages on the counter, and led the men into the castle and downstairs to the east wing and the Generals' Hall.

"I am sure there is nothing you will find there," Becker explained. "It has been the same as it was for several decades now. Empty. We hardly ever use it."

No one responded to Becker's statement. They walked in silence to their destination. On reaching the wooden doors of the Hall, Becker searched for the appropriate key on a large ring. Finding the one he needed, he opened the doors for his unusual visitors.

Rausch led the way through with Christof, Günther and their German police confederate in tow. The men spread out in the now brilliantly-lit great Hall, looking at everything. Two things caught Rausch's eye. The first was an infrared security camera mounted at the top of one of the far columns. Then he looked down on the Black Sun, inspecting it closely.

"Herr Becker, is the floor in this room swept or polished often?"

"*Ja*, it is kept in perfect condition at all times. Why do you ask?"

"I notice some dirt here on the *Schwarze Sonne*. Would you say that is normal?"

Becker ambled over to the mosaic and peered at it closely. His eyebrows shot up.

"No, that is very unusual. I cannot account for it. I must take this up with the maintenance supervisor."

Rausch knelt down and noticed two small holes on either side of the center tile, and that the center tile clearly appeared independent of the surrounding mosaic. He looked up at the old man.

"Do you have two screwdrivers we might use?" he asked calmly.

Becker blinked while he considered the request. "There should be some in our janitor's closet just outside in the hallway. I will check."

In the meantime, Rausch went over to the grandfather clock, looking for any sign of the key mentioned in Himmler's riddle.

'The key swings freely to and fro,' he remembered. *That narrows it down to the pendulum.* Stopping the movement of the clock, Rausch looked at each of the rods, then ran his hand down each one, top to bottom. When he discovered the center rod having two protruding knobs behind it, he suspected that might be the key—right-sized pegs, right distance from each other for the floor plate. Looking up, he noted the hook on the suspension assembly, and lifted the rod free of its resting place.

As he did this Becker returned with two screwdrivers.

"We won't need those now, *dánke.* Jäger, can you check the video recordings for any activity in the past two days?" He pointed up at the security camera. "Start with today and go backwards. I have a feeling this dirt is fresh."

"Herr Becker, please show me your video recording equipment," Constable Jäger said. The two took off for the hostel office.

Rausch brought the rod key over to the mosaic, knelt down and inserted it into the holes. He began turning the rod counterclockwise, opening the tile plate. After four turns the lid came free. The safe was now visible, but locked.

Rausch looked up at Christof and the other man. "I doubt Becker or anyone even knows about this, so they wouldn't have a key. Obviously Dominic and his people have already been here by the looks of the dirt. I can only assume that he and his people must have picked this. Let's see those video recordings."

The three men ran out of the Hall, down the stairs and back to the hostel office, where Becker was just loading the recorded video on the computer for them to see.

"Wouldn't the night manager have seen activity in the Generals' Hall on this monitor?" the constable asked.

Becker was nonplussed. "No, we don't monitor live security feeds, they just record to the server for archival purposes. It's not like this is Deutsche Bank."

As the images appeared on the monitor, Becker dragged the timeline bar backwards, watching their own activity in the Hall first, all in reverse, then some period of time where no activity appeared.

Then it showed three men, walking backward from the door to the mosaic, where they knelt down and appeared busy over the mosaic. Their faces were unrecognizable in the dim light, even with the night-sensing infrared.

"Let me take over," Rausch said firmly. He sat down, advancing the scrubber to the apparent start of the men's activity, then hit the Play button.

They all watched as the three men opened the tile lid with the rod key. Then one of them, a long-haired younger man, fiddled with the safe using some kind of tools, obviously picking the lock, Rausch thought. The safe popped open, and one of the men extracted what appeared to be a white box, which he placed on the floor, then later into a red backpack.

Rausch stopped the playback.

Angry, he slammed his fist on the desk, startling Herr Becker.

"I did not even know there *was* a safe beneath that mosaic, much less a hole in the floor. It must be very old," the old man muttered to no one in particular.

Rausch considered the situation. Neither Dominic nor Hana Sinclair had appeared in the video. These men must be their accomplices, though. The time stamp on the video showed the event as happening late last night, so they may still be in the area. Maybe they even checked into the hostel.

Then he thought back to when they crossed the bridge coming in, passing four men, one of whom greeted Rausch's team carrying the same backpack shown in the video. *It was them!* He had a good memory for faces and would not forget the one who saluted them.

"Herr Becker, can you tell me, please, who were these men who checked in, and what car were they driving?"

"That information is private! We can't—"

"Ahem…" Constable Jäger interrupted him, reminding the old man this was 'official business.'

"Ah, yes, well then… let me see…" Becker opened up the guest register. "Herrs Karl Dengler, Lukas Bischoff, Milosh Lakatos, and Shandor Lakatos were the names registered. The only vehicle listed is a Jeep Wrangler under Herr Dengler's name."

"Let's go," Rausch said to the others.

CHAPTER 29

"*You got it!*" Dominic said excitedly as Dengler and Lukas walked into the hotel room. "I'm so proud of you, Karl, and you too, Lukas. Where are Milosh and Shandor?"

"They decided to return home since the job was finished," Dengler replied, "Milosh said to give you his regards, and to call on them again if you ever need their help on anything else. They were pretty excited to be part of this operation."

"I'll contact their father later to reward them for their efforts," Dominic said. "Well then, let's see what we've got here."

He took a pair of white conservation gloves out of his backpack as Dengler gently removed the alabaster box from his own pack and set it on the bed. They all stared at it as if it exuded mystical properties.

"The alabaster is in remarkable condition for being two thousand years old," Hana observed. "There's a surreal translucence to it."

"Most likely it's Oriental alabaster, quarried in Egypt," Dominic explained as he examined the box closely. "The ancients often used this type of stone for sacred and sepulchral objects, for carving large sarcophagi and even small perfume bottles.

Archeologists have actually found alabaster jars in the tomb of King Tutankhamun, thirteen hundred years before Christ. It holds up remarkably well over time."

His gloves now in place, Dominic carefully unfastened the bronze hasp and lifted the lid, which slid open smoothly on two stone hinges on the opposite side.

Resting inside the box was the thinnest of fabrics Dominic had ever seen. It appeared to be in magnificent condition, but so sheer that he was concerned any attempt to remove it might damage it. He lightly prodded the fabric, testing its resilience. Confident it could manage handling, he cautiously lifted it out of the alabaster box.

"This material is undoubtedly byssus," he noted. "Byssus fibers are derived from Mediterranean sea mollusks—you may know them as the 'beards' on mussels—and when harvested in bulk the filaments are finely woven into a soft fabric just like this, known as sea silk. It was a tedious process, and fabrics like this specimen are exceedingly rare."

Guardedly unfolding the veil, he let it fall open naturally. The fabric was surprisingly supple, and apparently had not been exposed to much light or handling.

It clearly revealed a man's face, evidently beaten in spots, with long stringy hair, a prominent nose, a beard, and eyes portraying a surreally calm look—and what appeared to be remnants of blood on various sections of the fabric.

The room was absolutely silent as each person beheld the image.

Dominic himself was moved beyond speech. As he held the veil, his hands trembled, and he said a silent prayer. Of all the incredible artifacts he had come into contact with over the years, this one alone exceeded any expectations he might have had. He could not take his eyes off it. It was as if Christ himself was looking into his very soul.

Hana's reaction was more visceral, tears gently falling down her cheeks as she gazed upon the sacred image. Both Karl and Lukas took to their knees, crossing themselves, their lips moving in quiet prayer above clasped hands.

After a few respectful moments, Dominic—his active mind

still working out the characteristics of such an artifact and the mystery of divine transference—noted a few things.

"Although this may look like a painting, byssus is believed to have properties preventing substances like pigments or oils from affecting its natural fibers, so it can't be painted on. There is some heated discussion about this in limited scientific circles, so for now, it comes down to a matter of faith.

"In fact, as I recall, this image looks nearly identical to the one I had the privilege of seeing at Santuario del Volto Santo, the Capuchin church in Manoppello, Italy, which claims to have had the Veil of Veronica for some four hundred years. There is also strong similarity here to the face on the Shroud of Turin."

"Well, in any event," Hana added, sniffling, "this is an incredibly moving experience, at least for me."

"As it is for me," Lukas said devoutly, looking at Karl, who nodded in agreement. "I can't believe we're looking at the face and blood of Our Lord."

"Alright," Dominic said quietly after a few reverent moments, "let's pack up and get back to Rome. I'll need to secure this in the Riserva until we can bring in specialists to analyze it."

He looked around at his friends. "I want to thank you all for your courage in making this happen. There were great risks, and you two…" turning to Karl and Lukas, "deserve special praise, along with Milosh and Shandor. I'll have to call Gunari with my appreciation for his sons' efforts."

Hana had been nurturing a festering concern, which she finally voiced.

"I know this is well after the fact," she said, "but do you think we'll have any problems having just taken it out of a museum like that?"

"I've thought about that," Dominic replied. "Nobody even knew about the safe, or so we have to assume, since Himmler himself placed the artifact there some seventy-five years ago. If they had discovered it earlier, it would have certainly made headlines, or even hold a place of honor today in the museum itself, not still buried beneath the floor. To my thinking, we simply liberated it from the Nazis."

Having boldly laid out his justification, Dominic noticed Hana's still questioning gaze. *Had he done the right thing?* he now wondered. *Was this really 'just' a matter of finding and seizing Nazi loot—or was it theft?* For now, he had to set those notions aside.

Then a more practical thought came to him. "Karl, did you notice any security cameras in the Generals' Hall?"

Dengler considered this briefly. Then, with an embarrassed look, he admitted, "Well, to be honest, I did not even look for them. But the room was totally dark except for our chem lights."

"Hmm," Dominic pondered. "I suppose we'll just have to wait and see then. Hopefully no one will be the wiser."

As he said this, his phone rang. Surprised to see it was Milosh calling, he answered.

"Milosh! I didn't have time to thank—"

"Father Michael!" the young gypsy interrupted, "you must help us. Shandor and I were arrested by the *polizei* in Marburg on our way back home!"

CHAPTER 30

"What was the problem?" Dominic asked.

"We don't have a vehicle registration for the BMW. They think we stole it! We need you to bail us out. Can you come?"

"Of course," said the priest, well-knowing the gypsies *did* steal the car a few months back, so they couldn't possibly have the registration. "How far away is Marburg?"

"It only took us an hour to get here, which is why they pulled me over. I guess I was speeding…"

"See you in about ninety minutes. Stay put until then."

"As if we have a choice," Milosh said glumly, looking at the cell awaiting him next to the grimy wall phone.

Dominic turned to the others, explaining the new development as he donned his black shirt and clerical collar.

"Karl, can I use your car while you guys wait here?"

"Well, you're not going without me," Hana said firmly. Dominic nodded.

"Sure, Michael," Dengler said, tossing him the keys. "Lukas and I will be here for you. You should be back in three or four hours, I imagine, so we'll extend the room for the day."

"Just keep that veil secure. Put it in the room safe or something."

"It's fine in my backpack. Lukas and I can handle ourselves if it comes to that."

"Alright, see you soon."

Dominic and Hana took off in the Jeep, heading south for the Gothic city of Marburg, Germany.

SITTING in the rented black Mercedes G-Class SUV, still in the parking lot of Wewelsburg Castle, Jacob Rausch had spent the past thirty minutes combing area hotels for a guest registered as Father Michael Dominic. Büren being a small town, there weren't that many to call, and he finally found his quarry at Hotel Walz in the nearby burg of Salzkotten. The clerk said Dominic was still checked in.

Turning to Jäger, who was at the wheel, Rausch gave him the address. "Paderborner Strasse 21, about fifteen minutes away."

"KARL, are you hungry? I'm starving," Lukas said to his partner. "Why don't I get us a couple *currywurst* from that truck down the street?"

"Mmm, yeah," his mouth watering at the thought of the traditional German street food. "Get some extra curried ketchup, too. And a couple Cokes."

"Breakfast of champions! You're on. Back in a bit," Lukas said as he grabbed his key card and left the room.

As he walked away from the hotel, Lukas paid no attention to the black SUV pulling into the parking lot.

Taking a spot beneath a thick green alder tree, Jäger shut the engine off while Jacob, phone in hand, called the hotel, asking to be put through to Father Dominic's room. The operator made the connection, and Dengler answered the phone.

"Yes?"

"Good morning, sir. This is room service, just confirming that your breakfast order will be up shortly."

"But, we didn't order room service!" Karl said.

"Is this not Room 237?" Rausch asked.

"No, it's 224. You've got the wrong room."

"My apologies for the intrusion, sir. Have a good morning." Rausch disconnected the call.

"Alright, they're in 224. Let's go."

The four men—Jacob, Christof, Jäger and Günther—got out of the SUV and made their way into the hotel, taking the stairs to the upper floor. When they reached Room 224, Rausch knocked on the door.

As he opened the door, Dengler was in the midst of saying, "I didn't think you'd be back this fas—" when he was suddenly and violently pushed back onto the floor by Günther. The others came in and shut the door."

"What the hell!" Dengler shouted.

Jäger pulled out his Glock 17 and aimed it at Dengler's head.

"Just give us the veil and you'll have no trouble from us," Rausch said calmly.

"I have no idea what you're talking about," Dengler said as convincingly as he could, getting to his feet.

"Günther, grab him."

As he tried to rise with Günther holding him, Jäger brought the butt of his gun down onto Dengler's head. Blood started oozing out behind his ear as he fell onto the bed and lay there unconscious.

"Look for anything resembling that white box," Rausch ordered. "Check the backpacks."

The men began looking through drawers, closets and the backpacks, until Christof, digging into Dengler's red pack, cried, "Found it!"

He pulled it out of the pack and handed it to Rausch, who flipped the fastener to check inside.

"This is it. Let's get out of here."

. . .

LUKAS WAS JUST APPROACHING the entrance when Rausch and his team came through the hotel's revolving glass door in a hurry, which kept him from entering until they had all come through. He looked at them suspiciously, thinking he knew them from somewhere. Then it came to him—their two groups had passed each other on the Wewelsburg Castle bridge just yesterday. *An odd coincidence,* he thought.

As they passed, just as he was entering the revolving door, Lukas heard the one in the lead mumble, "Dante will want to see this right away…" The turning door having closed behind him, before he could hear any more.

Dante?! It couldn't possibly be the same Dante. On high alert, he glanced back out the window but the men were out of sight.

Taking the steps two at a time as he carried the bags of food, Lukas finally reached the room. He opened the door with his key card and, seeing Karl on the bloody bed, dropped the bags on the floor.

"Karl!!" He rushed over to his partner, checked his pulse and breathing, then inspected the head wound. It wasn't too deep, but he had to stop the bleeding. He ran to the bathroom for a wet cloth, then ripped open his backpack and removed a small first aid kit. Stanching the flow of blood, he spoke softly to Karl as he applied pressure to the wound.

"I'm here for you, *Liebchen,*" he said quietly, urgently. "Come on, wake up now, Karl. You've got to get up. No more lying about."

Lukas was devastated, feeling guilty at having left the room, but his full attention was now on getting Karl awake. If he had a concussion he needed to be conscious. He thought of calling 112 but knew the wound wasn't as bad as requiring emergency assistance. Unless he had a concussion. He was torn, his mind indecisive, racing back and forth.

Just then Karl came around, moaning, his arm slowly rising, apparently trying to reach his head.

"It's okay, Karl, I'm right here," Lukas said with tears in his eyes.

The wound was no longer bleeding. As Karl lay there, his eyes fluttering open, Lukas gently washed the gash with warm soap and water, dried it off, then pulled out a thick patch of gauze and long strips of surgical tape from his kit. Prepping it, he carefully laid down the bandage on Karl's head, wrapping surgical tape around his skull to secure it for now.

As Karl came to, Lukas breathed easier, especially when he began speaking, quietly at first, but with anger rising in his voice.

"Those *bastards*…they came for the veil." At once he tried sitting up, anxious to see if it was still here. Lukas pressed him back down, looking over at Karl's red backpack, all items strewn about the floor along with the *currywurst* and spilled Cokes he'd dropped—and the alabaster box was gone.

"I'm afraid they must have taken it, Karl," he said. "But I did see them coming out of the hotel. They were the same guys we saw yesterday on the bridge at the castle. If I were to guess, I'd say it was Jacob Rausch. He's the only other one who knew the riddle, as Hana told us. And I heard him say something about 'Dante wanting to see this.' It has to be the veil!"

"They must have gone to the castle and tried finding it themselves," Karl muttered as he leaned into his partner. "I screwed up, Lukas. I should have heeded Michael's advice and put it in the safe."

"Don't blame yourself. How were we to know people were chasing us? Stay here and don't get up. I'm going down the hall to get some ice."

"I've got no place else to go right now, thanks."

CHAPTER 31

An hour and a half later, Dominic and Hana walked into the *Polizeistation* Marburg, just down the street from the famed Gothic castle Landgrafen Palace and the University of Marburg. A college town, the *polizei* were accustomed to rounding up young wayward students partying late into the night, but they rarely had to deal with Roma for any offenses—Roma who still carried the gypsy stigma as undesirable immigrants to Germany.

Approaching the reception desk, Dominic introduced himself.

"I'm here to liberate my two young wards, Milosh and Shandor Lakatos. I understand they got into some trouble here?"

The desk sergeant rifled through some papers until he came to the booking sheets for the boys.

"They were pulled over for speeding, Herr Pastor, and driving without vehicle registration. Plus, it's possible they are illegal immigrants."

"I can assure you they are not immigrants, Herr Inspektor," using the respectful form of address. "These boys live in France with their father. I am their guardian while we are here on a special mission to your country." Since that was a completely true statement, Dominic let the sergeant assume it could be some kind of religious mission.

"As for the registration, we can have that faxed or emailed to you once we return to France. And I will pay whatever speeding fine they have incurred. Would that be acceptable, Herr Inspektor?" Dominic gave him his most disarming smile, reaching for his collar to reinforce his honorable intentions. Hana stood next to him, her hands clasped in front of her as if an acolyte in prayer.

The desk sergeant looked steadily at both of them, then turned around to look at the Lakatos boys in the holding cell.

"The fine for speeding is one hundred euros." As Dominic reached for his wallet the sergeant wrote something on a card. "And this is our fax number. When you return to France, please send us the vehicle registration, and the matter will be closed."

Dominic laid out five twenty-euro notes on the counter. "*Danke schön*, Herr Inspektor, for your kindness in this matter. It will not happen again."

Grasping his key ring, the sergeant walked back to the holding cell and unlocked it. Swinging open the door, the two boys walked out with their heads hung low.

"I am so sorry, Father Michael," Milosh said as he approached him, "for making you come all this way."

The sergeant had Dominic sign a release form, then handed over the keys to the BMW.

"That is too nice a car for *these* kind to have," he said, emphasizing the attribution.

Ignoring the prejudice, Dominic defused the tension. "I will make sure they control their speed, Herr Inspektor. *Auf wiedersehen*." He ushered them all out of the station.

Addressing the boys when they got outside, Dominic said, "We got real lucky in there. Watch your speed on the way back now, okay?" They both nodded.

As Dominic said this, his cell phone rang. It was Lukas.

"Michael!" he pleaded, clearly distraught. "They beat up Karl and left him unconscious!"

"*What?!* Who did?"

"I think it was Jacob Rausch and his men, four of them altogether. I stepped out to get some food and passed them coming out of the hotel in a rush. It can only be him, Michael. He's the only one who knew we were going after the veil!"

"Slow down, Lukas. How is Karl?"

"He's okay. A little loopier than he normally is. I've dressed the wound and have him resting in the room. How soon will you be back?"

"We're leaving now. It should be another ninety minutes or so. Did they take it? The veil?"

Lukas was silent for a moment. "I'm afraid so, Michael. It's gone."

Dominic was crushed. After all the work, the planning and execution. And to be used and betrayed by Jacob! He felt he should have known better than to trust that man, but he'd wanted to believe his story. To believe the best in people. Quiet fury gripped him.

"Alright, Lukas. Take good care of Karl, we'll see you soon."

"One more thing, Michael," Lukas said. "The one in charge, Jacob, I guess, said 'Dante will want to see this.' It can only mean the veil."

Dante again! Dominic thought, his anger rising further.

"That's the last thing I expected to hear," he said to Lukas. "Okay, we'll be back there soon."

Explaining to the others what had happened, anger flared among them as well. The gypsies cursed in Romani, and Hana didn't hold back her feelings at all, especially upset that her cousin Karl had been injured.

"What can we do to help, Father Michael?" Milosh pleaded. "Anything you need. We owe *you* now, but we would help catch those bastards anyway."

Dominic thought a moment. "I don't know that there's

anything any of us can do right now, Milosh. We need to get back, see how Karl is, and consider our next steps.

"Meanwhile, you two get back home. If you *can* be of help, I'll let you know. Promise me you'll drive safely, alright?" He handed him the card the sergeant gave him. "And have your father use his network to work up that vehicle registration document, then have it faxed here. I'm responsible for this, so please don't fail me."

With Milosh's sincere assurance, they parted after a round of hugs and farewells.

Sitting in the Jeep, Dominic and Hana looked at each other.

"What now?" she asked.

"I just don't know yet. Maybe something will occur to us on the drive back. Somehow, Jacob must answer for this. And we *must* get that veil back. Then there's Dante."

With that thought hanging in the air, he put the car in gear, headed up the street to the onramp, and sped north on the Autobahn back to the hotel.

Having considered what may be needed in the hours ahead, Hana pulled out her phone and called her grandfather, Armand de Saint-Clair. They required flexible transportation and quick access to visas for all of them.

CHAPTER 32

Sitting in the waiting room of the Bariloche *Kinderklinik,* Hilda Fischbein was anxious. It wasn't the fact that, at twenty-four, she was five months pregnant with her first child that had her concerned. It was the clinic itself and the people working there she found disconcerting—especially its peculiar director, Dr. Kurtz—and her husband Günther's insistence that their baby be born here. If he were not out of town now on some kind of business, he would be here with her.

As she sat there, her thoughts turned to what had brought them here. When she and Günther moved from Berlin to this Argentine alpine village just five months ago, at first she loved it. It was a much smaller city, the neighbors were friendly and they all spoke German. The surroundings were beautiful, and the town's architecture reminded her of home. She enjoyed the same kinds of shops she frequented in Berlin and had access to familiar foods. But having to learn Spanish and adapt to such a different foreign culture proved to be challenging, though she adjusted more quickly in Bariloche than she had imagined she would.

But there was something obscure here, something hidden or unnatural, that she couldn't quite put her finger on. And though she was certain Günther knew what it was, he avoided the topic whenever she brought it up. He was a stern man, after all, and very rigid in his views on life and politics. But he also had secrets. She just knew it. There were evenings he would be gone for hours to private meetings with this Ahnenerbe group, where other men in town would discuss their ancestral heritage, or so she was told. She thought nothing more about it at the time.

Exacerbating her anxiety was this clinic. Hilda had done her homework, researching as much as she could on the internet when Günther was at work or away at night, and she grew more uncomfortable the more she discovered about the clinic's history, and indeed, about the Ahnenerbe itself.

The *Kinderklinik*, or Children's Clinic, was housed in a nondescript brick building set well back from the road on the outskirts of Bariloche. No signs announced its name or purpose, as it was known only to certain residents of the largely German enclave. Admission was exclusively by appointment and offered only to 'qualified' parents. Günther had assured her they were qualified and had made all arrangements himself. He had seemed quite proud of their acceptance there.

Though it had most every accommodation of a hospital, its primary purpose was as a maternity and birthing clinic, staffed largely by German obstetricians and midwives, with a larger than usual newborn nursery.

In fact, she found, childbirth and post-natal care were the *Kinderklinik's* only purposes. The reasons for its obsessive secrecy were apparent to those who knew of its existence—it was exclusively intended to birth and raise Aryan children in a program known as *Lebensborn*. The children born here were carefully nurtured from birth, with specialized *Kindermädchen*, or nursemaids, closely guiding their development along with parents through educational programs in private schools. Eventually these children were destined to become "Red Falcons"—the neo-Nazi equivalent of Boy Scouts and Girl Scouts —with their minds shaped accordingly.

Initiated in 1935, *Lebensborn,* literally "Fount of Life," was an SS-initiated program with one singular objective: raising the birth rate of racially pure infants in conformance with Nazi health and hygiene ideologies. Supposedly dissolved in 1945 with the end of the war, Hilda had discovered in private German chat rooms that many such clinics continued to exist, spoken of in discreet and ambiguous ways among thousands of other pregnant women in her position—most of whom admitted to having strict, overbearing husbands with far-right political ideologies.

What am I to do?! she worried. Leave Günther? I do not want my baby boy growing up to be a neo-Nazi!

"Frau Fischbein?" the burly nurse with a clipboard called out to the women in the waiting room.

Her stomach in knots, Hilda stood up, snatched her purse, and dutifully followed the nurse into the examining room.

CHAPTER 33

Entering the hotel room back in Büren, Dominic and Hana rushed over to Karl lying on the bed. Lukas was sitting by his side.

"Karl, I'm so sorry I got you into this mess," Dominic said, pressing his friend's shoulder sympathetically. Hana bent over and gave her cousin a kiss on the forehead while grasping his hand.

"Don't worry, Michael," Dengler replied. "We're all in this together, come what may. We know the risks. But I do want to have a close-up chat with your friend Jacob Rausch when I see him again. And one of the goons they called Günther. He's the one who held me while the other guy pistol-whipped me."

"He's no friend of mine—but I agree, Jacob does need a reckoning, especially now. We'll find them, Karl. In the meantime, are you alright to travel?"

"Oh, sure. Lukas has taken good care of me. I'm fine."

"Good. Let's get on the road, then. It's a six-hour drive to Paris, where Hana has arranged for us to use her grandfather's jet. We're going back to Buenos Aires to deal with Dante first. I've spoken with Cardinal Petrini about my need for your help, and he'll clear your extended holiday time with your commander."

WITH THE TEAM now on board the Dassault Falcon 900, the baron's jet lifted off smoothly from Paris–Le Bourget Airport for the transatlantic flight. It stopped briefly for refueling in Dominican Republic, then headed south for Buenos Aires. Tapping his diplomatic connections, Hana's grandfather had arranged for expedited Argentine visas for the team, helpfully bypassing the normal waiting period.

The two young Swiss Guards had never flown on a private jet before and marveled at the efficiencies such luxury travel afforded them, especially given the immediacy of their new mission. But they were all pretty tired, and with a long flight ahead of them, they both took comfortable seats where they could find some rest.

Except for Dominic. Anger had such control over him he could not find comfort in any position. He got up and walked the length of the cabin, then back again, and again. Even pacing and prayer weren't tamping his emotions. That he had fallen for Jacob's whole story in the first place, historically compelling as it was, shook him. *Why would he steal the veil, hurting one of us in the process, when we considered him part of our team? I'd assured him they would be well compensated. What was his real agenda?*

Dominic now doubted it was something as simple as selling the artifact to help Christof's father save his vineyard. Rational people don't act in this manner. No, there was something else going on here.

He sat down in the leather seat facing Hana's. She had been staring out the window, her own mind reflecting on the events of the day, when her gaze turned to Michael.

"I don't buy it," she said firmly. "Jacob's story of wanting to sell the veil for Christof's father."

"That's *just* what I was going to say," he replied. "'Great minds think alike.'"

"'—Though fools seldom differ,'" Hana responded, finishing the axiom. "How is it we were so taken in, Michael? I like to think we're both smarter than that."

"Jacob had a credible story. And I gather he told us a great deal more than he probably meant to. But what's his end game? What do they have planned for the veil? *And how is Dante involved?!* Still, too many questions."

"Is this something Cardinal Petrini might help us with?"

Dominic considered this for a moment. "We don't have enough to take to him yet for him to be of real use. He'll be there for us when we need him, though."

It was 7 p.m. when the Dassault touched down at Ezeiza International Airport in Buenos Aires. After disembarking the aircraft, Hana led the way to the VIP lounge in Terminal A where Customs and Passport Control handled private jet arrivals. She had arranged for limousine service to take them all back to the Alvear Palace Hotel, where they checked into three reserved rooms, with Karl and Lukas sharing one.

"Why don't we each just call room service for dinner, then get some sleep for tomorrow?" Hana suggested as they rode up in the elevator. Everyone silently nodded in agreement, tired from the long trip.

As they emerged from the elevator and headed for their rooms, Hana noticed a strikingly handsome man walking in her direction. *Definitely military*, she thought, admiring the fitness in his step. As they passed each other the man made direct eye contact with her.

"*Bonjour*," he said pleasantly as he walked by.

Hana blushed as she returned the greeting. *French. Nice.*

. . .

DURING BREAKFAST in the hotel's dining room the next morning, Dominic laid out the day's agenda.

"First, I'd like to meet with Javier Batista again, to see what more he knows about this Ahnenerbe organization. Then we should try to get in to see Dante, and ask him directly about his associations with that group and specifically Christof Prager. I don't expect anything more than his twisted version of the truth, but it may be worth the effort."

He turned to the two Swiss Guards. "Karl, why don't you and Lukas enjoy some time off today, take in the city and see the sights, while Hana and I attend to these things? You're still on holiday, after all."

Karl grinned and looked at Lukas. "I was kind of hoping that would be our assignment here. At least until you needed us for anything."

With breakfast finished, Karl and Lukas took off to explore the city on foot, while Dominic made a call to Batista's local Interpol office. After speaking briefly to his assistant, he ended the call.

"Javier can see us in an hour. After we're done there we'll just drop in to Dante's office later for a surprise visit, hoping he'll be there. I'd rather not give him a heads up that we're coming."

"That's probably wise," Hana said. "He probably already knows we're here anyway, given his penchant for spies."

After heading to their rooms to freshen up, they met again a few minutes later in the lobby and had the doorman hail a taxi.

"THANKS FOR SEEING us on such short notice, Javier," Dominic said, greeting the agent warmly. "We've come back to Argentina on the same mission as before, though much has happened since we last saw you."

He explained to Batista about eventually finding all three fragments—without going into specific details as to how—and ultimately discovering the sacred artifact they were seeking, and the incident where Karl was injured during the theft of the object, presumably by Jacob Rausch and Christof Prager along with two associates—which meant that the artifact had most likely been brought back to Argentina for whatever nefarious purposes the thieves had in mind.

"That's quite a story, Padre," Batista said, "and after all your hard work to obtain this object. I am sorry to hear of it. How can I be of help?"

"Javier," Dominic began, "what more can you tell us of Jacob Rausch and his associate Christof Prager? There was also someone named Günther involved, surname unknown, and a fourth man we know nothing about. We are not looking for vengeance. We just want the return of the artifact we found, and which was brutally stolen from us."

Batista got up, closed the door to his office, then took his seat again. Pulling out the keyboard tray from beneath his desk, he tapped in a string of words on a screen form, and a few moments later Jacob Rausch's record appeared on Interpol's Individual Nominal Database display. If Rausch had had any interaction with police anywhere in the world, at any time, it would appear here.

"It seems our young Señor Rausch has a clean record. No known crimes are listed in our database."

Peering closer to the screen, reading the smaller details noted, Batista sat back in his chair.

"As you may know, he lives in Paris, though he also has a home in Bariloche. He inherited millions from his grandfather, the Nazi SS Colonel Walther Rausch. Such cases, as you might imagine, are rather complicated. The imposition of strict secrecy in Swiss banking laws after the war had prevented even Interpol from knowing where many suspicious fortunes originated, though it's fairly obvious to even the casual observer that the assets of Jews and other victims of Germany's dominion were at stake.

"The notes here indicate that Colonel Rausch had amassed a

great fortune in gold, which was claimed by Jacob at a Swiss bank branch in Santiago, Chile, just a few months ago."

"Yes," Dominic said, nodding, "Jacob did mention this to me when we first met, that he had inherited money from his grandfather and was attending to his estate at the time. He too believed the funds were of dubious origin, but distanced himself from exploring it further. That's how this all started, in fact. The existence of the fragments and the artifact came to his attention through his grandfather's belongings."

"There is another thing here that causes me some concern, which I had not noticed before," Batista said, pointing to the screen. "Young Rausch seems to be affiliated with an active spinoff of the Ahnenerbe we have only recently started to investigate."

The agent stood up and slowly paced his office, both hands scrubbing his face as he gave thought to something. He stopped in front of a secured file cabinet, turned the combination dial several times, and opened the top drawer.

"This is a recently declassified CIA document discussing German Nationalist and neo-Nazi activities in Argentina, something you need to be aware of. There are two paragraphs in particular I want you to read."

He handed the paper to Dominic and Hana. They read the two sections Batista had pointed out.

CENTRAL INTELLIGENCE AGENCY
SECRET

...The situation in Argentina is peculiarly favorable for such a revival. A well-entrenched stay-behind organization was established before the recall or expulsion of German officials and known Nazi agents. Both the neo-Nazi movement in Argentina and the radical and nationalist organizations in Germany lack unity and dominant leadership. They are generally guided, however, by a single basic aim, which is to destroy or invalidate democratic capitalism…through the agency of strong totalitarian governments.

The scattered neo-Nazis also have in common a certain optimism as to the future and appear to have ample financial backing. Evidence of intention to carry on Nazi activities and of belief in Nazi resurgence in many parts of the world has been apparent among Germans in Argentina since 1946. A substantial stream of German immigration including Wehrmacht and SS veterans, Nazi economists, propagandists, intelligence agents, scientists, and military specialists has flowed into Argentina since 1945…

"WHAT I AM ABOUT to tell you must be treated as highly confidential. We have had suspicions for some time now that a neo-Nazi element in our country, specifically centered in Bariloche, has been involved in a eugenics program to produce children of pure Aryan conception. There are no specific laws here against doing so, but what concerns us, of course, are their intentions over time. Such a vile concept was quietly undertaken during World War II by Dr. Josef Mengele, the 'Angel of Death' at Auschwitz, with disastrous results for his trial subjects.

"The *Kinderklinik*, as they call it, has rigorous 'membership' qualifications, where those selected must produce hereditary documentation proving Germanic or Nordic ancestry going back many generations. And apparently those credentials are scrupulously verified.

"We are trying to get someone on the inside of this clinic so we can more subjectively monitor their activity," Batista concluded offhandedly. "But we've not had much success. None, in fact.

"Now, let's look into this Prager fellow."

Returning to his seat, Batista keyed in the information needed to call up database details on Christof. Confirming what

Batista had already known, he too was closely involved with the Ahnenerbe movement, the particulars of which his assistant, Rosa Cruz, had previously explained to Dominic and Hana in their last meeting.

"Hmm…this is interesting," Batista said as he stared at the display. "Christof Prager also appears to be connected to the *Kinderklinik*. These are some well-funded, locally influential people. As that operation has been handled by one of my colleagues, this kind of intel wouldn't have come across my desk before now."

He paused, thought a moment, then turned to Dominic and Hana.

"Do you suppose the interest in your artifact may have something to do with the Ahnenerbe's eugenics program?"

CHAPTER 34

"**E**ugenics?" Hana exclaimed, questioning its relationship to the veil. "How could that possibly be involved?"

The room was silent as Dominic and Hana considered the question.

As the possibilities dawned on them, each turned to the other, their faces drained of color.

"Are you thinking what I'm thinking?" Hana asked, fear in her eyes.

"Could it be the blood?" he wondered nervously, holding Hana's gaze.

"It's just not possible! Can DNA even last that long?" she replied, her mind racing.

Dominic nodded as his voice grew urgent. "Yes, it can. We know DNA can last as long as a million years."

Batista felt something significant had just occurred. "Wait! What are you not telling me?" he pleaded. "What DNA?"

Now it was Dominic's turn to stand and pace the room. He took a deep breath.

"The one thing we hadn't disclosed to you yet, Javier, was the nature of the artifact. Not out of any particular fear that you couldn't be trusted, believe me. It just didn't seem necessary up to now. Pieces of Jacob's scheme may be coming together, thanks to you.

"Have you ever heard of the Veil of Veronica? The *sudor*, or sweat cloth, that a woman in the crowd of onlookers handed to Jesus as he carried the cross to his crucifixion? The one on which his holy image had been imparted in full detail, and which legend tells us ended up in Mary Magdalene's possession?"

"Yes, of course, we were all told the veil story as children."

"*That* is the artifact we found, Javier, and which was stolen from us by Rausch and Prager! It had been hidden in a secret Nazi vault in a castle in Germany once occupied by Heinrich Himmler. We rediscovered it only a few days ago, having found all three fragments of a location riddle Himmler had written in 1945."

Dominic gave Batista further background about the original Ahnenerbe's sponsorship of the 1937 French expedition resulting in Otto Rahn's discovery of the veil, and the details of their own recent exploits at Wewelsburg Castle.

"When we opened the alabaster box and looked at the veil, there were clear indications of blood on it—blood from which DNA might possibly be extracted. The blood and DNA of Jesus Christ!"

Dominic was speaking quickly now, growing more animated.

"Adolf Hitler himself was convinced that Jesus was an 'Aryan fighter,' hailing from a long line of ancient Israelites, descendants of Abraham, Jacob, and Isaac. Rausch and Prager would have known this, of course, which obviously fueled their determination to acquire the veil by any means.

"But its potential use in an Aryan eugenics program is unthinkable!"

"All the more reason to get it back," Hana asserted. "Javier, we could really use your help on this."

"This isn't something Interpol can do on its own, I'm afraid. We are basically a law enforcement information coordinator, not a policing agency. But if we can get local authorities to work with us, we'll stand a better chance."

"We did meet with the chief of police for Bariloche, Ramón Santos, when we were here two weeks ago," Hana added. "He seemed helpful at the time. I'm sure we could rely on him."

"You must keep in mind," Batista cautioned, "that in a small town like Bariloche—with such a large and prominent German population—you might get some resistance to raiding one of their legitimate operations. We do not know how deep the Ahnenerbe's connections are there but must assume they are not without powerful political influence."

"Then we may need to just act on our own," Dominic said with an edge of anger to his voice as he took a seat. "If this is in fact what they're planning, it's an unconscionable undertaking."

"I do agree something must be done, Michael," Hana said as she placed her hand on his shoulder to offer assurance. "If local authorities can't or would be unwilling to help, then we should take the matter into our own hands. That veil should be in the Vatican, not in the possession of neo-Nazis in such a profane scheme. Maybe my grandfather and his 'Team Hugo' colleagues can help us."

Team Hugo referred to the triumvirate of Baron Armand de Saint-Clair, French President Pierre Valois, and Vatican Secretary of State Cardinal Enrico Petrini—all close comrades in battle during World War II in the *Maquis*, a special operations branch of the French Resistance movement.

With Saint-Clair being Hana's grandfather, Valois as her godfather, and Petrini acting as Michael Dominic's mentor throughout his life, they had access to a mighty army of combined resources.

Dominic was suddenly encouraged.

"Yes! Pierre Valois would certainly know the president of Argentina, if it came to that. And the power of having the Vatican at our back officially would be invaluable, though their involvement would need to be completely discreet. At this stage we don't want publicity about the veil's existence until it's gone through exhaustive analysis, lest the Church come out looking foolish."

"Javier," Hana asked, "Max Colombo once mentioned you had close ties to the Mossad. Wouldn't this kind of activity be something the Israelis would want to see suppressed? A production line of neo-Nazis having the blood of Abraham coursing through their bodies?"

"Well, now you put it that way, it does present a terrifying notion," the agent admitted. "I think we can count on Mossad to support our efforts, though as with the Church, discretion would be paramount. Mossad does not seek credit for nor publicity in its actions, working largely in the shadows.

"For that matter," Batista asked, "what would you think our next steps should be?"

"This will require some careful thought. We're heading to Bariloche tomorrow for a few days. Are you able to join us? We've got our own plane so transportation is taken care of."

"I'll need to move some things around, but yes, I can come with you. We can work out some kind of plan in the meantime."

Dominic stood and looked at each of them.

"Let's just pray we get this right. The Italians have a saying: *Quando Dio vuole castigarci, ci manda quello che desideriamo.*"

Hana raised her eyebrows thoughtfully, then translated it for Batista. "When God wishes to punish us, He answers our prayers."

CHAPTER 35

Walking the cobblestone streets of San Telmo, one of Buenos Aires' oldest and most lively barrios, Karl and Lukas found themselves rummaging through a street fair, with hundreds of trinket hawkers, art and antique dealers, and dozens of eateries serving *asado* barbecue, empanadas, and other regional specialties. A handsome couple in colorful formal attire danced the tango to the accompaniment of a street orchestra, an *orquesta típica*, comprised of two violins, flute, piano, double bass, and two accordion *bandoneóns*.

This was a rare treat for the Swiss Guards, whose duties at home were all-encompassing, and especially confining since they both lived and worked inside the Vatican. Though Rome had its own similar outdoor festivals, enjoying them in another country, especially one so romantic as Argentina, made for a special moment.

Karl pulled his partner toward the nearest bus stop. "The Metropolitan Cathedral isn't far from here, Lukas. Let's go visit the church of our Holy Father!"

The bus ride was a quick ten-minute trip, and as they stepped out and onto the curb, they were greeted by what looked more like a Greek temple than a Catholic Cathedral, with twelve golden-capped Neo-Classical columns, representing Christ's twelve apostles, supporting a massive triangular frontispiece carved in bas-relief.

Entering through one of two main doors, they took in the first captivating visual above the sanctuary—an impressive 1871 Walcker organ built in Germany, boasting more than 3,500 pipes. The breathtaking artwork on the floor—featuring various religious symbols and Venetian mosaics—held their gaze as they entered the 41-meter high vaulted space. First constructed in 1593, the *Catedral Metropolitana de Buenos Aires* was truly the city's architectural and historical crown jewel.

There were surprisingly few people inside at this time of day, but it provided good opportunity for Karl and Lukas to light a candle and spend time in reflection. They moved toward the front side of the main altar and knelt silently in the shadow of a large marble column, heads bowed in prayer.

After a few moments both young men sat back in the pew, silently taking in the sacred splendor of the space, when they heard low talking from the rear, voices approaching up the center aisle in the nave. It was as if someone were giving a tour.

Curious, Karl glanced over his shoulder to see the small group of men, four of them, as they approached the sanctuary. He froze when he saw who it was.

"Lukas!" he whispered, nodding his head toward the group when Lukas turned to him.

They both instinctively shrunk in their seats, as if in deep prayer, as Cardinal Dante led Jacob Rausch, Christof Prager, and Günther toward a private door off the South Transept and went through it, closing the door behind them.

"As if we needed any more evidence of Dante's involvement!" Karl said, his anger mounting. "God has brought us here for a reason, Lukas. Come, we must tell the others."

Walking down the darkened north aisle of the nave, they left through the main door where they had entered and headed back to the hotel.

. . .

"But, Your Eminence," Jacob faltered, "I'm certain Dominic and his people will spare no effort to recover the veil. I'm telling you, they need to be dealt with. Isn't there someone at the Vatican you can ask to recall them to Rome?"

"I'm afraid Dominic already has recourse over anything I might be able to do there," Dante grumbled. "You'll just have to deal with them in your own ways. You certainly have my blessing.

"The most important thing you can do right now is to make sure that veil is secure. And get your people started on the DNA extraction," he continued testily. "Do I have to make all the decisions?!"

"The veil *is* secure, Eminence," Christof assured him. "And no, we don't expect you to make these decisions at all. We were only hoping there would be a less forceful way to eliminate the problems these *Schweine* pose. But we will attend to it ourselves."

Dominic and Hana stepped out of the taxi in front of the administrative offices of the Metropolitan Cathedral, which were on the opposite side of the building from which Karl and Lukas had just exited.

Entering the gilded Baroque doors, they walked up to the reception desk.

"My name is Father Michael Dominic, Prefect of the Vatican Apostolic Archive. Would you please announce me to Cardinal Dante?"

"Do you have an appointment with His Eminence, Father Dominic?" the older Spanish nun asked him.

"No, I'm afraid I don't."

"Please let me call his secretary and inquire."

"Of course," Dominic said. He and Hana took a seat in the

waiting area.

THERE WAS a brief tap on the door, after which Dante's secretary walked into his office holding a small piece of folded paper. He silently passed it to the cardinal, standing by for his instructions.

"It looks like our meeting must end, gentlemen. Father Dominic and presumably Hana Sinclair are waiting to see me as we speak. Please leave by the same entrance we used, back through the church, and try not to let anyone see you."

"I knew it! They are here already," Christof snarled. "We're going back to Bariloche now, Eminence. You can reach us there if needed."

DANTE'S SECRETARY, the tall and gangly Father Vannucci, emerged from Dante's office and approached Dominic and Hana in the waiting room.

"Despite not having an appointment, His Eminence will see you now." He held out a bony hand directing both of them to the cardinal's office, hovering behind as they approached the closed door. Coming forward, he opened the door and beckoned them in.

"Do you wish me to stay and take notes, Eminence?"

"No, Bruno, they won't be staying long. So, Father Dominic. Miss Sinclair. To what do I owe the, um, pleasure?"

"May we sit down, Eminence?" Dominic asked.

"Of course, but I don't have much time." Dante took a seat behind his desk and sat, steepling his fingers as he waited to hear the nature of their business.

"This will only take a few minutes," Dominic began. "We understand that you know and are somehow involved with men named Jacob Rausch and Christof Prager. May I ask if this information is correct, and what that business might be?"

"I meet a great many people in the course of my daily affairs,

Father Dominic. These particular names mean nothing to me, but of course it is always possible that we have met. I do find it rather presumptuous that you ask about my business, though. Can you do me the honor of explaining the nature of this inquisition?"

Dominic leaned forward in his chair. "These two men stole something of considerable importance from us—an artifact possibly containing the blood of Jesus Christ. And we have good reason to believe they will be using DNA extracted from that blood in an abhorrent campaign to produce Aryan children."

Dante bellowed with laughter. "You cannot be serious! That is the most absurd thing I've ever heard, and coming from a man of God makes it even more preposterous. Have you lost your mind, Dominic?"

Hana stepped in defensively. "Believe it or not, Eminence, what we are saying is true, incredible as it sounds, and even unthinkable as an actual plan by these crazed ideologues. As a man of God yourself, I would expect a modicum of belief coming from such a man as Father Dominic, who has only ever acted in good faith on behalf of the Church."

"I could argue with that last point—but, be that as it may, what has all this to do with me? I am but a simple parish priest in the backwaters of South America."

Dominic leapt up and slammed his fist on the desk.

"*Dammit, Dante!* You know good and well these people are tampering with the devil's work, and you have the power to stop it!"

"Do not take that tone with me, young man," Dante exploded, rising from his own chair. "I will not be spoken to in that manner. Now get out of my church!"

"I'm warning you, this isn't over," Dominic threatened, pointing at the cardinal. "His Holiness will hear about your obstinance. You think you're in a backwater *now*?! Just wait."

With that, Dominic reached for Hana and escorted her out of the office, down the hall and out of the building. They both walked down the street in silence, Dominic still fuming over the exchange.

After a few minutes, Hana spoke up. "We tried, Michael. But we really didn't expect much from him anyway, did we? We'll deal with this ourselves. Javier will be of great help, and my grandfather and his friends will do what they can, you know that."

"My anger with Dante has been building up for some time," he confessed, "and that gave me the chance to vent, if nothing else. I feel much better now." He looked at her and heaved a sigh, then smiled.

"He deserved that, and much more," she admitted. "It's pointless to rely on him for anything. Can you really have him moved to another 'backwater,' as he put it?"

He looked at her. "That depends. If the veil is never recovered and its existence is disputed, there would be no basis for any retribution. But Cardinal Petrini can't stand the man himself, and once the Pope learns of what's happening, I wouldn't give Dante's career much hope. That's assuming the veil can even be found again."

"Let's head back to the hotel, have some dinner, and leave for Bariloche in the morning. Maybe Karl and Lukas are back and they can join us. Everything we've been through will be for nothing if we can't retrieve that veil."

CHAPTER 36

The Alvear Palace Hotel was bustling with travelers checking in and out, and as Hana and Dominic entered the lobby, they heard her name being called out from the adjacent lounge. She turned to look.

"Hana!" Karl was standing and waving from a table in the bar. They walked over to join him and Lukas.

"We've been waiting for you, with news. But first, what to drink?" The waitress had just arrived, waiting for their orders.

"I'll have a dirty martini, thanks," Hana said as she took her jacket off.

"And I'll have a beer—uh…Quilmes, please," said Dominic.

"Lukas and I visited the Metropolitan Cathedral today, and guess who we saw!"

Hana took the bait. "It wouldn't be a stretch to say Cardinal Dante, right?"

"Not only Dante, but he was talking to Jacob and Christof, and Günther was there, too! Right there in the nave as we were praying."

Lukas jumped in. "It was all I could do to restrain Karl from taking Günther down right there, in the house of God!"

"Actually, we just came from there ourselves," Hana said,

grinning. "Michael really got into it with Dante in his office. Another minute or so and there might have been bloodshed. But we didn't see the others, they must have left just as we arrived."

"No surprise that he outright lied to our faces," Dominic charged, "claiming he didn't know them."

"Well, if you listened to his careful choice of words—that *'these particular names mean nothing to me'*—it was just a clever sidestepping of the truth."

"We did have better luck with Javier Batista, though," Dominic said. "He shared with us a previously classified CIA report confirming the growing neo-Nazi presence in Argentina. Batiste further shared that he believes their aim is to expand the brotherhood by use of what they call a *Kinderklinik*—the Ahnenerbe's Aryan birthing operation in Bariloche. There are probably scores of these worldwide, I imagine.

"But our immediate goal is to retrieve the veil from Jacob and his people. Hana proposed we solicit help from Team Hugo—if they're up to such a mission, of course—and Javier even hinted that Mossad might offer some support. Now, we just need to formulate a solid plan, once we know where the veil is being kept, and bring in the reinforcements."

"For now," Hana said, "let's eat and turn in for the night. I've alerted the pilot that we leave for Bariloche in the morning."

CHAPTER 37

I t was just before noon when the jet landed at San Carlos de Bariloche Airport, and the large SUV Hana had arranged to meet them collected the team and their bags and drove them to Hotel Cristal in the city center.

"Do you always travel in such a stylish way, Señorita?" Batista asked her.

Hana laughed. "No, Javier, far from it. My grandfather doesn't use the jet all that often, yet he still pays for the crew. So he'd prefer to get some use out of his investment. And knowing this trip would have many travel requirements, it does make it easier for us to be able to stop and go when and where we need to."

"I have been to Bariloche many times, but never in such luxury. One could get used to that."

As they checked in at the front desk, Batista happened to notice an old priest sitting in the lobby.

"Father Castillo!" he exclaimed, approaching the older man. "What are you doing here?"

"Señor Batista! I might well ask you the same thing! What brings you to Bariloche?" the priest asked.

"Oh, just some business with friends. Let me introduce you."

Batista went around the group, introducing each person. "And this is my old friend Father Juan Castillo. He leads a small parish at the south end of Bariloche, fittingly called Our Lady of the Snows. It is a modest church with a little black steeple, burrowed deep among the pine trees overlooking the lake and snowy peaks of the Andes beyond. It is truly a beautiful sanctuary."

Dominic stepped forward. "It's so good to meet another man of the cloth here, Father," he said, shaking the priest's hand. "I would love to see your church while we're here."

The old man's face lit up, sensing an opportunity.

"As a matter of fact, Father Dominic, I could actually use your help if you have the time." Then the old priest's expression dimmed. "Sorry, Father, I was presumptuous to ask. Besides, most of our congregants are German and the help I would need would require knowing their language."

"But I am fluent in German. Just tell me how I can help."

The old man's weathered face lightened and his eyes glowed with gratitude. "Oh, what Providence! Well, with Easter just a few days away, my flock is coming to confession in droves, saving up all their sins for this one special holy day of the year, as they usually do. And with so much else to be done in preparation, I would get little else accomplished by sitting in the confessional for days on end. Perhaps you could help by hearing confessions this evening? I hope that won't be an imposition on your time here."

He looked at Hana and the others. "Think I might be able to get a few hours away from our work to help out Javier's friend?"

Javier spoke up for them. "I'd be happy to take them out for dinner, Father Michael, giving you time to do God's work."

Dominic turned to the priest. "Father Castillo, your timing is perfect," he said eagerly. "With so much travel lately, I have been remiss in my priestly duties. So yes, it would be a privilege assisting you later."

"Excellent! I'll see you at five o'clock, then."

Done checking in, the team went to their rooms to unpack and freshen up, then met back in the lobby half an hour later.

"I can't tell you how excited I am to get back in the confessional tonight," Dominic said to the group. "It's been a while since I've done that."

"Well, until then," Javier pointed out, "we have work to do. How about we start with the chief of police, Ramón Santos, and see what we can get out of him?"

"All five of us might be too intimidating a crowd for him," Hana pointed out. "Michael, why don't you and Javier take a taxi to visit Santos, and I'll take Karl and Lukas with me in the SUV to see if we can find anything resembling that *Kinderklinik*?"

"Sounds like a good plan," Dominic agreed. "Just don't raise any red flags if you do find it. And try to avoid being seen by Jacob and his ilk, if they're back from Buenos Aires yet."

Slightly chagrined, Hana pursed her lips and tilted her head as she chided Michael. "I think I've got this."

Hailing a cab from the hotel, Dominic and Batista took off for the Bariloche police headquarters, while Hana, Karl and Lukas took their chances with a list of hospitals, clinics, and their vehicle's GPS.

"It's good to see you again, Capitán," Dominic said, addressing the chief of police as they shook hands. "I'd like you to meet my colleague from Interpol, Javier Batista." The agent withdrew credentials from his coat pocket and presented them to the chief.

"*Interpol?!*" Santos repeated, surprised. "What is Interpol doing in my city? Is there some investigation I should know about?" He gestured with his arm, inviting them to take a seat.

"Actually, Capitán, we are investigating an international organization known as the Ahnenerbe. Have you ever heard the name before?"

The chief resettled himself in his chair, clearly discomfited. "And why is it you ask about this group?"

"We have reason to believe," Dominic explained, "that certain members of the Ahnenerbe are involved with the theft of an artifact that rightfully belongs to the Vatican and was stolen from us in Germany just a few days ago.

"When we were last here—I was with my colleague Hana Sinclair then—you may recall we inquired about one of your citizens, Christof Prager. He is directly related to this crime and we need to find him and retrieve the object. Can you help us locate him?"

Santos grimaced, weighing the political calculations of his response.

"We are aware of this Ahnenerbe group, but to my knowledge they are nothing more than a benevolent society, like Rotary Club International. I believe their mission is to improve the lives of children, or something like that."

Dominic and Batista looked at each other. *He's not far from the awful truth*, Dominic thought.

"The only odd thing about them is that their membership qualifications are quite rigid," Santos huffed. "They wouldn't even allow me to join! You need to be German and have young children or be expecting one in order to be a member. And I don't qualify on either count.

"As for Señor Prager," he added, a more official tone to his voice now, "if you have evidence that he committed a crime, I would like to see it. We cannot simply arrest him on an accusation. Have you such proof? And what is this item you claim was stolen?"

Knowing their evidential options were limited, Batista tried intimidation.

"Capitán, if necessary I will have Interpol issue a Red Notice for this man's immediate arrest," he said. "Your cooperation in this matter would look more favorable than appearing to be obstructive, and once resolved the matter will be closed."

"I assure you, gentlemen, I am only doing my job. Show me your evidence and I will be obliged to honor your request."

Batista was growing impatient. "You mean, you won't take the word of a Vatican priest from whom this object was stolen?"

"As I said, if you can show me—"

"I think we're done here for now," Dominic interrupted the chief, standing to leave. "Thank you for your time, Capitán, we will be back in touch, I'm sure."

"So what now?" Dominic asked Batista in the taxi heading back to the hotel.

"I think Santos is afraid. The German community here must have some hold over him. For all we know he may even be in the Ahnenerbe's pocket. Corruption is rampant throughout the Argentine policing system, especially in smaller cities like this one, where oversight is minimal. I think we're on our own on this one, Michael."

"I'm afraid I have to agree." Dominic sighed, looking at his watch. "Javier, why don't you just drop me off at Father Castillo's church, since it's close to five now anyway. I'll catch up with you later."

CHAPTER 38

"Bless me, Father, for I have sinned. It has been about a year since my last confession…" The young Latino man on the other side of the confessional screen went on to describe a slew of venial offenses—not praying every day, his use of profanity, being disrespectful to women—none of which merited more than minimal penance.

And so it went, with at least two dozen penitents waiting patiently in the pews just outside the confessional booth in Our Lady of the Snows chapel, with more streaming in by the hour.

The sacrament of reconciliation was one of Dominic's most cherished rites as a priest. He was a good listener and believed helping people to be one of his most sacred obligations, both as a priest and as a human being.

There were few things that ever surprised him hearing confessions. Yes, people would tell him what they did or didn't do in certain situations, but he always tried delving deeper into what drove an individual, what motivated them to take the actions they confessed to as they unburdened themselves to him in the anonymity of the dark little booth.

Dominic heard the door to the confessional open and close. The next penitent was a young German woman who was clearly struggling with Spanish. Hearing her Teutonic accent, the priest assured her they could speak German if she preferred, and he immediately sensed her relief that she could confess in her native tongue.

He also heard her sobbing as she struggled to find the words.

"Please, take your time, my child," he said comfortingly. "There is no clock in here."

She let out a nervous little laugh, then took a deep breath as she wiped her tears and began to speak. She started out by confessing to a few minor sins, as most people do, but then broke down again, obviously in deep sorrow. Then her voice descended to a whisper as she admitted what was really on her mind.

"Father, I am so sorry. I have no one else I can turn to about this. I am five months pregnant now with my first baby, but I am already afraid for my child's life. My husband Günther is involved with an organization that raises our children as *neo-Nazis!* They call themselves the Ahnenerbe. I did some research on this, Father, and…"

As she continued speaking, Dominic was staggered by the young woman's mention of her husband's name—*Günther*—and her reference to the *Ahnenerbe! Could it be the same guy who grappled with Karl and stole the veil?!*

"…they bring up these children in special schools where they are indoctrinated into God knows what. They call the children Red Falcons. Can you imagine, Father? *NaziKinder?!* I know this sounds unbelievable, but it's all true. I am afraid and do not know what to do."

"Where is your husband now? Do you feel you are in any danger?"

"He is at home, sleeping, but he just returned from Germany," she said. "He told me he had business there, but he is a butcher! I ask you, what kind of business would a meat butcher have in Germany? He never tells me anything about his activities. No, I don't feel I am in danger. But…" She let the thought linger. Clearly, she was in fear of something.

Though the odds seemed incredible, Dominic felt certain this *Günther* must be one and the same man. And his relationship to the Ahnenerbe would clinch it.

"What you have told me is protected by the seal of confession, so your story is safe with me. As for what to do, I must give this some thought. May I ask your name?"

"My name is Hilda. Hilda Fischbein. My husband must never know what I have told you, Father. He can be a cruel man. I don't even know that he would make a good father. He has hardly been a good husband." At this, she broke down again.

"Let me pray on your situation, Hilda. I'll do what I can to help you, you have my word. I am assisting Father Castillo here just for this evening, but I am staying at the Hotel Cristal for a few more days. Is it possible you can call me there tomorrow?"

"Yes, Father," Hilda said, sniffling. "I would be so grateful to talk with you again. I have no one else I can turn to in this awful place."

"Alright, we'll speak again tomorrow. Until then…" He dispensed her penance, said the prayer of Absolution, then gave her his blessing.

"Thank you, Father. Thank you so much." She got up and left the confessional, closing the door quietly behind her.

Günther Fischbein. Dominic would have to ask Batista to learn more about this man. Maybe Hilda was the way into his operation. He offered a quick prayer of gratitude for God's hand in assisting him. But he knew full well there would be more help needed along the way.

CHAPTER 39

As he sat in his motorized wheelchair looking out over the shimmering Lake Nahuel Huapi, Dr. Johann Kurtz —former decorated colonel in the Gestapo and one-time genomics assistant to Dr. Josef Mengele at Auschwitz—was waiting for the arrival of a very special delivery from his Ahnenerbe colleagues.

At ninety-two years old, Kurtz's mind was still sharp and lucid, though as eager as he might be waiting for delivery of the sacred artifact, he could only exhibit the weakest of misshapen smiles after the latest in a series of strokes.

His younger brother would also be arriving soon. That would please him similarly.

Kurtz's heavily-guarded Brick Gothic mansion on the northern edge of Bariloche was well prepared for the task ahead, boasting a modern, fully-equipped genetics lab and the most qualified German geneticists gold could buy. That and the promise that they would literally be making history in their work.

"Herr Doktor, would you like your tea in the library?" Kurtz's nurse asked.

"*Ja*, Inge, I am coming now." Kurtz rested a bony hand on the wheelchair's joystick drive control and maneuvered his way out of the sitting room, down the wide hall and into the oval-shaped library comprising two open floors of books, thousands of them. Between tall Dalbergia bookshelves surrounding the room, the heads of various trophy animals from the Bavarian backwoods looked down upon visitors: Black Forest red stags, roe, chamois, antelope—and that most recognizable symbol of the Third Reich, the golden eagle. A raised platform in the very center of the room featured a large West African lion attacking a blue wildebeest. Death in nature was the dominant if unintended theme.

As Kurtz rolled up to his desk, Inge set down a silver tray and began the steeping process. Kurtz favored the smooth and creamy Guayusa, a rare tea from the Ecuadorian Amazon rainforest which he had grown fond of since arriving in South America some sixty years earlier.

As he was taking his first sip, the doors to the library opened and his secretary stood at the threshold.

"Herr Doktor, the two gentlemen you have been expecting have arrived, Shall I see them in?"

"*Ja*, of course, Hans. See them in."

Jacob Rausch and Christof Prager, both dressed in dark business suits, entered the room and approached the old man. Jacob was carrying a leather briefcase.

"Please, gentlemen, have a seat," Kurtz said, his low voice breathy and guttural. "I understand you had some trouble in the Fatherland getting hold of this object. You do have it with you, I assume?"

"Yes, Herr Doktor, we brought it to you as instructed," Jacob said, "As for the trouble, it was not something we could not handle."

"Good. Well, I must see the veil," his voice croaked. "Now, please."

Jacob set the briefcase on the desk, unlocked the combination to it, and raised the lid. Reaching inside he withdrew an object wrapped in a thick red velvety fabric. He set the object on the desk in front of Kurtz, then slowly peeled back the covering, revealing the alabaster box.

Kurtz sat there staring at the object, the sunlight from the windows behind him giving the alabaster a diaphanous glow, as if it were emanating light itself.

He reached up, unfastened the bronze hasp, and lifted back the lid.

"Hans, please fetch my gloves and a loupe."

Prepared for the request, the secretary produced a pair of white conservation gloves and a small jeweler's magnifying loupe and set them on the desk. Nurse Inge approached, picked up the gloves and fastened them onto each of the old man's hands.

With trembling fingers, Kurtz withdrew the veil from the box, letting it fall open naturally. He showed no emotion whatsoever in front of the others, simply stared at it for a long while, taking in the image, the varied colors on the fabric, the sheerness of the byssus itself. Picking up the loupe he closely inspected the portions of the cloth which appeared to show blood, lingering over several areas that looked promising for the work ahead. The room was completely silent as the others watched the doctor analyze the artifact.

"Good," he finally said, returning the veil to its box. "Very good. Thank you, gentlemen, you have done well. Go back to your duties now. Our work shall soon begin."

"*Danke schön*, Herr Doktor. *Auf wiedersehen*," both Jacob and Christof said in lockstep unison, as they turned to leave the library.

As Jacob and Christof headed up the long drive back through the estate gates, a chauffeured black Mercedes S550 sedan with tinted windows passed them coming in.

Parking at the front door, the driver exited the vehicle and opened the rear door for the sole occupant, who was granted immediate entry into the mansion.

Hans knocked on the library door, then opened it.

"Herr Doktor, your brother has arrived."

"Oh, yes, please show him in, Hans."

A tall man with aquiline features entered the room and made his way to the desk. He bent over to give his half-brother an awkward embrace.

"It is wonderful to see you again, Johann," said the man as he sat down.

"And you too, Fabrizio," Kurtz said, looking up with his crooked smile. "I have something very special to share with you."

The old man had Cardinal Dante's full attention.

CHAPTER 40

The Noble Calf butcher shop on Avenida de Julio was busier than usual. The owner, Günther Fischbein, was sawing through a primal cut of Argentine beef for several waiting customers when his wife stepped out from the back room.

"Günther," Hilda said, "I must go to the market now, then I have my ultrasound at the clinic. Is there anything in particular you need while I'm out?"

"Yes," Günther groused, "more help. Get your errands done quickly so you can help me back here."

"Yes, *schatz*. I'll be back soon." She hurried out the front door.

Hilda walked briskly in her sensible pumps, not to the local grocer but several blocks away to the Hotel Cristal, where she and Father Dominic had arranged to meet while her husband was managing the shop. *Many customers are good*, she thought. *They will keep him occupied.*

It was a cold day so she had worn a thick cable-knit sweater beneath a dark overcoat. Not wanting to be recognized, she donned a pair of sunglasses. Thankfully the sun was bright enough—and there were many skiing tourists in town also wearing shades—that it would not make her stand out. She did not want word of her visit to the priest getting back to Günther.

Fifteen minutes later the doorman at the Hotel Cristal pulled open the door and she entered the lobby. She saw Father Dominic and a woman sitting near him in the corner of the lobby. She hesitated until the priest motioned her forward.

"Good morning, Hilda!" Dominic said.

"Hilda Fischbein, I would like you to meet my colleague, Hana Sinclair. We both came to Bariloche for a very special purpose, which I believe is related to the things you told me about.

"I have not divulged anything we spoke about to Hana, but she is among my closest personal friends, and I'm confident she will also be able to help. With your permission, I'd like the three of us to go to my room to share what we discussed in private, so all three of us have the same understanding and the same goal, which is to lighten your burden—but only if you feel comfortable doing so. I would never reveal anything you said in the confessional, of course, unless it was with your full permission. How do you feel about that?"

Hilda nodded, grateful that she wasn't meeting the priest alone in his room and that this way they could also speak in private, not in the open lobby.

At her nod, Hana thanked her in fluent German for allowing her to help. Hilda smiled now, even more comfortable with this associate of the *padre*. The three of them took the elevator to Dominic's second floor room.

Once inside she explained quickly, "I'm...I'm not quite sure how anyone can help change my husband's mind, Father. I've given this a great deal of thought, and I've decided I want a divorce. This pregnancy was not planned, and it was the only reason we married in the first place. I realize now I do not even love the man, for God's sake, and I do *not* want Günther in my child's life if he wants him to grow up as a neo-Nazi! No, that will not happen. I am only concerned what Günther might do when I tell him. He can be very violent." As she said this, her hand reached up to her face, as if recalling something of her husband's past temper.

"But I see no reason why you cannot share what we spoke of to Fräulein Hana," she added. "Just leave out the sins." She gave Hana a pleasant little laugh, which Hana echoed.

"Please have a seat, Hilda," Hana said, gesturing to an adjacent chair. "It is a real pleasure meeting you. May I get you some tea or coffee?"

"*Nein danke.*" Hilda took off her jacket, lay it on the bed and took a seat next to Hana.

Dominic related to Hana what Hilda had told him in the confessional booth, about Günther's activities with the Ahnenerbe and the *Kinderklinik*, and the indoctrination of young children into the Red Falcon program from birth.

"Goodness," Hana responded after Dominic had finished. "This all sounds so monstrous! You poor woman." She reached out her hand and placed it over Hilda's. Hilda began tearing up, finally able to talk to someone sympathetic to her previously unvoiced predicament.

Hana found the moment to inquire more about Günther. "How do you know your husband is involved with the Ahnenerbe, Hilda? Does he meet with associates at your home, or...?"

Hilda dabbed at her nose with a tissue. "There is a large barn on one of the member's properties where they meet each week. Günther told me their next meeting is two days from now, on Wednesday."

"Where is this barn?" Dominic asked.

"I can draw you a map if you like," she said. Hana nodded, then reached for pen and paper from the desk drawer and slid it over to Hilda. She drew a map of the area showing various points of interest as guides, then where the property was located.

"Hilda," Dominic said, "there is something I need to tell you about Günther which you may not like hearing, but I feel it's necessary given the decisions you have made.

"Hana and I were in Germany last week with other colleagues when your husband was there, at the same time and place we were. Without going into too much detail, Günther was involved in the theft of an object of great interest to the Vatican. He even injured one of our colleagues, a Swiss Guard and a very good friend, in order to steal it. This is why we are here in Bariloche, to take back what should be cared for by the Church."

Rather than tears or shock, which Dominic might have expected, Hilda's face grew hard, her eyes piercing.

"That is an unforgivable act, Father," she scolded. "I apologize for his behavior. It only makes my decision that much easier."

"You see now why we need to know more about the Ahnenerbe and its activities here. As young as he is, Günther is mixed up with some very dangerous people. And while we cannot influence their ideologies, we must not let them keep the artifact they stole from us. The consequences are far too important to the Church and society."

"I will help you however I can, Father, and you, Fräulein Hana. What is it I can do?"

Hana looked up at Dominic, then said, "Michael, what if Hilda and I were to visit this *Kinderklinik* first? See if there's anything there to be seen. We can do that today, yes, Hilda?"

"I do have to go in for an ultrasound this afternoon. You can accompany me—say, as my sister, from Heidelberg, so they do not get suspicious. They are very careful about security there."

"Then today we shall be sisters," Hana smiled at Hilda and saw a single tear of relief and gratitude on the woman's cheek.

CHAPTER 41

H ow far along are you?" Hana asked as she drove Hilda to the *Kinderklinik* a few miles away.

"I am five months now," she sighed. "The first ultrasound revealed I'm having a boy. But oh, the hot flashes, the backaches, and the leg cramps. I was never told pregnancy would be this painful before the birth itself. My mother died soon after I was born, and I have no friends here to help, so all this is new to me. I'm learning as I go along, I suppose, which is why I don't need Günther's obstinance. I know now marrying him was a mistake." She looked out the window at the passing landscape, thinking back to more pleasant times.

As they neared their destination, Hilda pointed out the road they needed to take. It was unmarked, not even a street sign, which Hana found unusual. Another half kilometer or so and she pulled up in front of a red brick three-story building in the midst of a thick pine forest—again, with no signage whatsoever—and parked the car.

Looking around, Hana saw many other cars parked in the lot. When she pulled in, she happened to notice the one next to her had one of those oval white country code stickers, simply marked with an "88" on it. *What country is designated as "88,"* she wondered. Looking around at the other cars, nearly all of them had the same "88" sticker on their rear windows. *How odd.*

"Hilda, what do these '88' stickers stand for?"

"I have no idea. I've never noticed them before now. Maybe they are parking permits?"

Entering the clinic, Hilda signed in at the reception desk, indicating her sister was here joining her. The older German nurse at the desk looked sternly at Hana, saying nothing, but handed both of them visitor passes. "You are permitted on the premises only with an escort. Do not leave your assigned area."

Assigned area?! Hardly a comforting bedside manner, Hana mused. She looked at Hilda and rolled her eyes, then they both took a seat in the waiting room.

Twenty minutes later another gruff nurse entered the room and called out "Frau Fischbein?" Hilda and Hana rose and followed the woman down the hall and into an examination room.

"The doctor will be with you shortly," the nurse said curtly, handing her a gown. "Take everything off below the waist and the gown opens in the front." She then closed the door as she left the room.

"I don't get a very welcoming impression from these people," Hana said, taking a seat as Hilda changed into the gown.

"Even for Germans, they do seem cold and indifferent," Hilda noted. "I have a different doctor every time I come here, too. Is that normal?"

"Well, not having experienced what you're going through, I can't say I'm an expert, but from what I understand women normally have one doctor who sees them through the entire pregnancy. I'm sure that helps breed familiarity with their patients. But as you said, this is a rather unorthodox clinic."

Just then the door opened, and a radiology nurse came in, followed by an old man in a wheelchair. The man spoke first, in German, introducing himself.

"Good afternoon, ladies, I am Doctor Kurtz, director of this clinic. How are you doing today, Frau Fischbein? I understand your sister is visiting you, hmm?" He looked curiously at Hana.

"Yes, Herr Doktor, this is my sister Hana. She is visiting from Heidelberg."

"Heidelberg! What a coincidence. I am originally from Heidelberg," the old man said with a twisted smile. "Are you here to help your sister during this joyful time, Fräulein?"

Hana was suddenly chilled in the presence of this man, though she couldn't reason why. She replied as enthusiastically as she could.

"Yes, Herr Doktor, I have not seen my sister in quite some time. I hear she is having a boy!"

"That she is," Kurtz said, giving Hana an appraising look, one tinged with suspicion.

"Your accent..." he said hesitantly, one eyebrow raised. "I find it curious. It does not sound at all like the Pälzisch dialect of our region. Did you grow up in Heidelberg?"

Hana collected herself quickly. "My father moved us around quite a lot. He was in the army, you see, so we lived in many parts of Germany. I suppose I experienced dialectic differences along the way."

"Herr Doktor," Hilda pleaded, sensing peril, "could we get this done, please? My husband needs me back at the shop, so I do not have much time."

Kurtz kept looking at Hana, uncertainty in his eyes. "Of course, Frau Fischbein, let us see what we have here today." He turned his attention to Hilda.

The nurse had set up the ultrasound equipment and, while the doctor remained in his chair, she performed the procedure. Everyone looked up at the sonogram display situated next to the table.

"Everything looks normal," the doctor said matter-of-factly. "We will be giving you a new vitamin regimen today, and a list of exercises to keep you and the baby as comfortable as possible.

Please take these seriously. We want to make sure your baby boy grows up to be a strong young man."

Hana felt a shiver up her spine hearing the old German say these words, now knowing what he actually meant. She folded her arms in closer to her body to ward off the unexpected chill.

Kurtz fiddled with the wheelchair's joystick, turning to Hana again.

"How long will you be staying in Bariloche, Fräulein?" he asked.

"Oh, just another couple of days, I expect," Hana replied.

"Well, do enjoy our city while you are here," he said, "and take good care of your sister, too."

With that, the nurse opened the door, and Kurtz turned and wheeled himself out of the room, the whirring sound of the chair's motor diminishing the further away he got. The door closed.

"That was the strangest man I've met in a while," Hana said as Hilda changed back into her clothes. "Does he know Günther? We wouldn't want them exchanging stories about 'your sister.'"

"I don't know," Hilda said worriedly. "They might know each other from Ahnenerbe meetings, if the doctor is part of that group. I can't imagine he wouldn't be, would you? I do hope he doesn't mention anything to Günther if he is. I suppose I should have thought of that earlier."

"I wouldn't worry about it, Hilda. You have enough going on as it is."

As they turned in their passes and left the clinic, Hana observed a large Mercedes van pass by them. Inside the back sat Dr. Kurtz in his wheelchair.

On the rear window was an oval sticker with the number "88" on it. She stared at the van as it slowly crept down the tree-lined drive and out toward the city.

Getting into the car, as Hilda got settled in the passenger seat, Hana checked the rearview mirror by habit, when she noticed a man sitting in the car behind hers. Sitting in the driver's seat, to her shock, was the handsome Frenchman she had passed in the hall of the hotel in Buenos Aires!

He noticed her recognize him, smiled at her, then pulled his green BMW out of his own parking space and exited the lot.

CHAPTER 42

The Nebbiolo Restaurant, not far from Hotel Cristal, was just the dining oasis they had all had been hoping for after a long day—true Argentine flavors with Italian overtones.

Dominic, Hana, Javier, Karl and Lukas were all seated at a large table with an attentive service staff. Two waiters set down plates each ordered from the ample menu: fresh grilled rainbow trout; pork with peaches and elderberry sauce; Locro, the traditional Argentinian stew with beef, beans, corn and potatoes; Milanesa schnitzel with broccoli and corn pudding; and Matambre Arrollado, flank steak stuffed with vegetables and hard-boiled eggs. Sample tastings made their way around the table as they all reveled in the tastes of South America.

The team had decided to meet up over dinner to exchange notes about their days' activities, and since the restaurant was packed, their discussion would be lost among the din of other patrons' conversations.

"I met the strangest man today," Hana began. "A Dr. Johann Kurtz, the director of the clinic where Hilda went for an ultrasound. Talk about weird vibes. This guy is in, I'd say his nineties, and runs the place with an iron fist.

"I posed as Hilda's sister visiting from Heidelberg. Coincidentally, he's from Heidelberg himself and questioned my accent, which made for an unnerving moment. But we got through it. I wouldn't be surprised, Javier, if he's involved with the Ahnenerbe."

"Johann Kurtz?!" the agent exclaimed. "We absolutely do know something about this man—a former Gestapo geneticist who we believe worked with Josef Mengele in his depraved human experiments at Auschwitz. Mossad has been hoping to find him for some time, but they did not know where he has been all these years. I have no doubt they'll be thrilled to learn you've found him, Hana. I'll let them know tomorrow."

"Another thing," Hana recalled. "Nearly every car in the parking lot had one of those oval country code stickers which just read '88.' Any idea what that means?"

Batista put his fork down and looked at Hana earnestly. "You say, every car had it?"

"Yes, nearly all of them. Why?"

The agent looked around at other tables nearby before answering in a low voice. The others leaned in as he spoke.

"Eight represents the eighth letter in the alphabet, H." he said darkly. "88, then, equates to 'HH,' which is neo-Nazi code for *Heil Hitler*."

Everyone fell silent taking in this new and unsettling detail.

"Clearly, Hilda's clinic has close affiliations with the right-wing extremists here," he remarked. "Not particularly unexpected given the city's history, but to be so boldly public about it like that is surprising. They're certainly not trying to hide the fact."

"Even the doctor's van had one," Hana added. "He's in a wheelchair and uses one of those specially adapted Mercedes wheelchair vans."

"I suppose when your organization pretty much controls the politics of the city," Dominic observed, "there's no reason to be afraid. The Ahnenerbe must have its hooks in deep places here."

"Meaning," Batista added supportively, "that we need to be very careful making inquiries. Neo-Nazis are prevalent throughout South America—especially here in Argentina—and they have no fear of consequences because there are none. You might compare them with Mexican drug cartels, who even control governments."

"So what are we going to do about getting the veil back, Michael?" Karl asked.

"I've been thinking about that," Dominic replied, "and we should all meet when we're fresh in the morning so I can lay out my thoughts. What Hilda told us will be part of our plan."

"This veal is superb, Johann," Cardinal Dante said as he took a sip of the Pinot Noir. "My compliments to your chef.

"So, when do you plan to start the DNA extraction? And are you certain it will work?"

Kurtz, sitting at the other end of the long candlelit dining table, set his own glass down, then paused before replying to his brother's question.

"Nothing about this particular process can be certain, Fabrizio," he said. "But the prospects are good. DNA persists for a very long time, but we must first test for carbon dating on the byssus fabric itself. And we can never be certain this is the blood of Christ himself, as you must realize. But given Himmler's, or should I say Otto Rahn's, perseverance in finding it where he did —given the historical legends of Rennes-le-Château—it looks quite promising.

"I think in the end we may never know. But we shall experiment nonetheless. We have many trial subjects in the clinic to test it on, though of course, I may not live long enough to see the results of my own work."

"Nonsense," Dante said chidingly. "Our mother lived to 103, and each of our fathers lived well into their nineties. Didn't yours die at 99? And you live well and eat healthfully. I predict many more years for you, Johann. Besides, I've always looked up to you. You can't possibly die yet. There is too much at stake. So enough of that talk."

The old man croaked out a phlegmy chuckle, then coughed to clear his throat. He took a sip of the wine.

"I should tell you, Fabrizio, that I plan to administer the extracted Jesus DNA on myself first. If there is *any* chance Christ had some form of divinity before his life was cut short, who knows what that could mean? Perhaps eternal life? What have I got to lose, given my advanced years already?"

"Johann, that could be a risky procedure at your age! Shouldn't you try it first on the infants in the clinic, to see what kinds of responses they exhibit?"

"As I say, I have nothing to lose in doing so. And the thought of having the blood of ancient Aryans coursing through my veins gives me a feeling of power and connectedness like no other. I have no doubt that is what Hitler himself was hoping for, which is why he wanted the veil so desperately. We shall know soon enough, won't we?

"And if it doesn't go as planned," Kurtz added, "this will all be yours when I die, little brother," he said wistfully, setting the glass down with a shaky hand. "When that happens you must abandon all that Church business and make sure our work here continues. You are the only one I trust to see that it does, and you will have substantial assets to carry things out, as you are my sole beneficiary."

"You have my solemn promise, Johann. I will take good care of your legacy," Dante said, looking admiringly around the opulent mansion. "But, God willing, that will not be for some time yet."

"You are staying for Wednesday's meeting, aren't you?"

Dante took another sip of his wine then dabbed a napkin to his mouth. "I'll be here for another couple of days, so yes, I'll be at the meeting."

CHAPTER 43

The wind was whipping off Lake Nahuel Huapi as Dominic, Karl and Lukas made it back to the hotel after a long early morning run. Their faces were flushed red from the cold, and the warmth of the lobby was a welcome relief from the onset of winter outside.

"It's not even June here and it's freezing," Karl noted. "It's all backwards from how it is at home."

"That's the Southern Hemisphere for you," Dominic said. "Seasons here are literally the polar opposite of ours. Don't you find it invigorating?"

"Apart from skiing, I'll take a warm Italian beach any time over cold weather," Karl moaned, shivering. "Growing up in Switzerland was enough, thanks."

"Okay," Dominic said, heading for the elevator, "Let's get showered, have some breakfast, then meet up back in my room for the day ahead."

"WE'LL USE Hilda's map to the barn and drive out there now to explore the area a bit, so we know the layout better for tomorrow's meeting.

"Karl," Dominic continued, "you and Lukas need to find a way to listen to what's going on inside. I doubt they let just anyone attend those meetings, but you'll have the cover of darkness in your favor tomorrow night. Just be careful not to arouse attention. We have no idea how serious these people are with others poking around, so don't take any unnecessary risks.

"Hana and I will drop you off from one of the nearby roads then and wait there for your return." He pointed out a side road on the map that was fairly close to the property. "It's a short walk through the forest to get to the barn; that looks to be the best course. Javier, do you have anything to add?"

Batista reached behind his back and produced a fully loaded Glock 17, sliding it across the table to Dengler.

"Pray you don't have to use this, Karl, but I'd be more comfortable knowing you had defensive protection if it comes to that."

Handling the weapon expertly, Dengler checked that the safety was on, then reached behind him and wedged the pistol in his inside waistband.

Hana reached over and put her hand on his shoulder. "You be careful out there tomorrow, Karl. You too, Lukas."

Dominic stood to leave. "Alright, let's load up and take a ride."

"I'll stay behind," Batista said. "I've got some calls to make. Mossad needs an update on Hana's news about Kurtz, and maybe they'll be willing to give us a hand if we need it."

A LIGHT SNOW had started to fall as the team headed out in their rented SUV. Looking out at the Alps across the lake, Karl could see skiers making their way down the mountain runs at one of the local resorts.

"Too bad we don't have more time to get some skiing in, eh, Lukas? That's the only good to come of winter, in my opinion."

"I'll say. That powder does look inviting." Growing up in the

Swiss Alps, both of them had skied since they were young children, and even more so as Mountain Grenadiers in the Swiss Army.

"Who knows," Lukas posed, "once our job here is done maybe we can get in a day or two on the slopes."

"Not likely," Dominic said. "We've all been away for longer than I expected already."

"We're coming up on the road to the property, Michael," Hana said, riding shotgun with the map. "It should be just up here, at the next turn."

Reaching the designated road, Dominic turned onto it, heading deeper into the forest. The day was dark with clouds as it was, but the thick canopy of trees made it seem like it was nighttime.

A few minutes later they arrived at the property Hilda had identified, with "No Trespassing" signs posted in Spanish. Dominic turned into the drive anyway. He saw nobody standing guard. Nobody at all, in fact. He drove up to the barn and let the engine idle.

Suddenly two German Shepherds rushed toward them, appearing from nowhere, barking ferociously as they surrounded the car. Hearing the commotion, a large man wearing a cowboy hat came out of the adjoining house on the property carrying a shotgun.

"*Esta es propiedad privada!*" he shouted, waving the rifle.

Dominic rolled down his window enough to speak to the man.

"I'm sorry," he said in English. "No hablo Español. We're lost."

"I said," the man repeated in English, "this is private property. Turn your car around and leave before the dogs get angrier."

"Sorry! Gracias," Dominic smiled as he rolled up the window. "Karl, you and Lukas get a good look around as I turn the car back." Dominic took his time doing a three-point turn of the car, giving his companions an opportunity to survey the lay of the property.

"Got it. We're good," Karl said.

"Now let's find another road nearby where we can let you out tomorrow."

Peering down at the map, Hana found what looked to be an ideal location.

"Let's try here, Michael," pointing to a road a short distance behind the property. "It's probably a five-minute walk to the barn from there."

Driving to where Hana directed, Michael found a flat turnout off the main road where the four-wheel drive SUV could easily be hidden in the trees. That would be their drop-off and meeting point.

BACK AT THE HOTEL, Javier Batista had reached his primary contact at Mossad headquarters in Tel Aviv, a man he had served with on clandestine missions during the Gulf War.

"Eli, it is good to hear your voice again, my friend," Batista said.

"And yours, Javi, *shalom*. But, as it's been so many years since we last spoke, I expect you are calling for a good reason, in which case you have my attention."

"Always cutting to the chase," Batista acknowledged. "That's what I like about you, no small talk.

"Eli, I think I may have stumbled onto something here in Argentina your people may find of interest. Are you familiar with Dr. Johann Kurtz? We believe he worked with Mengele at Auschwitz."

"Familiar?!" Eli asked without hesitation. "He is on our most wanted list! Why do you ask?"

"I am in Bariloche, down in Patagonia, on another mission here helping some friends. But it seems we have found your Dr. Kurtz running a neo-Nazi children's clinic, and from all appearances they've been doing this for some time. I assumed this is something you might want to know about. But I also have a favor to ask."

"Javi, if it is within my power to arrange, you shall have it. And yes, we do want Kurtz. Badly."

"Good. Here is what I have in mind…"

CHAPTER 44

Nestled among the gnarled Planatus trees on the shore of Lake Geneva near Cologny, Armand de Saint-Clair was hosting French President Pierre Valois and his wife Jacquelin as they vacationed in Geneva as guests of the baron at his château, La Maison des Arbres.

Agents of the GSPR—the presidential Secret Service unit—were spread throughout the vast property with cordons set up on the main street on which the property lay, creating its usual disruptions to the entitled expectations of Saint-Clair's upscale neighbors.

"I always feel as it I must apologize for my presence wherever I go, Armand," Valois sighed. "Such is life for the likes of politicians in this day and age. Threats seem to be everywhere."

"It is not just you, Pierre," Saint-Clair replied. "Anyone of celebrity or significant worth must take extraordinary precautions these days. It comes with the territory."

"If my granddaughter Hana would allow it, I would have a security detail on her at all times. But she is obstinate and refuses such accommodation."

"*Alors*, but she is an independent one, *oui*?"

"Yes, she is," Saint-Clair agreed, shaking his head. "But still, I do take protective measures for her, even now as she is in Argentina."

"Argentina? Is she on assignment for *Le Monde* down there?" Valois asked.

"She is onto some story, yes, but I think it has more to do with another adventure of Father Dominic's. His work as an archivist is far more compelling than one might imagine. And as we have seen, often hazardous. That is why your goddaughter needs protection, Pierre."

Saint-Clair's personal aide appeared. "Excuse me, Baron?"

"Yes, Frederic, what is it?"

"It is Mademoiselle Hana for you on the telephone."

Saint-Clair looked at Valois with surprise, then went to the phone.

"My dear, we were just talking about you! Pierre and Jacquelin are visiting."

"Grand-père! It's so good to hear your voice. And when we're done, I would love to speak with them—but first, I need to tell you what is happening here. We may need your help."

Hana went on to tell her grandfather about their discovery and the provenance of the Magdalene veil, its theft in Germany, their following the thieves to Buenos Aires then Bariloche, and Dominic's plan to recover it, which, she admitted, was still being formed. She also revealed having encountered Dr. Johann Kurtz, and his sordid activities with the *Kinderklinik*.

"He might be someone you could look into for us, pépé. He has Nazi connections that go back to the war, and we believe he intends to use DNA from the veil for perpetuating an Aryan birth line."

"You simply can't take it on face value that the veil is even authentic, my dear, can you? Really?"

"Yes, I agree there are many factors to be considered. But let's give it the benefit of the doubt for the moment and base our actions on its veracity. If we're wrong, so be it. But what if it is authentic to some degree? Shouldn't that artifact be in the hands of experts in such things, rather than neo-Nazis?!"

"As always, you do make a good point," her grandfather admitted. "Let me discuss it with Pierre and Cardinal Petrini, and I'll get back to you shortly. In the meantime, Hana, I insist you stay out of any dangerous situations. You may be dealing with fanatical fascist elements there and I won't have you in jeopardy."

"Yes, Grand-père, I love you, too," she responded with affection. "Now, let me speak to my godfather. I'll be waiting for your call soon. *Au revoir.*"

CHAPTER 45

I t was just after 9 p.m. when Dominic extinguished the headlights of the SUV. He had pulled off the road onto the turnout and into the forest a few minutes' walk away from the barn. A quarter moon hung in the dim sky, lending no light beneath the canopy of trees as Karl and Lukas emerged from the vehicle.

"You boys be careful now," Hana pleaded in a whisper. "Don't take any risks."

"You mean, apart from this one?" Dengler said, smiling as he rechecked the Glock. "We'll be fine, cousin. See you inside half an hour."

As Dominic and Hana waited in the dark car, the two Swiss Guards crept through the forest toward the barn, which they could see from this distance had only one light over the front entrance.

Slowly making their way through the trees, the two were careful where they stepped, recalling their mountaineer's training in stealthy maneuvers on forest underbrush. One snap of a twig could give their presence away, and a German Shepherd would certainly hear that.

They could see people, all men by the looks of it,

approaching the entrance, and a guard with a rifle slung over his shoulder holding a clipboard, apparently checking names.

The old redwood barn was large, two stories tall, with light seeping out of open cracks between most of the wallboards. Karl led the way toward the rear of the building, where they might have a good chance of hearing the goings on inside. Finding a suitable spot next to a tall woodpile, they held their position and waited, listening to the murmuring crowd inside.

A few minutes later the murmuring died down as footsteps on wood were heard just on the other side of the wall, which they reasoned would be where the speakers would stand. A moment later they were startled when two men shouted *"Heil Hitler!"* followed by the respondent crowd rising and returning the salute.

"Think we're in the right place?" Lukas whispered to Karl rhetorically.

One of the men on the stage began speaking in German, not ten feet away from where Karl and Lukas were crouched.

"My friends, our mission in the Fatherland was a great success! We have acquired Himmler's sacred artifact, and it is now in good hands at Dr. Kurtz's genetics lab in the mansion. Soon he will be initiating the true *Lebensborn* program begun by our forefathers."

Rousing applause followed his statement, together with shouts of *Seig Heil!, Seig Heil!* as the attendees grew frenzied by the news.

"That is *Jacob* speaking!" Karl acknowledged quietly. "He's obviously one of the leaders."

They tried peeking through cracks in the barn wall but could only make out parts of the audience, not the speakers.

"We do have a problem that has come up, however," Jacob continued. "A Vatican priest and his three companions have come to our city and are nosing around our business, looking to steal our rightful property. We are distributing photographs of each of them now. If you see them anywhere in town, let us know. They must be dealt with."

Karl and Lukas looked at each other in the dim filtered light, worry on their faces. But right at that moment, they realized they had a more immediate problem.

Just a few feet behind them they heard a large dog emitting a low menacing growl. They slowly turned to find one of the German Shepherds, her tail lowered between her legs, her ears flat, her posture firm and unyielding.

The men froze. Lukas slowly turned, then began backing up away from the animal, drawing her attention away from Karl.

Slowly reaching into his jacket pocket, he grabbed the last handful of dog treats he had used for Fritzi a few days earlier. He slowly bent down on his knees, coaxing her gently in German, and held out his hand for the dog to inspect.

Smelling the treats and sensing Lukas was less a threat than a source of food, she slowly crept forward, sniffing his hand. Her snout approached the hand, then wolfed down the treats. Her tail started wagging, and Lukas reached out to pet her. He looked up at Karl and smiled.

"Good girl," he said to her, as he played with her a bit more, stroking her head.

"I think it's time we leave," Karl whispered. "We've got what we need." He too slowly backed away from the dog, but it was clear by now she didn't perceive them as a further threat, her tail still wagging. She had seen dozens of others come into the barn and figured they must be part of the activities, too.

Retreating into the forest and away from the barn, both men made their way back to where Dominic and Hana were waiting for them.

"When could they have possibly taken photos of us?" Lukas asked as they walked, incredulous. "Have we been spied on the whole time we were here?"

"I'm sure word got around pretty quickly. We weren't exactly hiding our presence here, asking questions and all."

The trees were thinning out as they approached the vehicle on the turnout, but they noticed both front doors were wide open. *Maybe they just needed air*, Karl thought.

When they arrived, the SUV was empty. Both men looked around, quietly calling out their friends' names.

Dominic and Hana were gone.

CHAPTER 46

"Where could they have gone?!" Karl asked. "There is no place to go!"

"Do you think they might have followed us to the barn?"

"No, that wasn't the plan. They should be here waiting for us."

Lukas noticed the keys were still in the ignition. "I'm worried, Karl. Why would they just leave the car doors wide open with the keys in it?"

Karl was deeply concerned now. "I think we have to assume the obvious—that they've been taken."

As he spoke a car was approaching them quickly from up the road, which then pulled into the turnout, slowly coming toward them through the trees, lights turned off, and stopping next to the vehicle. Karl reached for the Glock.

A man stepped out of the green BMW, his hands raised in submission.

"You must be Karl and Lukas," the ruggedly handsome man said, stepping toward them cautiously. "My name is Marco Picard, I'm on the Personal Security Detail for Baron Armand de Saint-Clair and have been keeping a distant eye on his granddaughter at his instructions, both here and in Buenos Aires. I'm afraid she and Father Dominic have been captured."

"You say you know the baron?" Karl asked warily, his hand still on the Glock's handle.

"I have been on his PSD for seven years now."

"What's the name of his personal aide?"

"Frederic."

"And the name of his château in Zürich?"

"La Maison des Arbres. But it's in Geneva, not Zürich."

Karl paused for a moment, considering.

"Listen, I would do exactly what you're doing," Marco admitted hastily. "For what it's worth, I was a *Bérets Verts* with the French Marine Commandos before working for the baron. I can certainly hold my own and would be honored to work with you. But we need to act soon."

That was all Karl needed. "Welcome to the team," he said as the three shook hands. "What happened?"

"I had been parked just down the road a bit, across the street and hidden in the trees like you, watching what took place after you all arrived. Once you left the car, about ten minutes later a dark van arrived, and four armed men got out and apprehended your friends. There were too many for me to take on alone, so I followed them at a distance. They were taken to one of the mansions on the lake. Once I knew where they were, I raced back here, knowing you would return to find the car empty and have questions.

"So, what do we do now?" Marco concluded.

As they stood beneath the trees, Karl filled Marco in on the basics of the situation, the people involved, the events at the barn, and the probability that Michael and Hana had been taken to the home of Dr. Johann Kurtz, the apparent leader of the Ahnenerbe, who also possessed the artifact they were there to recover.

"Yes," Marco acknowledged, "the baron informed me that Hana called him last night about the veil and this Dr. Kurtz. I believe he is now assembling Team Hugo for their influence in helping you out. Or rather, helping *us* out."

"Yes, that means we'll have a lot more firepower, politically anyway," Karl said. "But I fear that may come too late."

Lukas said, "I know you want to charge over there to rescue them, but without a plan that could only endanger them all the more."

Marco agreed. "I saw numerous security guards stationed at the mansion beyond the four men who had captured them."

Reluctantly Karl nodded. "Let's get back to the hotel and coordinate a plan with Javier."

"YOU HAVE YOUR GO-AHEAD, JAVI," Mossad's Eli Raziel said, calling on a secure line from Tel Aviv. "It may interest you to know that the prime minister himself got a personal call from Pierre Valois, the French president, requesting a Shayetet 13 ops team to assist yours in Bariloche. Their flight arrives tomorrow morning—six special operatives trained in both land and sea assaults. The team leader is Yossi Geffen. We've arranged for a Chinook helicopter to transport his men and their gear to Bariloche, and he'll meet you at the Squadron 34 Gendarmería Nacional Air Base on arrival, then on to the safe house to coordinate the op. I'll send you the address.

"Valois also called the Argentine president for authorization to operate in his country, which he approved reluctantly. We want Kurtz, Javi, and the S13 team will take him dead or alive, preferably the latter, to stand trial here in Israel. His work with Mengele will not be forgotten, and this new mission of his to breed Nazi mongrels is unthinkable.

"Lastly, and this is classified, we currently have a Dolphin-class submarine patrolling off southern Chilean waters. It will provide extraction support in the Bay of Puerto Montt once we have Kurtz."

"I'm impressed, Eli," Batista said, "especially at how quickly this all came about. I'll keep you apprised of developments here. Thanks, and *shalom*." They ended the call.

Batista sat back, torn between the good news of the support from so many and the call he'd gotten from the Swiss Guards about the kidnapping. Time was of the essence and he wondered if even now it was already too late for the good Father and Hana Sinclair.

CHAPTER 47

Dominic's body stirred, then his eyes slowly opened. He was in a dark quiet room, that much was clear. Then he remembered the injection one of the men had given him and Hana.

Hana! Where was Hana?

A small window at the far end of the long room he found himself in provided little light, but enough to see that Hana was a few feet away from him, still unconscious and lying on an army cot, as was he.

He slowly sat up and realized he had a slammer of a headache. After a few minutes of stretching his neck for relief, he got up and went over to Hana.

"Hey, wake up," he whispered, gently shaking her shoulder.

After several seconds Hana started to moan, then tried to move. Her hand reached up to her head and she opened her eyes.

Seeing Michael, she looked at him quizzically. "Where are we? Is there anybody else here?" She started to get up, then also felt the effects of the anesthetic, and lay back down again.

"Good God, how long have we been out?" she groaned.

Dominic stood up and started walking around the room to stretch his body and clear his head.

"I have no idea, but it's dark, so it must still be Wednesday night. Unless it's Thursday night already. My brain is cloudy. What do you remember?"

"I remember four men, none of them recognizable but all spoke Spanish, talking about trespassing. Then being tossed in a van, and one guy opening a medical kit and injecting us with something."

She looked down as she rubbed her neck.

"Those were fairly small syringes, so I'd say we got a dose of maybe 150 milligrams, probably ketamine. Which means we've been out less than an hour."

"How do you even *know* these things?!" Dominic asked in wonder as he arched his neck again.

"Well, besides writing about it once, I remember this feeling from a really bad date in college. Ketamine is one of the date rape drugs. There's little else like it. Are you feeling disoriented, too?"

"I am, yes." Dominic came back and sat on the cot next to hers. "It's like I'm having an out of body experience."

"That's Special-K for you. The effects shouldn't last much longer. But, where are we?" She looked around the room. "I hear a heavy lapping of water, like on the shore. We must be somewhere near that big lake here, and pretty close by the sound of it."

A noise came from the door to the room, as if someone were unfastening a padlock clasp. The door opened and in walked Jacob and Günther, closing the door behind them. Günther had a pistol aimed at them.

"I figured you were behind this, Jacob," Dominic scowled.

"Now, now, Father Dominic," Jacob chided with a sneering smile. "What are we going to do with you two? That is the question.

"Dr. Kurtz is considering his options as we speak," he added, "but I'm not sure you'll truly appreciate whatever outcome he has in mind."

Hana stood up awkwardly but approached the men resolutely.

"You already have the veil. What possible use can we be to you now?"

"I think you've answered your own question, Hana. You are of no use at all. But, you shall stay here as Dr. Kurtz's guests until he decides what to do with you. Food will be brought to you in the morning, and there's a bucket in the corner for when nature calls. And don't bother shouting for help. This estate is quite large and well-guarded, so no one will hear you or even care if they do.

"I do have one question, though. Where are the others, your Swiss Guard associates? We will find them soon enough, but why not be helpful and cooperate?"

"Obviously we don't have a clue where they are, since we're being held prisoners *here,*" Hana said heatedly. "And I wouldn't underestimate those two if I were you. They are trained killers and already have a score to settle with you, Jacob. Watch your back. They *will* come for you."

Jacob was slightly taken aback when Hana spat the words "*trained killers,*" and he briefly shifted his stance. "Let them try," he said unconvincingly. "We are well-protected here."

"In the meantime," he smirked, "make yourselves comfortable—and you might want to say a prayer or two."

With that, they both laughed, turned and walked back out the door, fastening the clasp and locking their captives in.

CHAPTER 48

I t was nearly 11:00 p.m. when Karl, Lukas and Marco returned to the hotel in both cars. Batista was waiting for them, anxious to relay the latest news from Tel Aviv.

After introducing Marco to the Interpol agent, Karl first related their activities of the evening—spying on the barn and what they heard, finding the SUV empty with Dominic and Hana gone, meeting Marco, and Marco's own observation of the abduction.

"What have they to gain by taking Michael and Hana?" Batista wondered. "I understand these are ruthless people and they see our friends as potential spoilers of their plot. My fear would be that they would have killed them, but it appears they were kidnapped instead. Why?"

"We did hear them distributing photos of all four of us to those assembled in the barn," said Karl, "and to be on the lookout for us. Maybe Kurtz must have some degenerate plan up his sleeve. I've got a bad feeling about this, Javier."

At that point Batista described his discussion with Eli Raziel at Mossad headquarters, and the S13 team that will be meeting them in the morning.

"Which means we raid the compound tomorrow night under

cover of darkness. Since Marco saw Dominic and Hana being taken there, we'll get them as well as Kurtz, assuming that is his residence and provided everything goes as planned. Yossi, the team leader, will lay out their mission specs when they arrive."

ARMAND DE SAINT-CLAIR WAS CONCERNED. He had been trying several times to reach Hana, but she was not answering his calls nor returning messages. He picked up the phone again and dialed another number.

"Marco," he said gruffly when Picard answered, "*where* is my granddaughter?! It's not like her to avoid my calls."

"Baron, things have been happening very quickly here, which explains why you haven't heard from me yet. I'm afraid Hana has been taken, sir, along with Father Dominic, we assume by neo-Nazis affiliated with Dr. Kurtz. I was widely outnumbered or else I would have stepped in. The rest of us are actually here now, discussing our plans for tomorrow's raid on Kurtz's estate. We believe Hana is there."

Marco went on to explain in general terms the pending S13 operation for the following day, somewhat alleviating Saint-Clair's apprehensions.

"I want a call immediately once Hana is safe," he demanded. "Have her contact me as soon as she can, Marco. I know you'll do your best in getting her back."

"Of course, Baron, I will. We're doing everything possible to ensure her safety, and Father Dominic's, too."

"I've put things in motion from here as best I can," Saint-Clair asserted. "And I've got another plan in mind about Kurtz. He won't get away with this."

CHAPTER 49

T he next morning, mostly recovered from the effects of the ketamine, Dominic was now moving around the large room in which they were confined. The high window at the far end was too small to pass through, but he had stacked two crates he found in order to get a look at what he could see outside.

They were indeed lakeside, on the shore of Nahuel Huapi, no doubt, and at the top of a long slope of neatly trimmed lawn leading down to the shoreline. To his left was a high brick wall, beyond which lay a thick forest of giant sequoia, with aged eucalyptus trees dotting the estate's vast landscape.

There were also armed guards patrolling the perimeter.

There would be no escape this way.

"I thought they said there would be food coming," Hana complained. "I'm famished." She began putting on and lacing up her boots.

Just as they heard sounds of the door bolt being unfastened, Dominic jumped down from his perch atop the crates and walked casually toward the door.

Again, it was Jacob and Günther, with a third man carrying an Uzi submachine gun waiting behind them in the hallway.

"I hope you both had a good night's sleep," Jacob said. "We have a special treat for you this morning. Dr. Kurtz has invited you both to join him for breakfast. He normally dines alone, so you must be very special. Let's go."

As Jacob led the way, Günther and the armed man followed them through the hall, then down a circular staircase built around an airy atrium with colorful native ferns and Chinese evergreens surrounding a pool at the base of a cascading rock waterfall. A few moments later they were escorted into an immense dining room featuring an oddly Scottish decor, with ancient suits of armor in each corner and an immense blue and green tartan tapestry on the main wall.

At the head of the table sat Dr. Kurtz in his wheelchair. Standing next to him was a portly woman, presumably the cook, pouring him a cup of tea.

"Ah, here you are," the doctor rasped as Jacob pulled out chairs for both Hana and Dominic, seated together several chairs away from Kurtz. "I trust your accommodations were suitable, given the circumstances?"

"Just tell us what we're doing here, Dr. Kurtz," Dominic said pointedly. "You have what you wanted. What more could we possibly do?"

"What more, indeed," the old man said, as he unfolded his napkin and laid it on his lap. "We shall get to that shortly, but first, I have a surprise for you."

There was the sound of heavy footsteps approaching them from behind, and the newly arrived guest took his seat at the foot of the table.

"Good morning, Dominic, Miss Sinclair," Cardinal Dante said with a mischievous smile.

Both Dominic and Hana were stunned to see their nemesis here in Bariloche, sitting at the same table with the infamous Nazi Johann Kurtz.

They were speechless.

Dante laughed vigorously. "Just the reaction I was hoping for, which is why I waited until you both were brought in and seated. Don't you find the element of surprise exquisite?"

"Wha…what the hell are *you* doing here?" was all Dominic could muster.

"This may come as a shock to a historical archivist such as yourself, Dominic, but I too have a history here. Johann, you see, is my half-brother. Different fathers, but the same mother—she was Scottish, as you can see around you." His arm made a flourishing gesture toward the tapestry and armory.

"But, my dear brother and I have much in common, including his abiding interest in genetics. There are few men on earth who possess the intellectual prowess of DNA extraction and sequencing better than Johann here."

"Oh, Fabrizio," Kurtz sputtered, coughing as he spoke. "You flatter me."

While listening, Hana had regained her composure and turned to Dante. "I might have known you were involved in this. You are the worst of hypocrites! A prince of the Church involved in *Nazi genetics?!* Subversive to your sacred vows and obligations? It's unimaginable!"

"Then *you* must broaden the limits of your imagination, my dear," Dante scoffed playfully. Clearly he was enjoying their reactions.

The dour cook entered the room again with a rolling cart containing four plates, each covered with a silver cloche. She set down Kurtz's plate first, removing the dome to reveal a sumptuous breakfast of scrambled duck eggs, Brätwurst sausages, and a fresh fruit melange. She went around the table performing the same ritual for each guest, then poured coffee for Dante, Hana, and Dominic.

"So, will this be our last meal?" Dominic quipped.

Neither Kurtz nor Dante laughed, leaving the question open as they silently dug into their breakfast.

. . .

"HERR DOKTOR," a newly arrived man in a white lab coat announced, "they need you downstairs in the lab, sir. Something to do with the new spectrophotometer you ordered."

His china plate clattered loudly as Kurtz threw down his fork. "Dammit, Franz, can you not see I am enjoying a meal here?!"

The little man trembled as he backed away. "I'm very sorry, sir. They did say it was urgent."

Kurtz sighed, tossed his napkin from his lap to the table, then backed away, heading for the elevator near the stairs. "I shall return shortly, Fabrizio. Please entertain our guests in my absence." The cook reappeared from the kitchen, placing a cloche over the doctor's plate to keep it warm, then folding his napkin and placing that over the dome.

In doing so she glanced at Hana, fear in her eyes, then nodded her head in the direction of the kitchen, to where she returned.

Uncertain what to do, but bolder now that Kurtz was out of the room, Hana took a chance. She glanced about the table as if searching for something, saying, "I'm just going to get some water." As she stood up, she caught Dominic's eye. He seemed to understand immediately that she was up to something.

"Could you get me a glass as well?" he asked her.

"Sure. And...do I still call you 'Your Eminence?'" she faltered, looking harshly at Dante. "Do you want water as well?"

"You may call me whatever you wish, Miss Sinclair. At this point it matters not. And no, I don't require water."

Hana walked through the large dining room, past the suits of armor and into the kitchen, where the stout cook stood quavering by the sink. They could hear Dominic engaging the cardinal in conversation—presumably, Hana thought, to cover her own discussion with the cook. *Good for you, Michael. You understood!*

"You must leave this house by whatever means possible, fräulein!" the cook whispered urgently, the crucifix around her neck glinting under the bright ceiling lights. "I overheard them earlier. They mean to kill you! That cannot be God's plan!"

"But, how can we escape?!" Hana whispered back desperately.

The poor woman was fraught with tension, trying to think how she might help. She reached for a sharp six-inch chef's knife and thrust it out, handle first.

"Here! Take this, it may be of some use. I am sorry I can do no more."

Hana accepted the knife, wondering where she could put it.

As she tucked it into her right boot, she asked the cook for two glasses of water. The woman complied.

"Thank you so very much!" Hana said quietly, her eyes reflecting grateful affection. She took the water glasses and returned to the dining room.

Setting a glass in front of Michael, she sat back down next to him and took a sip of her own water. With her other hand under the table, she reached over and squeezed Michael's leg as a form of affirmation. Not expecting it, he jumped a little.

"Hiccups, Father Dominic?" Dante asked, looking at the priest strangely.

"Uh, yeah. Hiccups." He feigned a few more for consistency, then took a sip of the water.

As long as Kurtz was still away, Hana pressed her luck. "You don't really expect to get Christ's DNA from that veil, do you?"

"I support my brother in all his endeavors, whether feasible or not," he declared. "It is not for me to say one way or the other whether it's genuine. But imagine if it is…" Dante looked out the window to the lake, his thoughts turning to the mere possibility of it. "Don't you think mankind could use a little more of God's divinity?"

"God seems to have gotten it wrong by leaving you with so little," Hana goaded him. "And we could all use less of your kind."

The cardinal chuckled as he sliced through his Brätwurst.

"Such tart language, my dear. But I'm afraid you'll have to put up with me here for another day or two."

The *ding* sound of the elevator opening down the hall echoed into the dining room, followed by the electric whirring of Kurtz's wheelchair as it approached them.

"I hope you have been enjoying Berta's fine cooking while I've been gone, not to mention my brother's stimulating gift for conversation."

"Berta has been most kind to go to the trouble," Hana replied. "Especially if it's our last meal."

"Oh, don't be so dramatic, Miss Sinclair," the doctor sputtered as he took his place at the table. "There may still be use for you yet."

CHAPTER 50

Thirty hours earlier, Swiss Air Flight 257 had departed Ben Gurion Airport southeast of Tel Aviv, bound for Buenos Aires with a scheduled arrival of 7:10 a.m. local after a stop in Zurich.

Six members of the Israeli Defense Forces' Shayetet 13 unit were on board, registered on the flight manifest under assumed names as military defense attachés with diplomatic passports. Accordingly, their weapons and operational gear containers were stowed in a secured section of the aircraft's cargo hold, visibly tagged with *"Diplomatic Cargo"* tape clearing it from Customs inspection or detainment.

As the Boeing 777 touched down at Ezeiza International Airport, Yossi Geffen, the S13 team leader, quietly prepped his squad at the rear of the aircraft for that morning's pre-op activity.

"A CH-47 Chinook will transport us down to Bariloche," he whispered in Hebrew to his men. "As in Zurich, observe all gear as it's being transferred to the bird, don't just trust the baggage handlers. Our landing zone is about five klicks from the target. Mossad has arranged a safe house for us to prep our gear for tonight's assault; another agent will meet us there with maps and further instructions. Tel Aviv wants Kurtz alive—if possible. A submarine is waiting for our exfil in the Bay of Puerto Montt in southern Chile, not far from Bariloche.

"Good thing you boys slept on the flight. It's going to be a long night."

JAVIER BATISTA MARVELED as the cumbersome camo-painted Chinook awkwardly settled down onto the landing zone at nearby Squadron 34 Gendarmería Nacional Air Base, not far from the Bariloche safe house he had arranged with Mossad's Eli Raziel.

Batista had also borrowed a deuce and a half truck from the Gendarmería to transport the men and their gear, including a Zodiac Milpro inflatable boat for use on the lake.

The agent well knew that Shayetet 13 is the most elite and secretive unit of the Israeli Navy, equivalent to other highly-trained commando forces such as the US Navy's SEAL teams or Britain's Special Boat Service. S13 operators are specialists in counter-terrorism and hostage rescue, sea-to-land incursions, sabotage, and unfriendly boarding missions. It took a lot of effort for him to coordinate getting an actual S13 unit, especially so far away from their primary field of operations. But with the assistance of Team Hugo's Valois, Petrini and Saint-Clair pooling their combined political muscle, accommodations were made quickly and agreeably. That, and Mossad's deep desire to arrest Johann Kurtz, made for a situation that was hard to turn down by all involved.

As the men disembarked the Chinook, with heavy tactical patrol packs slung over their shoulders, team leader Yossi Geffen headed straight for Batista standing near the truck, his arms folded over his chest.

"Batista, I presume?" he said, flashing a welcoming smile and extending his hand.

"Welcome to Bariloche, Yossi, and call me Javi. It's good to meet you," Batista responded, offering a firm handshake. As was typical for men of their training, each instinctively sized up the other, evaluating mutual got-your-back worthiness.

While the two men talked on the tarmac, the rest of the team offloaded their gear from the Chinook and stowed it onto the truck in an efficient matter of minutes. With everyone now on board, Batista drove them to the safe house to prepare for the night's operation.

DENGLER, Lukas and Marco were waiting for them when the team arrived. After introductions made the rounds, all ten men went inside to lay out plans for the night's operation, with maps and satellite images from Google Earth showing the layout of the Kurtz estate and surrounding vicinity.

"Our drone will help us determine how many external combatants we'll be up against," Yossi said, "but regardless, they will be no match for my team.

"We will approach the house from the lake, creating a diversion in the back of the property which should draw forces away from the main gate, allowing your team to enter from the front. I'll have a sniper in the trees adjacent to the property to take out as many as we find.

"As to that, I want each of you to wear these specialized arm bands so our teams' NVGs, or night vision goggles, can differentiate between the good guys and bad guys." He distributed olive-colored elastic arm bands with invisible fluorescers sewn into them.

"I understand they've taken hostages?" Yossi asked.

"Yes," Dengler confirmed. "My cousin Hana, and a priest friend, Father Michael Dominic. We have no idea what their plans are for them, or even *where* they are in the house, but I want to head up their rescue." He quickly explained to Yossi their own respective qualifications, as former elite Swiss Mountain Grenadiers and now Pontifical Guards, and, for

Marco, as a former green beret with the French Marine Commandos.

"Then I couldn't ask for better soldiers to serve beside as overwatch," Yossi commended him. "Your captured comrades are lucky to have you. Here are two more arm bands for when you find them." Lukas accepted them and tucked them in his pocket.

"We also need to find and retrieve a special artifact that Kurtz stole from us," Dengler added.

"Duly noted," Yossi confirmed. "We were told about this object and will help you get it back."

"Alright, we each have our assignments. The operation will commence at 2200 hours. Let's gear up."

CHAPTER 51

Returned by one of the guards to the same room they were kept in before, Dominic and Hana sat down on the cots, pondering their fate.

Hana removed the knife Berta had given her, telling Michael that Kurtz planned to have them killed, and probably soon.

"Great!" Dominic said, taking the knife and concealing it behind him under his belt, beneath his untucked black shirt. "Not the killing part, just the knife. But, why would she do that?"

"I take it she's a religious woman and can't abide Kurtz's plans for us. I'm just grateful we had the opportunity. And thanks for engaging Dante while I was in the kitchen."

"I figured something was up when you gave me 'The Look,'" he said with a grin.

Hana looked past him as her mind worked something out. "I've just got to believe that Karl, Lukas and Javier must be planning *some* kind of rescue, knowing them," Hana said. "But how would they even know where we are? We've been in a few jams together, Michael, but this one doesn't look so good."

"I'm still wondering about Dante's involvement in all this," he said, irritation edging his voice. "How could someone so highly placed in the Church even remotely consider an alliance with neo-Nazis?! Remember, he was once Vatican Secretary of State, and not that long ago. That kind of power is nearly limitless, and global. One wonders how long he's been using it in support of his brother's diabolical mission."

"Well," Hana said, "at least we know the lab is downstairs, somewhere below the first floor. I imagine that's got to be where the veil is."

"Given Kurtz's ultimate 'plan' for us, we don't have much time to act," Dominic reasoned, looking at his watch. "It's about noon now. Whenever the guard returns, I'll use the knife to distract him enough while you grab his gun. After that, we'll just have to wing it."

Hana looked at him in rapt concern. "Do be careful, Michael, please. I'd hate to see anything happen to you." Her eyes started glistening.

"Don't worry about me, Hana. I don't want anyone hurt and I can handle myself. We will get out of this. Alive."

CHAPTER 52

A heavy cloud layer obscured what little reflected light the quarter moon provided, and a light rain had begun to fall over Bariloche. Lake Nahuel Huapi was dark and calm, and a light onshore breeze was the only sound heard as it blew in over the still water.

Four armed guards patrolled the back of the Kurtz estate, one at each of two opposing walls some five hundred meters apart, with two more reconnoitering the rear side of the large mansion.

None of the guards observed the six black helmeted heads that slowly and silently emerged from beneath the placid surface of the lake, their M4 carbine rifles raised in shooting position as the S13 team stealthily made their way onto shore. They had beached their Zodiac inflatable a hundred feet up shore for quick exfiltration when needed.

While the others held their position, crouched low on the sand, one of the men, a sniper scout, quickly made his way over to the tall sequoias on the other side of the estate's western wall. Mounting one of the giant trees, he positioned himself with a clear view of the entire property using his NVGs. Once settled onto a thick, sturdy branch, he pulled a Black Hornet PRS nano drone out of his tactical assault pack and let it fly.

Ultra-light and virtually silent, the tiny drone made its way high over the property, its wide night vision camera lens surveying the landscape below. As it flew, it fed live streaming high-definition video feed back to the sniper in the tree, who in a whisper transmitted the visible data back to his team on a secure comms channel built into their headgear.

"Four tangos spotted in back. One on each wall, two sentries behind the house." Then the slight sound of channel static as he released the Talk button.

He guided the silent drone over the house to the front of the property.

"Five more tangos in front. Two at the gate, one at the door, two roaming the fence line. Two vehicles parked in front of the house." Another static squawk. He guided the drone back to his position in the tree, returning it to his tactical pack.

Equipping an SR-24 sniper rifle with an OPS silencer from his pack, the treed soldier took aim at the guard closest to him near the wall. Pulling back the bolt, he took a deep breath, then gently squeezed the trigger. With a nearly silent puff, one target went down.

He did the same with the guard along the far wall. Two tangos down.

Relaying current status to his teammates, it was now clear for them to approach and take out the remaining two guards nearest the house.

Moments later, four tangos down.

A loud buzzing sound suddenly erupted from inside the mansion, bleating every second. Apparently, someone saw what was happening outside and tripped the security alarm. Several armed men appeared out of nowhere, and since all the activity seemed to be happening on the lake side of the house, the guards in front came to their comrades' defense in back—leaving the gate undefended.

Dengler, Lukas and Marco, each armed with Heckler and Koch .45 caliber handguns, silently stormed the front gate, easily jumping over the wrought iron fence. Spread out in tactical fashion, alert to their surroundings, they watched for any sign of enemy combatants.

Finding none, they checked the two cars parked near the entrance then headed inside the mansion.

HEARING THE COMMOTION, Dominic and Hana ran to the lake side of the house. The priest stood up on the crates to look out the little window to see what was happening. He spotted several soldiers in camouflage gear making their way from the lake toward the house. He turned to Hana.

"There are soldiers out there! Find something I can use to break the glass and let them know we're here."

She quickly scanned the room, seeking anything suitable. She found nothing.

"How about using your elbow?!"

"Why didn't *I* think of that?!" Dominic bent sideways, away from the window, then pulled his arm back and thrust his elbow through the glass. It shattered in small shards, enough to let him alert whoever it was outside.

"We're in here!" he shouted. "Up on the second floor!"

Just then a guard burst into the room, swinging his Uzi at both of them.

"Get down from there!" the man shouted in Spanish, agitated by the pandemonium outside.

Dominic jumped down from the crates and headed toward the man, his arms slightly raised. Speaking in Spanish, he talked to the guard.

"You should be out there, helping your *amigos*. We are no threat to you!"

The man was nervous and shaking, as was the Uzi he was pointing at both of them. He was uncertain what to do, but since they were being held captive they were probably on the side of those raiding the mansion. He made his decision.

He raised the submachine gun, taking direct aim at Dominic.

Hana shouted, *"No!"* just as a loud explosion behind the guard instantly felled him.

Dengler and Lukas ran through the door, weapons drawn, scanning the room for any other targets. Finding none, Lukas turned back to the doorway, guarding the entrance for anyone else approaching from the hallway.

"Karl!" Hana cried out. She ran up to him, giving him a fierce hug. "You came just in time!"

"More of that later," said Dengler, all business. "For now, put these on." He handed each of them one of the S13 arm bands. "Javier and Israeli commandos are raiding the house. We need to get you out of here."

"That's great, Karl," Dominic said, "but I'm not leaving without the veil."

"Where is it?"

"We think it's in the lab, somewhere beneath the main floor. That's probably where Kurtz is, too."

"The Israelis want him taken alive, for obvious reasons. Let's get down there and look for it."

Yossi and two of his men were in the atrium, fanned out in a tactical defensive posture, waiting for Dengler to bring out the hostages. They all ran across the balcony and down the stairs to join the team below.

Dominic moved to the elevator. "This leads to the lab downstairs, I hope." After he, Hana, Karl and Lukas crammed into the small wood-paneled car, Yossi and his team discovered a set of stairs behind a closed door for getting there faster.

Dominic punched the button marked "L" and the doors slowly closed. Though it seemed to take forever, the car inevitably reached the floor below. Dengler and Lukas had their pistols aimed at the doors while Dominic and Hana remained behind them, their backs against the side walls.

The doors opened. Yossi and his men were already there waiting for them, guarding each end of the hall. Standing beside Yossi was Marco.

Hana was taken aback. "That's the man who's been following me! Who are you?!"

"I'm sorry, Ms. Sinclair," Marco said rapidly. "I should have introduced myself at some point, but your grandfather gave me strict instructions to keep a low profile…that you wouldn't like being protected."

They all headed down the hallway toward a door that appeared to be for a lab.

"You work for my grandfather?" she asked as they moved. "Well, I wasn't expecting that. But I'm glad you're here now."

Marco quickly explained that he was the one who saw Dominic and her being captured, but that he couldn't take on four men and decided instead to alert the others.

"That's when I came out of hiding, so to speak. And I'm glad I did."

"Me, too," Hana said, giving her best smile to the handsome man.

"Okay," Dominic cut in abruptly as they approached the door, "let's find that veil and get out of here."

THE LAB WAS behind a floor-to-ceiling glass wall. Going through the door, they found various machines and scientific equipment, but otherwise the room was empty of people.

Dominic and his team searched everywhere for the alabaster box, or any other receptacle that might serve to hold the artifact. They opened every machine, cabinet, drawer, and even checked inside the refrigerator. There was no veil.

"Dammit!" the priest cried out. "Where could it be?"

Dengler found a door to an adjacent room off the lab. Opening it he found it led to a richly appointed office, probably

Kurtz's, he assumed. Making his way to the desk, he sat down and began rifling through the drawers.

Right behind him, the tall door of a wooden closet slowly opened, and Günther quietly stepped out. Holding a gun at Karl's head, the barrel nudged up against his hairline, he quietly whispered, "We meet again, little man."

Just as he was about to pull the trigger, Marco flew into the room, his pistol poised to shoot. Günther looked up. Without thinking, Marco took quick aim and shot Günther in the chest. As the German fell back, his gun went off, the bullet flying across Karl's head, grazing his hair.

Karl ducked and fell to the desk, unharmed but shaken, the thunderous explosion over his head causing temporary hearing loss.

"That was way too close," he chuffed, shaking his head to clear the ringing in his ears. "Thanks, Marco." The two men glanced at each other as the rest of the team ran into the office. Seeing Günther's body on the floor behind Karl, they imagined what had happened. As a precaution, Marco approached Günther and kicked his gun away from the body, then felt for a pulse. He was gone.

JUST THEN ONE of Yossi's men approached him, speaking in Hebrew, then pointed toward an open door at the end of the hall.

"It looks like the others have escaped through a tunnel. I'd bet two shekels it leads to the lake," the team leader said. "Follow us."

As they all ran through the doorway, Yossi pressed the Talk button on his comms, directing his team to assemble back on the shore, and for two of his men to retrieve the Zodiac and bring it back to the beach.

The underground tunnel was well-lit and did indeed lead to the lake. Eventually exiting a camouflaged door built into the hillside, they found a path leading to a wooden dock—but there was no boat.

Looking out over the lake, Yossi saw the retreating lights of a speedboat in the distance—a green light on the right, red on the left—moving away from them at speed.

A few minutes later, the Zodiac roared up to the dock.

"Wait here," Yossi commanded the others. "We're going after them."

The six S13 operatives piled into the inflatable and it flew away from the dock, its nose high in the air as it headed toward the escaping craft. With a top speed of 55 knots, the Zodiac Milpro would reach them in minutes.

CHAPTER 53

The Bertram 50 Express speedboat carrying Kurtz, Jacob, Christof and the doctor's bodyguards hurled away from the shore, heading east toward the road to the Bariloche airport. A van was waiting for them at a pre-arranged shoreside pickup point in case of attack, plans that had been set in motion once the mansion alarm was tripped.

"Who was that attacking us?!" Jacob asked Kurtz once they had all gotten aboard and sped away from the dock.

"It *has* to be the Israelis," Kurtz sputtered as he feebly gripped his wheelchair as the boat flew over the water. "That was too efficient an operation, probably Mossad. I doubt they want the veil more than they want me, but they shall have neither."

"Captain," he rasped to the driver, "how fast can this boat go?"

"Up to 44 knots, Herr Doktor," the man at the helm replied confidently. "We should be able to outrun anything on this lake."

Kurtz was unconvinced. "We must get to the airport," he screeched again. "My plane is ready to go. How long before we get to the pickup point ahead?"

"I'd say another ten minutes, sir."

Jacob and Christof were looking behind them, well beyond the boat's wake across the dark waters. "I don't see anything. Maybe they didn't have a boat."

"They came in from the water, so we must assume they do," Christof said. "And if it's an inflatable, it won't have running lights. They could be out there right now and we wouldn't see them."

As they watched the inky blackness behind them, they caught the muzzle flash of a rifle. A millisecond later a bullet hit the stern of the boat.

"There they are!" Jacob shouted, pointing to where the flash originated. "Maybe five hundred meters back!"

They could now hear the lusty high-frequency whine of the Volvo Penta's D6 engine on the Zodiac. It was growing louder.

More shots came. Standing on the aft deck, Jacob and Christof dove beneath the Bertram's railing, leaving only Kurtz and the captain exposed.

Kurtz's three guards came up from below and took positions on the side rails and in the cockpit, bracing themselves while firing behind them blindly in the dark, hoping their rounds found purchase in a target.

One by one, all three guards fell as Yossi's snipers hit their marks. The Zodiac was now a mere hundred meters behind the speedboat and gaining.

From out of the dark, a bullhorn blared behind the Bertram: "Stop your engine immediately and prepare to be boarded!"

Kurtz yelled at his driver, *"Keep going!"*

A few moments later, another warning: "We will keep shooting unless you stop the boat now!"

Ten seconds passed. The boat did not slow down. Instead, the captain put the boat on autopilot, picked up the Uzi the felled guard next to him had been using, and turned to fire.

One bullet from the approaching S13 team put him down. The speedboat was now out of control, racing forward on autopilot across the black surface of the lake, heading for the shore.

Kurtz, in his wheelchair, could do nothing. In a panic he shouted at Jacob, who was crouched on the floor of the aft deck next to Christoff, avoiding bullets.

"Come up here and take the wheel! *Take the wheel!*"

The roaring sound of the Bertram's Caterpillar engine was too loud for them to hear him from the cockpit. They had no idea the captain was dead. The boat raced on.

As the Zodiac approached, it was clear to Yossi there was nothing they could do now. Speed and gravity would take its own course in resolving the situation.

As Kurtz sat in the cockpit, unable to reach the wheel or even disengage the autopilot, he watched in terror as the shore rushed up to meet them at full speed.

In a matter of seconds, the massive fiberglass hull of the fifty-foot Bertram slid up onto the sand and crashed into the trees, throwing Kurtz through the windshield and into the forest. Smacking into a giant sequoia, the old Nazi was dead on impact.

At the same time the bodies of Jacob and Christof flew off the aft deck, went through the boat's overhead canopy and into the tree branches, meeting a similar fate.

The Bertram did not explode, but with the electronics cut from the mangled fore section, the engine eventually died, and the craft's propellors spun down to a halt.

The arriving Zodiac rapidly beached itself next to the speedboat's hull and five men jumped out, weapons drawn for any unseen survivors, while the sixth operator hauled the boat ashore.

"You two, look for survivors or bodies in the woods," Yossi directed his team. "The others with me, onto the boat."

While two men searched among the trees, their helmet lights engaged, Yossi and two others climbed aboard the Bertram, tactical flashlights in hand. Apart from the dead guards and captain, there was no one else aboard what was left of the yacht.

. . .

AFTER DOMINIC and the others watched the Zodiac tear away from the dock in pursuit of Kurtz, they headed back through the tunnel and into the mansion. On their way, they passed several dead bodies from Kurtz's security team. Once inside the atrium, Dominic turned from the others and began his prayers for the dead, knowing each fallen man was still one of God's own and deserved his blessing. After that prayer, he also said a prayer for the safety of the team who had sped off in the Zodiac.

When he turned back to the others, he saw Karl look outside the tall windows through to the front entrance. "Wait," he said, his voice tinged with suspicion. "Weren't there two cars parked there when we came in?"

"Yes, there were," Lukas confirmed, now seeing that the front gate was open. "Looks like someone got away. Maybe it was just one of the guards, too afraid to tough it out."

"Yeah, but hopefully it wasn't Kurtz. Let's wait for Yossi to get back and see who was on that boat."

AN HOUR later Yossi's team returned through the tunnel and back into the house. It was clear the men had seen action on the lake; the adrenaline still coursing through their bodies animated their behavior, their movements sharp and constant, their eyes and minds on high alert.

Yossi set a waterproof leather duffel bag on the nearest table, in front of where Dominic was sitting, as the men filed into the room.

"We tracked the boat pretty easily, ultimately taking out the guards and the captain. Unfortunately, the driver had set the craft on autopilot, heading to shore. The boat finally beached itself at full speed, throwing Kurtz and the two German boys into the trees. None survived. We'll take care of cleaning things up there.

"I'm not looking forward to reporting this to Tel Aviv," Yossi added.

Dominic could see the man was disappointed that they couldn't have taken Kurtz alive.

"And Cardinal Dante? What happened to him?"

"Only seven bodies were accounted for—Kurtz, the two Germans, the captain and three guards. No one else was aboard."

Dengler turned to Dominic. "That missing car could have been Dante escaping during the melee, if he was here."

"Oh, he was here," Hana assured him. "We had a late breakfast with him this morning. And he said he would be staying another day or two. It was *he* who escaped, I'm sure of it."

"We can deal with him later. What's in the bag, Yossi?" Dominic asked.

"Open it and see for yourself," he replied, smiling.

Pulling the handles back and reaching for the zipper, Dominic opened the duffel. Inside was a mass of gray rubber foam split down the middle.

Peeling back the seam, Dominic found the alabaster box. Lifting the lid, he was overjoyed to see the veil was still intact.

"Yossi, what can I say?! This is *fantastic!* You and your team have done a great service here. I'm only sorry you couldn't take Kurtz alive to stand trial."

Yossi's discouraged look spoke more than the words he offered.

"Yes, I feel the same," said the commando sadly. "Having these *paskudnyaks* ultimately stand trial shows to the world we will never forget the Shoah. There is yet a great debt to be repaid for those still in hiding. Our job is to ferret them out, bring them to justice."

Dominic allowed a moment of reflective silence before standing up and reaching out his hand.

"Thank you, Yossi," he said, gazing into the man's hardened

eyes. "Thanks to all of you for what you've done here. We are so very grateful."

Dengler began to applaud the team's efforts, with the others following his lead.

"Alright," Hana said with relief in her voice. "Can we all get back to Rome now?"

"Actually," Dengler said, "my Jeep is still parked at the Paris airport! Can we go there instead? Besides, Lukas and I still have another two days left on holiday."

"We'll drop you boys off first, then head back to Rome. I'm sure my grandfather would like his plane back sometime."

Dominic smiled at his friends, but in his heart he knew they still had important tasks ahead. And those results could bring honor to the Church. Or another and deeper level of disquiet.

CHAPTER 54

I t was a beautiful spring day in Rome on Dominic's first day back. The Vatican gardens were flush with scents of honeysuckle and gardenia, and the sun filtered through the dense canopies of ancient, gnarled trees as the young priest walked to the Secretariat of State building in the shadow of St. Peter's dome, a backpack slung over his shoulder.

As Cardinal Enrico Petrini beheld the byssus veil, his eyes teared up as emotion overtook him, the mere thought of holding such a sacred artifact rendering him speechless. Dominic filled in the silence for him.

"While there is yet much to be done in establishing authenticity—or as much as that's possible—this is one of the very few artifacts that has ever affected me so deeply," he said reverently. "The mere possibility relies as much on faith as it does ultimate acceptance. I *want* to believe, therefore I do."

"I couldn't agree more, Michael," Petrini replied, finding his voice. "This is an extraordinary discovery. And to think it was about to be defiled in the name of neofascism is simply unimaginable. You have done well, young man. That was quite an adventure you had getting it, too."

Dominic shrugged modestly. "Many were involved, most enlisted through the efforts of your Team Hugo. But if I hadn't had the support of Sergeants Dengler and Bischoff, and Hana, I don't know that we'd be here at all."

"As for Dante's role in all this," Petrini said, his tranquility turning to anger, "I've recalled him to Rome to be laicised. He is unfit to continue serving Holy Mother Church and will thus be dismissed from his clerical state. This does take some time to process, so in the meantime you will see him here in the Vatican. Just know that, despite still being a cardinal, he has no real power in the interim. He will simply be in stasis, awaiting a final decision from His Holiness, which is just a formality at this stage."

"When does he get here?"

"Dante's flight was arranged for arrival tomorrow. I'll be curious to see if he honors even that."

Dominic thought for a moment. "It's not in my nature to wish ill on anyone, Eminence," he said, "but in his case, I'll make a glad exception. I can't abide being in the same room with the man now. He's as repellent as they come. The Church will be better off without him."

Armand de Saint-Clair sat at the dining table in his suite at the Rome Cavalieri Hotel, enjoying breakfast with his granddaughter, when his butler approached him.

"Baron, you have a call from your bank in Geneva. Shall I take a message?"

"No, Frederic, I'll take it now. Excuse me, Hana." Saint-Clair rose to take the call in his study.

"Good morning, Baron." It was the director of Banque Suisse de Saint-Clair on the line. "My apologies for disturbing your morning, but I can confirm that account holder you requested details on has assets on deposit of nearly two hundred million US dollars, all from a single account at one of your subsidiaries, Banco Suiza de Argentina. What do you wish done with the account, sir?"

"Freeze it immediately, François, on my personal order. Is there a named beneficiary?"

As he listened, Saint-Clair made notes on his desk pad.

"Thank you, François. This is all very good. *À bientôt.*"

Returning to the table, Saint-Clair sat down as Frederic was pouring hot coffee into his empty cup.

"How is your story coming along, my dear?"

Happy to oblige him, Hana replied enthusiastically.

"It will be a wonderful piece, pépé. I'm nearly finished with it. My editor says it has all the elements of a dark historical thriller: old Nazis, neo-Nazis, the Ahnenerbe, the *Kinderklinik* and its grotesque assembly line of Aryan fledglings. It's all there. It will be a fantastic exposé, just the kind of thing our readers love."

"And will you be mentioning the veil?"

Hana sighed. "No, in respect to Michael's wishes, I'll be omitting that delicious detail. But he has, of course, given me first rights to the news before an announcement is made, if that ever happens. You know how secretive the Vatican can be."

"Indeed, yes. Oh, speaking of big news: Enrico is defrocking Cardinal Dante this week. Apparently he's had enough of his impetuous conduct."

Hana's eyebrows shot up, astounded at the news. "If anyone deserves *not* to be in the priesthood, it's that revolting man. Good for Enrico. I'm sure Michael will be pleased. I'm having dinner with him tonight, may I tell him?"

"Of course, though he probably knows by now, I would imagine."

CHAPTER 55

E njoying his scotch in the first-class cabin of his Alitalia flight from Buenos Aires to Rome, Cardinal Dante was anxious to get on with whatever business Petrini had in mind so he could catch the next flight to Geneva and attend to his brother's estate.

Or at least the financial part of it. He was aware, of course, that Johann had made him sole beneficiary in his will. He just needed to find the proper estate attorney to claim his rights in the matter and ensure that he had control of what he assumed would be a vast fortune sitting in Banco Suiza de Argentina, for he knew Johann to be a wealthy man.

But what does that pesky Petrini have in mind, I wonder? Probably a spanking for Johann's holding Dominic and that Sinclair woman as his 'guests.' Nothing I can be blamed for, certainly! After all, I am not my brother's keeper. What he did was his own business. Poor Johann. What a sad way to go.

"Another scotch, Your Eminence?" the flight attendant asked. "We'll be landing in an hour, but there's time for another if you'd like."

"Of course, my dear," he said. "By any chance, do you have a Macallan 18 back there?"

The petite young Italian woman laughed. "Not on these flights, I'm afraid. The Dewar's 12 will have to do for now. But it does have a nice finish, suggesting wood spices and salty caramel with just a hint of pepper, don't you think?"

"Yes," the cardinal said smugly, "I suppose it does get the job done."

AS AN ACCOMMODATION TO ITS PROMINENCE, Father Dominic had had a special wooden case made for the alabaster box containing the veil. The Vatican's special *sampietrini* carpenters have a fine woodworking shop on the premises and had lovingly fashioned a beautiful custom container lined with a rich red padded moiré fabric for holding and presenting the fragile artifact.

Until the appropriate technicians and analysts could be chosen to begin their work on the authentication process, however, Dominic had determined the best place for the veil would be in the Riserva, the most secure room in the Secret Archives.

Placing it inside the large 17th-century Borghese *armadio*, he looked up at it fondly, recalling the effort it took to get it here, then closed the cabinet's doors and left the Riserva, locking it behind him.

"WHAT DO YOU MEAN, *I'm being laicized?!*"

Dante was outraged, pacing the Secretary of State's office as Petrini calmly sat at his desk after delivering the verdict.

"You *cannot* do this to me, Enrico! I am a goddamn cardinal of the Church, for Christ's sake!"

"Yes—exactly *for His sake*. You've brought this upon yourself, Fabrizio, and watch your sinful language in my presence. Collaborating with neo-Nazis, your obvious involvement in the kidnapping and imprisonment of Father Dominic and Miss Sinclair, your participation in a bizarre scheme to use a possibly sacred artifact in evil and disgraceful ways. These are serious charges, and they merit serious action. You're lucky you won't be sent to prison!

"I've had enough of your odious handiwork over the years, Dante. The Holy Father will make it official shortly, but as of this moment, you are stripped of your stations and responsibilities, and all of your priestly duties. You will remain here in the Vatican until His Holiness renders his final decision, at which point you are free to leave, dismissed from the clerical state."

"You *will* regret this, Petrini!" Dante said in a rabid fury as he headed toward the door. "I am hardly finished with you and Dominic yet. Remember what I know, Enrico. I *will* bring you down with me."

With that, Dante slammed the door behind him.

Petrini got up from his desk and walked to the window, looking down wistfully at the gardens and the people milling about, then up at the great dome of Saint Peter's basilica.

I expect I must prepare for the worst now, he sighed. Please forgive me, Michael.

CHAPTER 56

T he ninety-minute Alitalia flight to Geneva couldn't be fast enough for Fabrizio Dante. He felt his power slipping away as he nursed a neat scotch in Seat A1, looking out over the rolling alpine landscape below.

Remain in the Vatican, indeed. I will do as I please.

Dante had called his law firm's Swiss branch office earlier, alerting them to his imminent arrival and having them prepare the essentials they would need for him to access his brother's accounts immediately. Banco Suiza de Argentina's corporate parent was a Geneva-based conglomerate called Banque Suisse de Saint-Clair, which is where he had to go to stake his claim.

Why does that name sound familiar?

The chauffeured Mercedes sedan that met him outside the terminal whisked Dante to the offices of Dreyfus & Bustamante in the fashionable Quai de l'Ile Building in Geneva city centre, tucked away on a small island on the Rhône River.

Wearing his black wool suit with the cardinal's scarlet rabat over a white clerical collar—and his pectoral cross to ensure a distinct impression was made—Dante entered the law offices and met with the branch director, Monsieur Henri Boudet.

"While there is still some work yet to be done in settling your brother's affairs, Eminence, as his sole beneficiary you do have immediate control over his financial assets, and the final paperwork for that has already been prepared," Boudet confirmed as they both took seats in the director's office. "Simply sign here and our notary will formalize the documents you will need at the bank."

With an exaggerated flourish, Dante's pen flew over the signatory line in great broad strokes, the fact of his instant wealth making him swell with a conceited self-esteem.

Now, on to the bank.

The Mercedes had been waiting at the curb for the cardinal, the address coordinates for the Banque Suisse de Saint-Clair already preset in the car's GPS.

Fifteen minutes later, Dante stepped out of the vehicle and into the bright Swiss sunlight in front of the bank on Quai du Mont-Blanc. The warm and scratchy wool suit was starting to irritate him, the heat an unwelcome sensation to a man in a hurry.

As he waited in the bank's client lounge overlooking Lake Geneva, Dante reflected on Petrini's abhorrent decision to defrock him.

Surely His Holiness will recognize and honor my work of over forty years in the Church. How dare Petrini take such unwarranted action!

"Cardinal Dante, I presume?" A short, impeccably dressed man in his sixties approached Dante, holding out his hand.

"Yes, and you are?" Dante asked, enveloping the man's small hand in a shake.

"François Trudeau at your service, monsieur. I am director general of the Banque Suisse de Saint-Clair. How might I be of service?"

"I am here as the designated beneficiary of my brother's estate, which was serviced by your Banco Suiza de Argentina."

"Ah, yes, of course," Trudeau said. "Will you follow me please to my private office?"

The two men walked down the gleaming marble corridor and into a corner suite with an expansive view of the lake and the Swiss Alps beyond.

"Please, do have a seat, Your Eminence."

Dante sat down in an elegant leather chair, then withdrew the papers provided him by his law firm and set them down in front of the banker.

Trudeau inspected the papers carefully, then looked up the account on his computer, and a few moments later, frowned. He paused, then tapped a few more keys, his eyes scanning the screen, before turning to Dante, the frown still in place.

"I am sorry to inform you, monsieur, but this account has been frozen."

Dante was not expecting this. At first he seemed disoriented.

"There is obviously some mistake," he said, his mind stretching for a reason, his voice rising in anger. "Can you check again? The account holder's name is Johann Kurtz, he was my brother, or half-brother, really, and these documents prove that I am his legally named beneficiary. His assets are now my assets! *What can you not understand about that?!*"

"Monsieur, please, keep your voice down. Let us be gentlemen about this."

"I am not a *gentleman*," he spat. "I am a prince of the Roman Catholic Church!"

"Be that as it may, Your Eminence, this account has been frozen on the order of the bank's executive chairman himself, Baron Armand de Saint-Clair, in accordance with laws regarding illegal activities in Argentina. That is all I can say. You must take up the matter further with your legal representatives."

Armand de Saint-Clair…? That's it! He's related to that Sinclair woman! I see how it is now.

Dante picked up the papers from the desk and threw them across the room, his face twisted with rage.

His deep voice grew menacing as he pointed a finger at Trudeau. "You tell Saint-Clair he won't get away with this...this outright *theft!* You will be hearing from my attorneys!"

Dante stormed out of the office like a petulant child.

Only now he was out for blood.

CHAPTER 57

The next morning Dominic and Karl had just finished a long morning run through the Suburra when they settled into a sidewalk table at Pergamino Caffè on the Piazza del Risorgimento.

"That's exactly what I needed after what we've been through," Karl said, taking a sip of hot espresso. "And this will help energize my day.

"Lukas and I had a great time in Paris before driving back yesterday. We also went to survey the fire damage at the great Cathedral of Notre Dame. It was just awful, Michael. Such a terrible waste."

"I've been meaning to make that pilgrimage myself, Karl. It's possible I could lend a hand to their antiquities specialists. The losses must be staggering. I think I may do that soon, in fact... maybe make a few days of it with Hana."

The early morning crowds had started to swell as the morning unfolded, with waves of black and white habits and cassocks appearing as various clergy—or what the children of Rome chided as *bagarozzi*, or black beetles—made their way to the Vatican.

Looking across the street, Karl noticed a tall man walking

north along the Vatican wall toward the taxi stand. He would otherwise have been lost in the sea of other priests and nuns were it not for his quick pace and the unusually large valise he carried.

"Isn't that Cardinal Dante?" he asked.

Dominic looked up, scowling as he answered. "Yes, it is. I wonder what he's up to. Petrini told me he's giving him the boot. It can't be too soon, if you ask me."

Having gotten into a waiting cab, the cardinal took off toward the east.

"Let's go," Dominic said, glaring at the cab as it left. "Time to get to work."

KNOWING Dominic would be out on his usual morning run, Cardinal Dante had earlier left his apartment in Domus Santa Marta, the resident guesthouse just south of Saint Peter's Basilica, well before the hordes of Vatican employees streamed in through Saint Anne's Gate to begin their workdays.

Along with a valise, Dante carried a special key to a very special door, one that only two other people in the Vatican possessed, though when he left his previous role as Secretary of State, he surreptitiously had a copy made—just in case the time came when he might need it.

That time was now, and as he made his way down the antiquated elevator in the Secret Archives to the secured Riserva below, he mentally applauded his prescience.

Stepping into the amber pools of automated lighting as he walked through the vast Gallery of the Metallic Shelves, Dante knew what needed to be done. He also knew there were no CCTV cameras—and as a cardinal he still had full access to the Vatican—so no one would be the wiser when they discovered the veil to be missing. And that would probably not be for a while.

Unlocking the heavy wooden door and entering the most

treasured room in the Vatican, he looked around on the shelving. Seeing nothing that resembled the alabaster box or any other object that might contain it, he went to the *armadio*, swinging back its massive doors.

Sitting on a shelf in the very front he discovered a specially crafted wooden box. Unfastening the metal clasp, he opened it, found the alabaster box within, then removed the veil from its container.

Gently placing it inside a small wooden box he had brought with him, Dante closed the lid to that then snapped the valise shut.

Back inside the *armadio*, he then let the lid fall on the alabaster box, closed the *sampietrini's* wooden case, reset the metal hasp, and shut the doors to the great cabinet and left the Riserva.

VINCENZO TUCCI UNLOCKED the front door of his antiquities shop on the Via del Governo Vecchio and flipped the door sign over to "*Aperto*"—open for business.

A stout man in his late seventies with a round face devoid of any hair at all—owing to an acute case of alopecia—Tucci was a recognized expert in the world of Etruscan art and antiquities, with a roster of world-class collectors who turned to him for the most coveted pieces he seemed able to obtain on a regular basis.

And though most of his inventory was legitimately acquired, Tucci was also known to a more discreet clientele who cared less about an artifact's rightful provenance and more for its singular rarity—and who were sufficiently well heeled and unburdened by conscience to deal under the table, regardless of price or murky pedigree.

For apart from Tucci's legal avenues for obtaining fine artifacts, he was also *capo zona* to the *tambaroli* of Rome—the regional head of black market tomb raiders.

As Tucci was attending to a recent shipment in the back

room, a little bell over the front door signaled the arrival of a visitor. Putting down his tools, he brushed himself off and walked out to the front of the shop to welcome his first customer of the day.

The little bell rang again as the door closed, and the tall man entering the shop turned to meet its proprietor.

"*Cardinale Dante!*" Tucci gushed with surprise. "It has been much too long since you have been to my humble shop of worldly wonders. How might I assist you today, Eminence?"

"*Buongiorno*, Vincenzo," Dante said furtively, assuming the presence of others in the shop. "May we meet in your private office, please?"

"Of course, signore, certainly," Tucci said, his smile fading as he led the way through the back room and into a well-appointed office filled with antique furniture.

"Now, what is it you require of me?" he asked as they both took a seat.

"I have something here which I feel would be worth your while finding a buyer for. Something most extraordinary. Something also…shall we say…highly sensitive."

Tucci's face turned solemn.

"I understand completely, Eminence. Tell me about this object."

As Dante withdrew the veil for inspection, he gave Tucci the necessary highlights of the artifact's provenance, its relationship to Himmler and Hitler's fascination with it, Otto Rahn's original discovery of the veil in France, and it's fabled relationship to Mary Magdalene.

"Yes," Tucci said, his eyes shining as he beheld the veil, "I have heard of these legends. This would be among the most, as you say, 'extraordinary' of artifacts I have ever seen."

"It belonged to my brother in Argentina, who passed away suddenly last week. As I am his beneficiary, I would like you to find a buyer for this magnificent piece. In complete confidence, of course."

"Of course. Complete confidence, yes. And I am sorry to hear about your brother. That is indeed sad news." With the obligatory acknowledgement out of the way, Tucci's gaze turned back to the veil.

"Naturally, such an item would be considered priceless, so I would not know where to start. But, I do have one particular client in mind, a Russian oligarch, to whom price is never an object. And something so unrivaled as this would surely awaken his envy. Of that, I have no doubt.

"Let me take some photographs of the veil, Eminence, while you retain possession. Then we'll see what I can do for you, yes?"

"No, Vincenzo, I must leave this here with you. I prefer you to have custody."

Tucci blinked, surprised at the request. "Alright," he said nervously, "I will keep it securely in the safe. And as always, no questions will be asked."

CHAPTER 58

Enrico Petrini had just returned from the Apostolic Palace and his daily meeting with the Pope when Michael Dominic appeared at his office door.

"Michael, do come in," the cardinal said, greeting him with a warm smile. "Your timing is fortuitous. His Holiness would like to see your veil, and he would like *you* to bring it to him!"

"*My God*, Eminence!" Dominic exclaimed. "He asked for me by name?"

"Of course, he did. He certainly knows who you are. The Holy Father knows everyone."

"Well, this is exciting! When and where does he want a viewing?"

"Actually, he has invited us to have dinner with him tonight in his apartment, so you can share your adventures with him. He'd love to hear about your exploits."

"Dinner with the Pope?!"

"Dinner with the Pope," Petrini casually affirmed. "And wear your best collar."

AT THIRTY-FIVE-HUNDRED METERS, the pistes of Chamonix-Mont-Blanc were still packed with fresh white powder as the end of ski season was approaching.

Dmitry Zharkov favored this time of year at his home in the French Alps, since he could have the best of two overlapping seasons rather than face the dependably constant gloom of Moscow. And after all, his vast business interests could be managed from anywhere in the world.

Zharkov and two bodyguards had just come off the slopes and arrived back at his chalet when an assistant brought him a list of phone messages taken while he was out. He selected several he would call back now, but the rest could wait until later.

Among those he chose was a call from Vincenzo Tucci. He would always take Vincenzo's calls, for he knew other collectors might get word of some newly discovered treasure before him, and that he could not chance.

Véronique DuPont, an attractive and intimidating French lawyer, or "fixer," under exclusive retainer to Zharkov, attended to all matters of legal or extralegal concern to the Russian oligarch. Often such services required the provision of forged passports, arranging for legal assistance on behalf of certain associates to Mr. Zharkov, or simply expediting the elimination of other nuisances, often in life or death situations. Nikki DuPont was not someone you wanted to go up against, in court or anywhere else—especially when the *death* part might be involved.

"Nikki, my love," Zharkov cooed as he entered the great room overlooking the Chamonix valley, "how about nice glass of champagne, yes?"

"That sounds lovely, Dmitry, thank you," she said as she lay on a crimson velvet fainting couch, reading a novel. "How were the runs today?"

"Agh, sun make for slushy powder, not good for best skiing.

Another day, maybe. I will be back soon with champagne. Keep reading."

Zharkov went into his study to call Tucci. The room was decorated with ancient symbols of warfare—swords, maces, ceremonial daggers…even a miniature trebuchet from the 17th century, which sat next to a large wooden globe of the world. The Russian loved military history and the weapons used in its development over the centuries.

But ranking second among his most prized possessions were the finest religious artifacts money could buy. And he had plenty of both.

He picked up the phone and called Vincenzo Tucci in Rome.

"Ah, Signor Zharkov!" the old man sang, his excitement in reaching the Russian evident in his voice. "Knowing you don't like small talk, I will get to the point of my earlier call.

"I have come into possession of the most extraordinary item, one I believe you will find of extreme interest."

Tucci went on to describe the veil and its history, as far as he knew it, until he could sense he had the Russian's undivided attention and fervent interest.

"As you know, Vincenzo, I cannot come to Italy now due to long-ago misunderstanding in Customs law. Ridiculous country. But I will send Nikki. She will look at veil and report back to me, yes?"

"Oh, certainly, signore, yes, Signorina Véronique is always welcome in my shop. I look forward to her arrival, then. In the meantime, I will send you photographs of this object."

The two exchanged goodbyes and ended the call. Considering this potential new acquisition, Zharkov went into the kitchen, popped a bottle of Roederer Cristal champagne and poured two glasses.

"Are we celebrating anything in particular, Dmitry?" Véronique asked.

"Not yet, Nikki," he uttered in a deep guttural voice, "but

you are taking jet to Rome tomorrow to look at something as old as Christ himself. Something truly extraordinary. If I like what you have to say, you will bring back to me, yes?"

CHAPTER 59

Two Swiss Guards stood at attention on either side of the door to the papal suite as Dominic approached it. Despite their knowing this was the well-vetted Prefect of the Apostolic Archives, they performed their ritual identification checks as soberly as they would for anyone else. They also required Dominic to open his valise for inspection. Seeing it contained nothing more than an alabaster box, they let him pass, opening the door and snapping their heels as they formally escorted him into the Pope's apartment.

Dominic was greeted by Sister Amelia, head of the papal household, who brought him into the sitting room, where Cardinal Petrini was chatting amiably with His Holiness. They both stood as he entered the room and set down his valise.

"Ah, dear Father Dominic," the Pope said, extending both arms in greeting and smiling widely. "I am so happy you could join us."

As if you could turn down an invitation from the Pope! Dominic thought nervously, taking both the Pope's hands in a firm clasp.

Dominic genuflected, head bowed, then kissed the Ring of the Fisherman on the Pope's right hand. The Pope pulled him up and embraced him, as he was known to do for nearly everyone. It was all pretty overwhelming for Dominic, who, in his routine duties, rarely saw the Holy Father.

Petrini poured a glass of Chianti for Michael, then they all sat down to chat before dinner. Sitting in a throne-like chair wearing a white, watered silk cassock, the Pope spoke on a variety of topics: his beloved San Lorenzo football team, the music of Mozart and Beethoven, the films of Fellini...there was little doubt the man's mind was clear and engaged—and he loved telling and hearing a good story.

At the Pope's request, Dominic shared his long adventure chasing down the veil, with the tone, colors and richness of a master storyteller. The Holy Father was on the edge of his seat as the tale unfolded, grimacing whenever gruesome details—or Dante's name—came up. He glanced at Petrini, and something unspoken passed between the two men. Dominic could only imagine it had to do with the Pope's pending decision on Dante's laicization.

"May I see it now? The veil?" the Pope asked Dominic.

"Yes, of course, Your Holiness."

Dominic stood and went to where he had left his valise, then brought it to the coffee table where the Pope and Petrini were sitting. Withdrawing the wooden case—commenting on how well the *sampietrini* had crafted the box—Dominic opened it, then placed the alabaster box in front of the Pope.

The Holy Father sat transfixed by the luminescence of the alabaster. Looking up at Dominic, then Petrini, with great expectation in his eyes, his hand reached down and lifted back the lid.

The alabaster box was empty.

The Pope looked up at Dominic quizzically, wondering if perhaps this might be a joke. Everyone knew this pope loved a good laugh, so it was not inconceivable they might be pulling a prank on him.

But Dominic was aghast. He *alone* had had contact with the

veil. He *alone* had placed it in the Riserva, in this very box. *Where was it?! How could this happen?*

He looked up at Petrini.

"Eminence, you and I are the only ones with keys to the Riserva, correct?"

"Yes, Michael. Just you and I." Petrini was equally confused by the absence of the veil.

Dominic's mind raced. Who could have taken it? There must be an explanation.

Then, almost as if a vision was being delivered to him, his mind's eye recalled Cardinal Dante walking to the taxi stand carrying a valise, earlier that very morning.

But...how could Dante have a key?

It came to him in a flash of understanding.

"Your Holiness, Cardinal Petrini, I may be going out on a limb here, but since Cardinal Dante was once Secretary of State —meaning the only other person besides the Prefect to have a key—is it possible he may have had a duplicate made?"

Petrini's face crumpled in anger. "That can be the only accounting for it, Michael, especially given recent events. I'm afraid you are probably right. Holy Father, I deeply apologize for this terrible embarrassment. We will make it right."

"Oh, dear Enrico, do not be embarrassed," he sympathized. "I am sure the veil will turn up. But I do believe now we must act promptly on this Cardinal Dante matter. He has gone too far, if this is indeed the case."

"Thank you, Your Holiness," Petrini acceded. "May I make a call before we sit down to dinner?"

"Of course," said the Pope, looking at him seriously, "and feel free to use my name if it can be of help."

The two men shared the briefest of smiles, then Petrini stepped into the Pope's private office. He picked up the white telephone and dialed the Commander of the Pontifical Swiss Guard.

"This is Cardinal Petrini. Find and arrest Cardinal Dante at once, on the orders of the Holy Father. Confine him to his apartment, under guard."

CHAPTER 60

K arl Dengler and Dieter Koehl were both guarding the door to Cardinal Dante's apartment in the Domus Santa Marta guesthouse when Michael Dominic approached them, intending to see the soon-to-be ex-cardinal.

"Hey, Karl, how's your prisoner?" he asked, a satisfied grin his face.

Despite their official capacity, both Dengler and Koehl were each smiling as well, happy that Dante was finally where he belonged.

"He's in a sour mood, Michael," Karl said. "Not at all happy to be confined to quarters."

"I'll bet. But, I need to speak with him. Shouldn't be more than ten minutes."

Dengler opened the door and allowed Dominic to enter, closing the door behind him.

Dante was standing, his tall dark silhouette framed against the sheer white curtains to the wide open balcony, arms folded in front of him. He turned his head.

"You," he spat accusingly. "*You* are the source of all my troubles. You and your meddling friends. How dare you ever take up arms against *me*, your obvious superior!"

"Oh, settle down, Eminence. I'm only here to ask *where* you've taken the veil. It's all over now. The Holy Father knows you are at the center of a great deal of trouble here, not to mention your association with that nest of vipers in Argentina. But that sacred veil must not be used as a bargaining chip. You have higher obligations here. What have you done with it?"

Dante turned around fully to face Dominic. His eyes were burning with hatred. "Really, young man, I have no idea what you're talking about," he lied.

"Playing coy won't help your situation, Dante. Everyone knows you had an extra key made to the Riserva, and given that your brother's bank accounts had been frozen, you were out of resources. That's why you stole the veil, isn't it? To pawn it off on the black market."

Dante was startled, first at the mention of the key, but mostly about Johann's Swiss bank account.

"How could you possibly know about my brother's accounts?!" His face quickly morphed from visibly shaken to one of dawning recognition.

"Ah, of course. That Sinclair woman. It was her grandfather who stole my legally acquired assets. Well, we'll see what the courts have to say about that.

"You know," he went on, now more animatedly hostile, his arms flailing dramatically as if he were on stage, "you really are an insufferable little bastard! And that *is* what you are, isn't it? *A bastard!* You don't even know who your real father is, do you?"

The cardinal caught Dominic completely off guard. This was the last thing he expected to hear from the man.

"It's *Petrini*, you fool! Enrico Petrini is your father! I had DNA tests done on you and him last year for leverage I needed at the time, and it's conclusive. Didn't know that, did you, you little bastard? Yes, that hypocrite Petrini. At least that's one thing I can clear up for you."

Dominic stood there, shocked, unwilling to believe such a

scurrilous liar as Dante. The man was just goading him, reaching out to hurt anyone in his darkest time.

And yet, Dominic's throat tightened as if more than a grain of truth, even a lump of unexpected facts, had lodged in it from what he had just heard. His mind raced as he reconstructed his entire life: his mother Grace denying he had a living father, changing the subject whenever it came up; Petrini—Uncle Rico —always being there for him, paying for his education, guiding him on his path through life and into the Church. It all made sense now. Of course, Petrini couldn't come out as the father of a child. It would have ruined him.

But what about me? All these years of not knowing…

"I see I've opened a page of gospel truth for you, haven't I?" Dante cajoled malevolently.

Dominic snapped out of his reverie for the moment.

"Where is the veil?" Dominic was now shouting, angry for all kinds of reasons now. He felt unsteady in the presence of this menacing creature.

"I'm sure I have no idea what you mean," Dante muttered finally, folding his arms inside his cassock sleeves and turning back to the balcony window. "You shall get nothing more from me."

Dominic turned away angrily, swung the door open, and without a word marched past Dengler and Koehl toward his own apartment in the building.

CHAPTER 61

Colonel Benito Scarpelli of Italy's *Tutela Patrimonio Culturale*—a special unit of the Italian *Carabinieri* informally called the Art Squad—was savoring a robust demitasse of steamed espresso in his office when an aide knocked on his door.

"*Si, entrare,*" Scarpelli said, inviting the woman in.

"Colonel, we picked up something on Vincenzo Tucci's wiretap that might be important. From the sound of his describing an artifact to a Russian collector named Zharkov—you may remember his involvement in last year's Vatican reliquary case—well, it could be of similar significance."

She conveyed to Scarpelli the depth of the tapped conversation and details of the Magdalene veil as Tucci had passed it on to Zharkov himself.

A precise and orderly man in his sixties who previously worked as an antiquities curator for Sotheby's, Benny Scarpelli knew that if Zharkov was involved, it must be an important piece Tucci was offering. And if experience had taught him anything, there was a better than even chance it would be a questionable if not illegitimate transaction, since he was well aware of Tucci's role with the *tambaroli* of the black market community—hence the perpetual wiretap on the dealer's telephones and internet access.

He looked up at the aide. "What's the name of the new Prefect of the Secret Archives at the Vatican, do you know?"

"Yes, Colonel," she said, "it is Father Michael Dominic. He replaced the retiring Brother Calvino Mendoza. Do you wish me to get hold of him for you?"

"Ah, yes. I remember Dominic. No, I'll do it myself, *grazie*."

Scarpelli looked up the number for the Vatican switchboard and dialed it. One of six nuns on duty in the call center that morning greeted him pleasantly, "*Pronto, Vaticano*." After asking for Father Dominic's extension, the operator gave the colonel Dominic's direct line for future use, then put the call through. Dominic answered.

"Hello, Father Dominic, this is Colonel Benito Scarpelli of the Italian Art Squad. You may remember me from our work together last year on the Magdalene reliquary case."

"Yes, of course I remember, Colonel. What can I do for you?"

Scarpelli went on to describe the intercepted call between Vincenzo Tucci and the Russian collector Dmitry Zharkov about some artifact called a "*veil*."

At the mention of "*veil*" and "*Zharkov*," Dominic sat bolt upright in his seat. Scarpelli had his complete attention.

"Not only do I know Zharkov from our past dealings with the man," he said anxiously, "but that veil was stolen from the Apostolic Archives just a few days ago and *must* be returned to the Vatican!"

"That is all I needed to know, *Padre*," Scarpelli said, an official tone to his voice. "I will send a recovery team to Signor Tucci's place of business today. I will be back in touch with you soon."

THE BELL over Vincenzo Tucci's door jingled as a customer entered. The shop's proprietor came out of the back room to greet the new arrivals—a tall, striking woman and two men who were obviously bodyguards. When he recognized the woman, Tucci's pale face broke out in a wide smile.

"Signorina Véronique, what a great pleasure to see you again!" he gushed. "Signor Zharkov told me you would be arriving soon, but I did not realize it would be this quickly.

"Come, let me show you this new treasure. I am certain it will meet with your approval."

Tucci led the woman to his private office, where he opened the safe and withdrew the wooden box Dante had left with him. Setting it on his desk, he put on a set of white conservation gloves, handed a set to her, then lifted the lid and removed the byssus veil.

Véronique slid a glove onto each hand and reverently accepted the artifact from the old man. As emotionally hardened as she was from the sort of people and events she had to deal with, even she was moved by the spectral image of Jesus Christ on the sheer silken fabric, the apparent blood from his beatings clearly evident, the peaceful visage looking into the very soul of the viewer. She held it for several long minutes, completely enraptured, shivering under the visceral impact it had on her.

"Vincenzo, may I use your office for a private call, please?" she asked.

"Of course, Signorina. I shall return when you are finished."

After Tucci left the room and closed the door behind him, Véronique called Zharkov.

"Dmitry, you must possess this incredible artifact. The pictures he sent you do not do it justice at all. There is something... something so very special about it. Just gazing upon the image makes you feel as if you have literally touched the face of God.

"Pay what he asks, Dmitry. I will bring it back with me."

CHAPTER 62

Four Carabiniere squad cars, blue lights flashing, two-tone sirens blaring, blocked the entire Via del Governo Vecchio as the police pulled up in front of Vincenzo Tucci's small antiquities shop. A dozen officers poured out of the cars, weapons drawn, and stormed the shop's front door.

Tucci ran out from the back of his shop, thinking it was the fire brigade, terrified his shop might be consumed in some conflagration.

No, it was worse. He recognized Colonel Scarpelli from previous encounters. It was the Art Squad.

"Vincenzo Tucci," Scarpelli announced, "you are hereby being served with a search warrant, allowing us to conduct a thorough search of your property and records.

"However, it will serve you better if you simply come clean with us from the beginning—where is the Vatican's sacred veil?"

Tucci was immobilized, his hands raised in defense.

"Cardinale Dante said nothing of that being the Vatican's property! You must believe me," he pleaded. "I run a legal business here, Colonel, surely you must know that."

Scarpelli's eyes rolled as he let out a deep sigh. "Signor Tucci, what can you tell me of this veil? You said Cardinale Dante brought it to you? Where is it now?"

"Yes, Dante," Tucci lamented. "But sadly, I have only this morning sold it! I did not know it was stolen property. Surely I would not have accepted it had I known…" He gave his most convincingly earnest look to the colonel.

"To whom was it sold? The Russian?"

"Well, yes, the…" Tucci 's face turned perplexed. "How did you know it was a Russian?"

"Where is this Russian now? Tell me, quickly!"

"It was not he himself who purchased it. He sent his representative, a Signorina DuPont. I believe they came to Rome in Signor Zharkov's private jet. Perhaps you can find them that way?" Tucci only now began lowering his hands, still curious as to how the Art Squad knew a Russian was involved in his business.

Scarpelli went back to his official car and picked up the radio mic to call dispatch.

"Stop all private air traffic leaving from both Fiumicino and Ciampino airports. Find a private jet registered to Dmitry Zharkov or any of his companies. Call me back when you have this information, but send available squad cars to meet the departing jet's passengers immediately. Scarpelli out."

CHAPTER 63

The fast-moving motorcade of ten Carabiniere squad cars, blues and twos blazing, descended on the tarmac of Ciampino airport southeast of Rome's city center, surrounding the private jet of Russian oligarch Dmitry Zharkov.

Having been cleared for departure, with its passengers all boarded and engines set for taxiing to the runway, the plane was instructed by the tower to hold its position just moments earlier.

The jetway was repositioned back to the plane's door as Colonel Benito Scarpelli walked through the tunnel toward the aircraft.

"I am looking for Signorina DuPont," he said to the first person he met, obviously a Russian bodyguard by his look and build.

Véronique emerged from the main cabin to meet the agent.

"Yes, what is it?" she asked assertively. "Why are you holding us from departure?"

Scarpelli introduced himself, then explained his reason for being here.

"Signorina, I understand you have a sacred artifact you acquired from Vincenzo Tucci. Is that correct?"

"I don't see why that is any business of yours, Colonel. It was a legitimate purchase."

"Ah, but that is where you are wrong, madame," he said with official satisfaction. "That object was stolen from the Vatican itself, and the Church demands it be returned to them. Now. The Prefect of the Apostolic Archive, Father Dominic, told me so personally."

Dominic! she thought, shocked at hearing the name from their encounter in Chamonix the year before. *That sonofabitch!*

"I am Mr. Zharkov's attorney, Colonel. Does Father Dominic have proof to the Church's claim of ownership?"

"Do you or Signor Tucci have proof it was acquired legally?" he countered.

Appearing unperturbed, though at an obvious disadvantage in the negotiation, Véronique stood there, trying to figure a way out. She turned to look at all the people surrounding them.

"Colonel, could we have a moment alone, please?" She escorted the agent to the back of the luxurious cabin, far away from the others.

"My employer is a very indulgent man, Colonel," she purred in a low seductive voice. "Is there a generous contribution he might make to a particularly worthy cause of yours, so that we can resolve this amicably?"

"Ah, I see, Signorina," Scarpelli said in a knowing whisper of his own, his head nodding reassuringly. "As it happens, there is one that comes to mind, yes."

He reached behind him to produce a set of handcuffs, slapping them on her arms quickly and efficiently.

"He can make a generous contribution to your legal defense fund for bribing a state official," he declared. "Now, show me where the veil is, or I shall personally see to it there is no bail hearing."

Shocked, Véronique reddened at the mere thought of going to an Italian jail. She had misjudged this man. Badly.

CHAPTER 64

Michael Dominic sat despondently at his desk in the Prefect's office, repeatedly tapping the eraser end of a pencil on the red leather desk mat.

After reflecting for two days on what Dante had tortured him with, his emotions were raw. He hadn't been able to sleep or eat, and knew he must now approach Petrini for the truth.

He picked up his phone and tapped out a new text message to the cardinal: Can we meet, when convenient, in your apartment one evening this week? Sooner than later…

He knew that meeting his mentor, his father, on quiet, comfortable ground would be better than someplace public.

A few minutes later the response came back: **Does tonight work for you?**

Dominic confirmed that tonight would be fine. Great, in fact, he thought, since he couldn't take another day without confirmation from Rico's own lips.

As he sat there, now nervous about tonight's meeting, there was one person he wanted to talk to about this. Hana. He picked up the phone and called her in Paris.

"Hey there," she answered in a congratulatory tone, "I hear

you got the veil back! Sorry I haven't been able to call yet, but I'm on deadline for this story. How are you?"

He let a few moments of silence lapse before he said, simply, "I just found out Enrico Petrini is my real father."

Hana also allowed a quiet moment as she took in the leaden words Michael had just spoken.

"Oh, Michael…" she whispered quietly. "How are you taking this?"

"I've got mixed feelings about it, to be honest," he said, the edges of emotion creeping into his voice. "He and I are meeting tonight. He doesn't know I know yet."

"How did you find out?"

"Of all people, Dante told me. He let it out in a fit of anger two days ago, after he was arrested. He told me he had run a DNA analysis on both of us—which accounts for those stolen brushes last year, remember? I have to believe him. It all kind of makes sense now, anyway."

"Well, for what it's worth, you couldn't hope for a more wonderful father. Enrico has always been there for you, watching out for you, taking care of you and your mother. I can see it now, yes, there are certain similarities between the two of you. If you want my opinion, I think this is great news, Michael!"

"I think it's just the way it played out that hurts. I would have rather heard it from Rico himself, not that bastard Dante. That's what he kept calling *me*, a bastard."

"Don't for a minute listen to anything that fool says. His only goal was to hurt you, and it appears you're letting him. Don't allow him to win, Michael. He's not worth it."

Dominic was now in tears listening to his closest friend offer her loving support. He let them fall, and it felt good. He needed the release.

"You're right, Hana," he sniffled. "Rico is a good man, and I'm proud to be his son." The gates burst open now, emotion pouring out of him.

"I wish I could be there for you, right now, holding you tight," she offered. "But I'm so glad you called me, Michael. I love you, and I always will. I think you know that."

He wiped away the tears, trying to compose himself.

"Yes, I know. The feeling's mutual. And I think *you* know that. As I've said before, if things were different…"

"I understand," Hana said, her own voice cracking with emotion. "As for tonight, please go easy on him. Just imagine what *he's* been through. He has undoubtedly carried this burden your entire life, at the risk of forsaking his holy vows. And to be perfectly frank, he doesn't have that many years left. You are a wonderful, gentle and caring man. He must be so proud of you, seeing what you've accomplished and how honorably you've done it."

They were both now sniffling so much that they laughed.

"Look at us!" Hana giggled. "We're both a mess."

Dominic collected himself. "Thanks for being there, Hana, it means so much to me. I'll let you know how things turn out."

"Looking forward to it, Michael. Take good care now, and give Enrico my love."

OVERLOOKING the gardens of Saint Martha's Square, the Secretary of State's apartment in the San Carlo Palace was a short walk from the Apostolic Archive.

As he made his way there, Dominic felt much better after his conversation with Hana, bolstered by her confident support and ready to "meet" his father.

It was only a few moments after he knocked on the door that a nun answered, and after welcoming him inside, escorted him to the cardinal's sitting room. Petrini was relaxing in a burgundy Queen Anne chair nursing a brandy.

"Michael, it is so good to see you," he said warmly, standing. "Do come in."

As Dominic approached Petrini to shake hands, the young priest impulsively embraced the man in a great bear hug, one that was long and meaningful.

Then he spontaneously began sobbing.

After a few moments, Petrini gently pushed Michael back, keeping his hands on both his shoulders, watching him. The tears didn't stop as the young priest looked back deeply into his father's eyes.

"So. I see you already know, then," the cardinal said quietly, as his own eyes began to glisten.

Michael looked at him earnestly, a mixture of tenderness and affection in his eyes as he nodded his head.

"Yes. I know. I won't say how just now, but the fact is, I know you are my father. And I want you to know that I couldn't be prouder to be your son."

It was Petrini's turn to shed tears now. After thirty-two years of carrying such a great burden, the release was overwhelming.

Dominic moved to close the doors leading into the sitting room. There was no need for anyone else to know. This kind of news would make it around the Vatican faster than fire.

He poured himself a glass of brandy from a crystal bottle on the table, then took a chair across from Petrini.

The cardinal had recovered his composure, took another sip of the amber liquid, and looked anew at his son.

"I have watched you grow with such pride, Michael. I'm sure you understand why your mother and I could not reveal the truth to you, or to anyone for that matter. Times were very different back then, not to say it's permissible now, not by any means.

"Grace and I loved each other so very much, but we had to keep our passions hidden. Her surprise pregnancy was unplanned, of course, and abortion was simply not an option or desire. So we arranged a cover story that worked to protect you and your mother, and me, though I've often felt the coward by doing so."

"Does anyone else know?" Dominic asked.

"Yes. The Holy Father knows, in fact. And Dant..." Petrini didn't finish the name when he realized something.

"It was Dante who told you, wasn't it?"

"Yes. I visited him a couple days ago to ask what he had done with the veil, and he seemed to relish telling me, as if gutting me with a verbal blade.

"So, His Holiness knows?!"

"He does. Dante tried to blackmail me last year when he needed something—his usual modus operandi, I suppose—and seeking absolution on my own terms, I went to the Pope and confessed my sin. He's a good man, our pope, and came down hard on Dante then, telling him to back away and never breathe a word about it to anyone, especially you. I expect Fabrizio has nothing to lose now. He's a lost soul, that one."

"What is to become of him?"

"Being subject to the Church's canon law, he'll face a Supreme Tribunal which will undoubtedly find him guilty of conspiracy to commit murder, among other crimes, then he'll most likely be sentenced to imprisonment. And after the Pope laicizes him, his days as a practicing priest are over."

People sentenced to imprisonment by the Vatican serve time in Italian prisons, with costs covered by the Vatican.

"Well, he's brought all this down on himself. I have no sympathy for the man. But let's not waste another breath on Dante. Tell me more about you and my mother..."

The two men spent the next couple hours reminiscing about the woman so central to each of their lives, with Petrini revealing many intimacies Michael would have been unaware of as a child. Learning these new details about both of them gave him a renewed sense of family, a bond he had been missing for as long as he could remember.

As Petrini spoke, Michael watched him closely, taking in his father's speech and mannerisms in a new light, one offering a sense of renovation, and of closure.

He knew now he was home.

EPILOGUE

N ot far from the Vatican, on the muddy banks of the Tiber River in Trastevere, sits a massive complex of buildings known as Regina Coeli, or "Queen of Heaven" prison. Originally a Catholic convent built in 1654, it is now home to a thousand of Rome's most unrepentant criminals.

As he was being admitted, the new inmate was handed a set of cotton overalls and a towel, a bar of rough soap, a toothbrush with toothpaste, and a pair of slippers. Carrying all these items himself, he was escorted by one of the guards to his new fourth floor cell—one which, ironically given his former station in life, offered a distant view of the dome of Saint Peter's Basilica.

Fabrizio Dante, now known by his new identity Prisoner Number 45789, placed the stack of goods on his flimsy cot in his new home, and sat down.

With an imposed sentence of five years, he could be out in much less, given time for good behavior.

UNDER THE BANNER headline *"Nazi Genetics Network Exposed,"* Hana Sinclair filed her story for *Le Monde* to acclaim by all, but with the special gratitude of world Jewish organizations, for its impact on bringing attention to the growing Argentinian neo-Nazi community. The Argentine president saw to the disbandment of the *Kinderklinik* and dissolution of the Ahnenerbe, arresting its leading members and installing new police enforcement brigades in Bariloche.

Hilda Fischbein soon remarried, finding a good husband who worked for an international aid organization based in Patagonia. Her son, whom they named Michael, was delivered under the care of a local Catholic hospital.

IN ROME, Karl Dengler, Lukas Bischoff and Marco Picard were honored in a discreet ceremony arranged by Mossad, congratulating them for their assistance to and support of Shayetet 13 forces while in Argentina, and the resulting breakup of the fascistic Ahnenerbe. The Commander of the Pontifical Swiss Guard was present, as was Karl's cousin Hana who flew in from Paris for the event.

IN ANOTHER QUIET CEREMONY, the Pope consecrated the Magdalene veil as dedicated permanently to the sacred, removing it from the secular state. His Holiness approved examination of the byssus veil by a small team of respected scientists and scholars, work that will likely go on for years.

In the meantime the veil was given prominence in a public display in the Vatican Museum for the faithful to view and to worship, a crown jewel in the multitude of sacred artifacts the Museum features for historical and religious posterity.

FATHER MICHAEL DOMINIC, feeling more centered in his life than ever before, kept the knowledge of his father's paternity secret—except, of course, for the one person he'd already told, Hana Sinclair.

As he and Hana walked arm in arm through the Vatican papal gardens on the sunny spring day, sunlight seeping through the apple trees lining the Viale del'Oservatorio, they recounted their adventures over the past couple years.

"We make a good team, you know?" Hana prodded, a light breeze tossing her chestnut brown hair. "Where do you suppose we'll end up next?"

"Oh, it's hard to say," Dominic observed, looking up at the sky as he took a deep breath. "But I get the feeling something will come along soon, and you will surely need a new story or two. Let's see what life has in store for us.

"For now, I'm just happy to be here with you, safe and free of any other influence. Life is good, Hana. Life is good."

✳

AUTHOR'S NOTES

Dealing with issues of theology, religious beliefs, and the fictional treatment of historical biblical events can be a daunting affair.

I would ask all readers to view this story for what it is—a work of pure fiction, adapted from the seeds of many oral traditions and the historical record, at least as we know it today.

Apart from telling an engaging story, I have no agenda here, and respect those of all beliefs, from Agnosticism to Zoroastrianism and everything in between.

Many readers of *The Magdalene Chronicles* series have asked me to distinguish fact from fiction in my books. Generally, I like to take factual events and historical figures and build on them in creative ways—but much of what I do write is historically accurate. In this book, I'll review some of the chapters where questions may arise, with hopes that it may help those wondering.

PROLOGUE: Nazi SS *Reichsführer* Heinrich Himmler, one of Hitler's top generals, was indeed obsessed with the occult, and instigated activities which took place in Wewelsburg Castle (a real place, even today as a museum and youth hostel) including supernatural and strange rituals in the Consecration Hall. Himmler did send Otto Rahn on archeological expeditions in the mid-1930s, and Rahn was reputed to eventually have brought "something" back to Himmler from his discoveries in southern France. We don't know what that was, or even if it happened at all.

The *Veil of Veronica* is, as far as we know, a true *legend*, an oral tradition passed down through the centuries. I did take fictional liberties with the veil being passed on from Berenikē to Magdalene.

CHAPTER 1: I did base two characters on actual historical figures, but for prudent legal reasons I was encouraged to change their names in the book. In spite of these changes, the backgrounds and actions of these two people in particular are, for the most part, based on recorded historical events. Their families as portrayed in the book, however, are entirely fictional.

FOR FURTHER RESEARCH, SEE:
   https://en.wikipedia.org/wiki/Walter_Rauff
   https://en.wikipedia.org/wiki/Erich_Priebke

CHAPTER 4: The Thule Society, the Ahnenerbe, and "The Twelve" were all authentic groups during the Nazi era. The Ahnenerbe's mission was, in fact, to justify the Holocaust and its brutal extermination of Jews and other "undesirables" in the years leading up to and during the war.

Bishop Alois Hudal was a real-life figure who did oversee the Vatican ratline as a Nazi collaborator. More information on him is available at https://en.wikipedia.org/wiki/Alois_Hudal.

The 3-fragment riddle I composed is purely the result of my own imagination.

CHAPTER 6: Bishop Hudal's book *Roman Diaries* was indeed published thirteen years after his death. In it you'll find the actual passage, as quoted in this book, regarding his visit to Allied detention camps, where he felt the Nazis were being mistreated.

The *Schwarze Sonne*, or Black Sun, mosaic is genuine and can still be found today on the floor of the Generals' Hall at Wewelsburg Castle in Büren, Germany.

CHAPTER 7: The Vatican's *Riserva* is, in fact, the most sensitive Archives room in the Vatican, though I have no idea what it actually looks like—so I've had to improvise in describing it.

Himmler's journal and Hudal's letter to the Pope are both fictional devices.

CHAPTER 8: Heinrich Himmler did keep diaries since he was ten years old, and the latest one to be found had actually been confiscated by the Russian Red Army at the end of the war. The notations about Himmler's preternatural view of the Jews in concentration camps and the vicious dogs are all true, taken from his own journals.

The biblical passage I quote here, John 20-3:7, is correct as used in the book (notwithstanding my fictional use surrounding it). The Bible's various editions may vary in terminology.

CHAPTER 9: Simon Ginzberg's description of the extant veils in the various locations mentioned is accurate and factual, as is the discussion about the name *Veronica* (*vera icon* in Latin).

CHAPTER 14: Javier Batista's mention of *Operation Oriente Cercano* was an actual event—a police raid in which a horde of Nazi artifacts and memorabilia was discovered hidden in a secret room behind a bookcase in a house in Béccar, Argentina in 2017.

CHAPTER 29: The fascinating image of Christ's face is actually an existing overlay of the real-life Manoppello veil contrasted over the face on the Shroud of Turin, a discovery made by Sister Blandina Paschalis Schlomer, a German Trappist nun, in which the combined overlaid images were found to be identical.

The usage of the Manoppello and Turin Shroud image, depicted fictionally herein and slightly modified, is licensed under the Creative Commons Attribution-Share Alike 3.0 Unported license. With kind permission by Brother Benno, given August 6, 2006.

CHAPTER 32: The *Kinderklinik* emerged from my own imagination, though Bariloche *is* a German settlement in the Patagonia region of Argentina. Nine thousand Nazis emigrated there after the war, and their families still populate the region.

The *Lebensborn* program was an actual German program initiated by the SS, with the goal of raising the birth rate of Aryan children by those considered "racially pure" and "healthy" based on Nazi racial hygiene and health ideologies.

And the Red Falcons were, in fact, the highly-indoctrinated Nazi equivalent of the Boy Scouts and Girl Scouts, though with different agendas.

CHAPTER 33: The once SECRET, now unclassified CIA document is fully authentic, and widely available on the internet. By sheer coincidence it addresses verbatim the exact situation I needed for the story and fit perfectly.

MISCELLANEOUS NOTES: Descriptions of all actual buildings and roads is accurate, thanks to the marvels of Google Earth and other resources.

Referenced hotels, restaurants (even menus), airlines and flight times are all factual. Accounting for verified and presumed times, including travel, the book took place over a span of 41 days.

✳

Thank you for reading *The Magdalene Veil*. I really hope you enjoyed it and, if you haven't already, suggest you pick up the story in the other books in this series—*The Magdalene Deception* and *The Magdalene Reliquary*—and look forward to forthcoming books featuring the same characters—and a few new ones—in the next *Vatican Secret Archives Thriller* series.

When you have a moment, may I ask that you leave a review on Amazon and elsewhere? Reviews are crucial to a book's success, and I hope for The Magdalene Chronicles series to have a long and entertaining life.

You can easily leave your review by going to my Amazon book page.

If you would like to reach out for any reason, you can email me at gary@garymcavoy.com. If you'd like to learn more about me and my other books, visit my website at www.garymcavoy.com, where you can also sign up for my private mailing list.

With kind regards,
Gary McAvoy

ACKNOWLEDGMENTS

Throughout this series I have had the grateful assistance of many friends and colleagues, without whose help this would have been a more challenging project.

For this book, I wish to thank several contributors for their generous donation of time, careful editorial thought, and invaluable cleverness, among those Greg McDonald, Yale Lewis, Michelle Harden, Jeanne Jabour, and Fran Libra Koenigsdorf, along with my brilliant editor Sandra Haven. Special thanks to Kathleen Costello for her logical and intuitive copyediting talents.

I am also immensely thankful for the many readers of my work, and for their wholly positive reviews. I write for your entertainment and am glad to have you along for the adventures.

CPSIA information can be obtained
at www.ICGtesting.com
Printed in the USA
BVHW082338210323
660847BV00014B/704/J